EMOTIONAL RHAPSODY

By

Kenan Hudaverdi

Edited by

Leslie Angelocci

Emotional Rhapsody

ISBN: 9781717741479

Imprint: Independently published

First Edition Revision II

Table of Contents

3

Foreword

In every life there are storms. Thunder with lightning, torrential rains, earthquakes, hurricanes and the dreaded tsunamis, and when the winds subside, there will always be sunshine and rainbows, rebirth, new beginnings. As you gaze across the dark skies, do not look for ghosts or mysteries... Spirits are people who, while still alive, have suffered a spiritual death. Do not try to understand the mystery of life, for life itself cannot be realised while witnessing all the ugly actions of humanity. The secret of life can only be discovered, within your subconscious mind. In every life, there is a tragedy. A book, a film a play, a poem, a song, and above all else a longing to be accepted, a longing to be loved, a longing to be understood. For this is the way of human nature. There are periods of calm as we journey through life, also periods of choppy seas and storms that may leave one feeling hopeless, useless, and worthless. Storms will lift and calm will return. The unspoken grief of the broken heart that cannot be the same for any two people. Grief will generate beauty and joy in the soul when recognised as a life change towards growth and enlightenment. Each awakening is so unique and specific to every individual as is each loss. When that "special someone" is missing, there is always a place of aloneness that is in the corner of your heart. When things go wrong, you curl up and fall asleep in the tranquillity and the safety of your inner sanctuary and begin to heal your soul. Eventually, you will wake up to face another day filled with beautiful mysteries, surprises, and endless possibilities. Every day is a new beginning...

Kenan Hudaverdi, 09.06.2018

Chapter One

The Golden Cage

The rain was pounding on the windows of the large doors that open out into the garden area of Annabella's beautiful home. The garden is full of all kinds of fruit trees, as well as olive trees, flowers, and aromatic herbs. The large terrace is for entertaining guests amongst the smell of the fruit and flowers and a lovely and preferred spot to spend time with friends or alone with a good book and a cup of tea or glass of wine.

The inside of the house remains beautifully decorated with art and comfortable furniture. A feeling generated to make anyone that entered feel at home.

There is a large dining area, a large modern kitchen with marble floors and countertops kept impeccably clean at all times. Through the rest of the house, there are three large bedrooms, with adjoining bathrooms and walk-in closets and a powder room for guests.

Annabella's bedroom contained all of her treasures. Mannequin heads sit on a table under a big mirror adorned with Venetian masks that covered the mannequin faces. Loving all things that glitter, one mask was silver, the other gold and both hand painted with rhinestones for extra sparkle.

A few years ago, Annabella painted a nude woman lying on her stomach wearing high heels; the painting was hung on the wall as you enter the room.

The walk-in closet is filled with an abundance of clothes, high heeled shoes and boots, sunglasses and purses that matched her daily ensemble or a night out with friends. From fur to wool there were coats for every season as well as hats, scarf's and gloves. Fashion has always been one of Annabella's greatest passions, and Annabella always prepared for any important event or a casual day in the park.

It's been two weeks since Annabella returned from Paris. The trip was supposed to be exciting and intriguing, meant for two star-crossed lovers, much to Annabella's dismay the trip was to be one of Annabella greatest disappointment, leaving her feeling broken hearted and unworthy of "true love." After a year of communicating online, chatting for endless hours, falling deeply in love, Annabella left for Paris to finally meet the man of her dreams Santiago. Annabella had planned to run away from her loveless marriage and spend her life with Santiago. The excitement and joy quickly turned to sorrow when Santiago did not show up in Paris as they'd planned. Annabella returned to her home with a broken heart and the feeling that she was unworthy of love.

Detached from her dreams, Annabella sits with her beloved dog Fluffy watching her favourite film "Wuthering Heights." Ibrahim, Annabella's husband of twenty years, walks through the room with his cell in one hand and a glass of water in the other.

Annabella remembers meeting Ibrahim in Paris. Annabella found Ibrahim to be very enchanting and exceptionally intelligent, they married in Paris, and the first ten years were beautiful. It was the last ten that had changed their relationship. The love they had was gone, and they lived separately in the same home. Annabella wonders what will happen now that Ibrahim's business was no longer thriving much like their marriage.

It's been ten years since they shared a bedroom or much of anything for that matter and Ibrahim is now 70 years old and still working.

Annabella pauses, her attention away from the film for a moment as Ibrahim walks across the living area without saying a word, making his way to his bedroom.

As Ibrahim disappears, Annabella refocuses back to the film were Heathcliff and Cathy are on the balcony and Cathy remonstrates:

"I am another man's wife, and he loves me!"

Heathcliff responds with all the sincerity of his soul:

"If he loved you with all the power of his soul for a whole lifetime, he couldn't love you as much as I do in a single day!"

Annabella always has the same emotional response to these words. Always tears, for words she will never hear in her own life with Ibrahim. Wiping her eyes, Fluffy looks up at Annabella with a strange but familiar sense of concern.

Annabella picks Fluffy up, turns off the television, and walks towards her bedroom, turning out the light on the way out. Once in the bedroom, Anabella reaches into the nightstand where she keeps her sleeping pills and opens the bottle; she hasn't slept since Paris. Tonight she will sleep. Removing all of her various pillows and stuffed animals and dolls from her bed, Annabella is thinking about her loveless marriage.

The lack of kindness, the lack of intimacy and how her life had become as cold as the marble floors that consumes her thoughts. Another empty, dull day without hope of salvaging her previous life. Another day filled with loneliness and unhappiness, she feels herself like the wind plucked a leaf before its full colour had turned to red and gold wafting aimlessly, with no destination in sight, just a long and painful journey into the unknown.

On the little table, a picture of Annabella holding her beloved Fluffy catches her eye for a moment, this little dog is now the closest thing to feeling loved that she knows.

Annabella takes her Pyjamas and walks into the bathroom, turns on the light, and begins to prepare for bed. As she takes off her top and she loosens her slacks in front of the big mirror facing her, she starts to look at herself with a critical eye.

At 62 years old her hair is long and beautiful keeping the colour, blonde to hide the grey, she maintains a three-month regiment to keep her roots from showing, and it works for her. Still lingering in the mirror, Annabella is searching for some life, her beauty is there, but the emptiness seems to be sucking the life out of her. Between the situation with her marriage and the trip to Paris, Annabella feels her soul is gone altogether now.

Annabella examines herself before putting on her Pyjamas; her thighs are softer now, her hips rounded, her stomach is weak. She looks at her large breasts inside the black bra; they are big and soft they no longer hold themselves up without the support of the bra. Now glancing at the back of her hands the veins are showing, a sign of age that can't be corrected. Clothing will only cover her "not so perfect" skin. These days she often asks the question to herself what life is all about?" There are no answers.

Recalling to memory the days she lived in Paris as a fashion model. Those were the happiest days of her youth, while the modelling scene wasn't her thing; she enjoyed the attention and adoration.

The wealthy men that attended the Paris fashion shows were nothing more than vultures. Always looking for a liaison with young models even though they were married. It was a time that men would have multiple mistresses and purchase lavish gifts to try and win the favour of a young "twenty-something" year old model.

The insincerity of those men always made Annabella feel sick for the girls that fell for their games.

That happy and carefree life in Paris and those days were long ago and far away now, just memories of a happy time in her now miserable life. Annabella never imagined that her choice to leave Paris to be with her husband in Morocco would have turned into a life of quiet suffering and loneliness.

Annabella still has a few friends in Paris. Prior to now, she would travel to Paris for a few weeks at a time. The trips were a way to escape the boredom of her relationship with her husband, and the empty feelings of living in the big house full of expensive art, statues, and paintings that represented the life they had when business was good.

Now, business is suffering, and they are barely scraping by with the hard-hit economy. Annabella recalls that things were beautiful when they had money, now, just misery. Shaking herself back into the moment, she finishes her night time routine with moisturiser, and then slips on her Pyjama pants, turns off the light and heads into her bedroom.

On her way to bed, she turns a small lamp on and then turns off the overhead chandelier. Slipping into bed, Annabella takes the photo of herself and Fluffy and places it next to her on the nightstand.

Sinking gently into her bed, Annabella reaches for her phone, places her earphones in her ears, and chooses the album "Stone Gone" by Barry White presses play and begins to sift through junk mail, then emails. Clicking on the messages, she finds unopened emails from Santiago; suddenly Annabella was feeling a rush of mixed emotions and uncertainty.

Annabella kept all the messages between herself and Santiago. There were days that she would reread the words to be able to "feel" again, now she opens an email from six months ago…

Santiago 11/15/2013 5:55:29 PM

There is a longing in my heart for the imagined beauty of life, I wished to have had with you, and I could not."

"It's always with me, my love for you, and that persistent pain has been forever present in my soul. Confident of the happiness we could have had together, the pain grows even more significant because I do not have the money to provide you with the security you deserve in life… With my love XXX

Santiago 11/15/2013 5:58:29 PM

I wanted to speak a little about the situation between you and Ibrahim. I do not doubt that he is a good man and that he works hard, to ensure you have all the material things you like.

I do understand you still love him.

Annabella searches her thoughts for answers, but again, there were no answers to be found everything was now. She clicks open the reply she sent him.

Annabella Amir 11/15/2013 6:56:43 PM

"Yes, I do understand you. It is regrettable in a way. There are many people, like us. If our situations, were different we could still do something, we could have a new life together, but unfortunately, we are not young, and there is a long distance between us.

I know your desires, it's so easy to dream and believe that dreams can come true sometimes. Please consider how we would live our daily life. Being without money is not for me, not at my age."

With a deep sigh, Annabella stops reading, shuts off the music, removes her headphones, closes the old messages, and presses SEND on her email. For a moment she closed her eyes and faded back in time. A few weeks ago when she was in Paris alone. Paris was to be their first in-person meeting. Annabella was in love, and it was her greatest hope to meet the man that held her heart. Since he did not show up and had not left a message at her hotel, she never knew why. What was his reason? The not knowing was the reason that upon her return to Morocco she had ceased almost all communication with him with the exception of email. Annabella could not forgive Santiago but would allow him to email her once in a while.

Santiago was down to earth, funny, kind, tender-hearted and had all the qualities that Annabella admired and loved in a man. Tragically, Santiago was very poor financially. Living in a rented room, not a home of his own and being that he was 55 years old and time had passed him by for making something of his life, it was indeed a recipe

11

for more broken dreams and no hope of a future with security and happiness in place.

Annabella felt that Santiago would be a great love for her and her for him if only they had some security and could live without worry. Once again, Annabella had no idea where her life was going and how she could survive feeling broken and riddled with anxiety.

In Morocco, Annabella had a sense of security in her home, living there from day to day, but her soul was cold now and frozen in the wilderness of life, as she resigned herself to the fact that this was how it was going to be always; a life without a "true love" experience.

A life with no love, no hugs, no tender kisses, no I love you. It was all gone, and she had lost all confidence in humanity and herself. Visualizing her soul as a graveyard that she wandered through the daily listening of tweeting of birds that she did not see was what her life had become, such a harsh reality, a cruel joke. As she turns off the lamp and sinks into the in bed takes her sleeping pill, pulling the blanket close to her face, she silently begins to cry alone in the dark, alone in the world.

Annabella pulls aside the curtains on her large window to reveal a beautiful day outside. The soft glow of the morning sun hitting her delicate face, she stops there in the sunlight daily looking out the window. Beyond the garden and the flowers, above the rooftops, can see the Straits of Gibraltar that connects the Atlantic Ocean to the Mediterranean Sea and Spain in Europe from Morocco. For the past ten years, she felt homesick for France, a longing to return to Paris and lose the feeling of "not belonging" in Morocco.

Annabella walks into the large kitchen with a dining table in the centre Ibrahim is sitting there drinking his morning coffee and looking at his messages on his cell phone.

"Good morning" uttered Annabella while in casual stride walking towards the tea kettle on the counter. Ibrahim without looking at her in a casual voice replied, "good morning." Annabella fills the pot and flips the switch to "On." Annabella asks Ibrahim, "would you like some breakfast?" Ibrahim responds, "No, I will have something at work when am hungry and by the way I spoke to the gardener yesterday, he will be here this afternoon to prune the leaves of the palm trees."

"Adilah has some government stuff she is sorting out, and she will not be here today" replied Annabella in a disappointed voice. Adilah was the housekeeper that came to the house three times a week to help Annabella with the house.

"Well, I am sure she will be here tomorrow." said Ibrahim without looking at Annabella.

Annabella looked at Ibrahim with an expression on her face that her body drained of energy, from being taken for granted as well as being ignored and neglected as a wife. A look that had become familiar to Ibrahim, as usual as it was to ignore it and Annabella.

Annabella asks half-heartedly" Is there anything special you like me to cook for you tonight?"

Ibrahim, replies, "You know what I like, we've been married for twenty years" He finishes his coffee and puts the cup down while looking at his phone.

Annabella was very familiar with the tone of his voice, but felt compelled to challenge Ibrahim; "We have been married for twenty years, but for the past ten years we have not had a marriage! What has happened to us Ibrahim?"

"Right now is not the time to talk about this!" Ibrahim's voice was stern and sharp, but that didn't stop Annabella from responding.

"It is never the right time Ibrahim, and it has never been the right time! I have been trying to talk to you for the past ten years, and you ignore me! We have become strangers in a marriage that started as a couple! Where is the tenderness? Where is the love? Where is the happiness? What has happened to us?" Annabella's voice was pleading with emotion, and her eyes were searching his eyes. Ibrahim is losing his calm demeanour and replies with a sharp retort;

"We can talk about this another time! Right now, I am going to work!" Ibrahim gets out of his chair and walks out of the kitchen and out of the house. Annabella is now alone and feeling empty and lost.

Annabella gets up and heads into her bedroom where she had left her cell phone, picking up the phone she carries it into the kitchen, laying it on the countertop. The tea kettle is whistling, and she makes herself a cup of tea. A sharp pinging noise is coming from her cell phone; Annabella has a new email in her inbox.

Ignoring the email, Annabella turns on the stereo and plays a song by Sharif Dean it was a favourite entitled *"Do You Love Me"* This was a song dedicated to her by Santiago De La Cruz, he told her, "This will be our song forever!"

Annabella sits at the table, taking a slow sip of her tea; she picks up her phone and goes directly into her emails. There are some random and unimportant emails, but then she sees there she sees an email from Santiago, her expression changes to one of anger to curiosity. Thinking for a second, then opens it and reads it.

"What has happened to us, Annabella? Why are you always cold towards me? Why can't we speak like we used to? I would like us to have a serious conversation, give me a time we can talk on video chat and I will be there."

Annabella is infuriated by what she is reading as the song plays in the background of perfect love; she hits the reply button on the email and begins to respond feverishly.

"What is there to speak about? You go on about the same things all the time! I find you annoying as nothing ever changes with you! Every time I get an email from you I get so frustrated and unnerved! Since nothing is new or exciting, I think its best that you only write to me once a month."

Annabella looks at the email and then presses send! Placing the phone down, she takes another long sip of her tea. The song continues in the background.

Chapter Two

Broken Spirit

Four Years Later

Outside in the garden, Annabella is washing the floor of the patio with a hose and a broom. Once again, her longing for home has her distracted for several moments as she looks at the coast of Spain and Europe. As she resumes the cleaning of the patio, her eyes fall onto the little grave of her long-time companion Fluffy, who had just passed six months ago. There is a rose bush planted on her grave. Annabella walks to that sunny spot in the garden and kneels down she speaks clearly…

"I miss you! I miss you so much!" Annabella takes the time to sit for a while reflecting on the good times they had in the past. Fluffy had given Annabella unconditional love and companionship. Constant friends, they went everywhere together, and that sweet little dog followed her all over the property and the house like a child.

Later that evening when in the privacy of her room, Annabella spent some time watching video clips of Fluffy that she had taken with her cell phone. Fluffy was a precious girl, so beautiful when she ran and played. Fluffy was so close to Annabella that she was like a little human being, with a sweet and tender heart. Annabella was nearly brought to tears, but pulled herself back together, resisting the urge to cry. Annabella places her phone on the nightstand, opens the drawer, and takes a sleeping pill. Dozing off to sleep, she wonders what will happen to her if something happens to Ibrahim; she decides she must confront him to be informed.

The situation at home was coming to a boiling point; Annabella falls asleep before Ibrahim arrives home.

Most nights Ibrahim came home late, sometimes he did not come home until it was past midnight.

On this night, it was nearly approaching one in the morning; there was no noise when Ibrahim arrived inside. Walking into Annabella's room, he found her fast asleep, no TV or music, just a lamp on by the bed. Ibrahim looks at her for a few seconds without emotion, and then walked out of the room. A few moments later he returns with a blanket and covers her gently so as not to wake her. Ibrahim hears a slight snoring sound coming from Annabella he leaves the room, shutting off the light as he closes the door.

The following morning Annabella strolls into the kitchen looking worse for wear. Ibrahim had been already awake, dressed, and ready to go to work, drinking his coffee, she stops and looks at him

In a calm voice

"Ibrahim, we need to talk."

"Talk about what?"

"We need to talk about us, the house, the business, the finances, our future, and most importantly, what is going to happen to me if anything happens to you."

"This is not the time to talk about these things."

"I want to know what is going to happen to me if anything happened to you."

"What are you talking about?"

"I am talking about security! Annabella raises her voice. You've never said to me not to worry should anything happened to you!

You've never reassured me that I will be taken care of if you should die.

Understand that I too have put my life and soul into this marriage, into this house, into your business.

I'm totally justified asking questions and I expect answers! I want to know what is going to happen to me if anything happens to you!"

She waits patiently for an answer that does not come. Ibrahim looks at her thinking to himself that she is from another planet. Annabella's voice rises higher

"I have given you twenty years of my life! Our life was good when we lived in Paris, but ever since we got here it's been miserable! Everything has gone wrong! I asked you to sell the house as it's too big for me to manage! You've done nothing about that!"

"I don't want to talk about these things now!"

Annabella is seething with a severe look in her eyes. "You brought me here as your wife, but you treat me like a second-hand human! You treat me like the Moroccans treat their wives! You have become like all the other men in Morocco! I have supported you in everything, and you treat me like shit! You have two boys from your previous marriage. Both of them are lazy and entitled as you have given them everything; treating them like kings, teaching them no respect. They shit on you all the time, and you do nothing about it!"

Ibrahim is now clearly angry. "Don't you dare talk about my kids; my kids are none of your business!"

Annabella is aggravated and moves a step forward towards Ibrahim "Ok then, let's talk about business! I gave you two hundred and fifty thousand Euros to put into your business, have you ever once offered to give that money back to me?"

Before Annabella can continue, Ibrahim interjects "So, this is about money?"

"This is about my life, and what will happen to me if you die tomorrow! As far as I can see and guess, everything will go to your sons! The house, the business and God only know what else will all go to those ungrateful boys, and I will be on the street!

No home, no money and nowhere to go, this is what I'm talking about!"

As abruptly as the words came out of her mouth, the tears begin to fall, and Annabella is weeping.

Ibrahim tries to calm her down, "Annabella lets calm down now. We can discuss all of this another time, ok?"

Annabella looks at Ibrahim in disbelief, the crying stops and the anger is seething from her.

"Damn you! You haven't got the decency to say you're sorry! You haven't got the decency to say "don't cry". You haven't got the decency to tell me that I am right and that we should be talking about these things because they are important questions that deserve a clear and precise answers! Everything I have said about our situation is true. All I want to know is what is going to happen to me?"

"As I have said, we will talk about this another time!" Ibrahim replied calmly.

"You bastard!" Annabella lunges forward, stretching her hand out to scratch Ibrahim's face.

Ibrahim grabs Annabella by the hand to stop her. In the struggle, Annabella's long nail on her index finger breaks; she lets out a scream of pain. Ibrahim pushes her backwards; she falls helplessly to the floor. Annabella looks at her shaking bloody hand; her nail is missing. On the floor and bleeding, Annabella sees herself as a broken woman.

Ibrahim's voice is raised again "I told you we would talk about this another time!"

"No! I don't want to talk about anything, anymore. You have said everything with your actions here this morning. Just leaves me alone, leave me alone Ibrahim!"

Annabella sheepishly gets herself up off the floor. Wiping her tears, she slowly starts towards her bedroom.

With her finger bleeding, she goes directly into her bathroom and begins to wash the blood from her hand. Ibrahim looks at her without an ounce of pity and then leaves the house. Annabella turns on the tap in the basin, placing her hand under the running water. Glancing into the mirror, she sees that she is a mess.

Without any thought, she opens the cabinet door where she keeps prescription pills for sleeping and arthritis pain. Annabella places the pills on the counter and thinks to herself; "In thirty minutes I will have no more pain." Drying her hand, she places a bandage where her nail used to be. Crouched over the counter in front of the mirror Annabella breaks down into tears crying inconsolably.

A defeated and exhausted Annabella walks out onto the terrace, the air outside was fragrant as Annabella sat with a blanket across her knees. Feeling disoriented, lost and ultimately defeated Annabella stares out into the distance looking at the Straits of the Ocean, Spain, and her beloved France. Surrounded by the songs of the birds, this mortally wounded soul was alone in the world.

The house in spite of its beauty felt like a graveyard where she would bury all that she once loved and knew. It was over between her and Ibrahim. The last place she wanted to be was in Morocco with a house she didn't want, a husband that has become a stranger to her, and no money to plan her way out. The world had become so unkind and so unforgiving, Annabella wondered how many other women felt as she did…ALONE, EXHAUSTED, FRIGHTENED AND HOPELESS.

Once again Annabella resorts to travelling back in time. This time, she was eight years old, living with her mother in a very poor part of Paris. Annabella's mother worked long hours, holding two jobs to keep a roof over their heads and food on the table.

Even though her mother was young, being a housekeeper was still manual labour and hard work.

Often at the end of the day her mother would fall asleep after supper in the worn-out armchair. Soft music was always playing on the radio that she kept on the side table. One night Annabella was looking at her mother, fast asleep in her clothes wondering to herself why was it that some people have beautiful dresses and live in beautiful houses while my mother and I do not have these things.

The next day at school, she made up her mind that she would clean the house so that her mother could rest when she returned home from work.

After school, she began cleaning the house. Annabella knew she had about four hours before her mother returned home; she washed and put away the dishes, swept the floors, dusted whatever needed dusting, took out the trash, cleaned the bathroom and finally changed her mother's sheets for a peaceful night's rest. When her mother arrived home, Annabella was eagerly waiting to see if her mother would be thrilled with all of her hard work. Instead, her mother walked through the door and headed into the kitchen to make supper without a word of acknowledgement.

During supper, her mother never mentioned what a great job Annabella had done. Annabella was so tired and sadly disappointed. Mother seemed oblivious and slightly unaware of anything other than her exhaustion. After half an hour of eating, Annabella looked at her mother who had still said nothing and wondered how could her mother not notice all of her hard work?

Annabella was expecting a thank you, perhaps a cuddle or a kiss of appreciation. Much to her disappointment, Annabella received neither. Young Annabella went to her small bed, clasping her old handmade doll that she had named "Fluffy" she climbed into her bed in the darkness and silence and began to cry.

A theme that throughout her life that she would repeat many times.

The memory subsided, and Annabella came back into the moment.

There was a soothing breeze, and Annabella's eyes filled with tears. The memories proved to be as complicated as her present life. Would she recognise the pattern that started when she was only a child?

This night would consume Annabella with memories and melancholy. Unable to stay in the present moment, she slips off into the past again.

Vividly recalling when she met her first husband. It was during her modelling years, she was young and beautiful. Many fell in love with her but, it was through a friend that she met a man and fell in love. His name was Renee, and after a short year, they married. Renee was a successful businessman with a chateau forty kilometres outside of Paris.

The chateau was massive and came with a Heli-pad, swimming pool, sauna and ten large suites. There were ten outbuildings on the property for the grounds-keepers and a few collector cars that didn't fit in the garage. Renee also kept a penthouse in Paris and another house near Cannes in the South of France.

Annabella found it all very exciting in the beginning but, after five years of happiness, their life began to change.

Annabella discovered that Renee was having an affair with another model and ended the marriage without receiving anything in the divorce. Annabella left her marriage with only the money she made from modelling.

Suddenly she is the present moment again, feeling hopeless; she turns her eyes to the rooftops and the Coast of Spain in the distance, but only for a moment…

After her divorce from Renee, she rented a flat in Paris and began modelling again on a small scale. The industry no longer held her attention, but her beauty and magnetism were both charming and alluring, and few men could resist her. Annabella began to socialise with friends at nightclubs.

One night at "The Blue Oyster Club" all of her friends were celebrating one of the girl's birthdays. It was at this party, she was, introduced to a perfect looking Turkish man named Erol.

Erol was twenty years older than Annabella, but she was unaware of his age and his career as a drug dealer and a massive cocaine addict. Erol sent two bottles of champagne to the table where Annabella and her friends were at, and then he approached the counter and congratulated the birthday girl. In a moment he was chatting with Annabella. The two exchanged numbers and soon began dating. After six months they moved in together.

Erol was possessive and jealous, but continued his partying life, while Annabella preferred to stay home at night.

Erol loved to go clubbing. He was making so much money; he would take Annabella everywhere. There were several trips to Turkey, Greece, the South of France and other lavish trips where they stayed at lavish resorts every time. After three years together, things started to get crazy between them. Erol had begun beating Annabella when he was high on cocaine. Every time he hit her, the next day he would apologise and send dozens of red roses and gifts.

Annabella was not impressed by the apologies, the roses, or the gifts. Annabella tried to leave Erol several times; she realised the relationship was destructive and broken the only option was to leave. Annabella had kept her figure, but in the midst of this relationship ending she discovered that she was two months pregnant. The pregnancy was not visible, so, Annabella planned to have an abortion as soon as she could leave Erol.

With Erol being so possessive and crazy, Annabella was a nervous wreck. She hid the pregnancy with loose dresses and loose-fitting jeans for fear of him finding out.

One night a big drug deal went wrong. Erol came home far too high and began accusing Annabella of all sorts of things but most of being unfaithful and disloyal. The paranoia from the cocaine was talking and none of it was true but, Erol believed it. Erol beat Annabella so severely that she lost the baby. That was the end of their relationship. Once again Annabella was alone, feeling empty and unappreciated.

Sliding back for a moment from her memories with Erol, Annabella lowers her eyes in defeat.

The tea in the cup has become cold; she takes a sip and closes her eyes, feeling the breeze on her face her senses engaged. The smell of the fruit on the trees brings her to a place where she had met Ibrahim. It was a few years after Erol. Annabella was introduced to Ibrahim at a dinner party with some friends.

Ibrahim and Annabella got along right away. He was kind and gentle and a successful businessman.

Annabella continued to model. She was in her late thirties now, and she would mostly do older women's clothing modelling and was earning excellent money. Annabella was independent and single which made her even more attractive.

Ibrahim and Annabella dated for a while, three years actually, and then they married in Paris. They had lived in Paris for ten years when Ibrahim came home and announced they would be moving to Morocco. In the beginning, Annabella was against the idea because she would be isolated from all things familiar to her. Annabella did not know anyone in Morocco; this was a big step and a personal sacrifice, but, she gave in, and they moved to Tangiers in Morocco.

Over the years, she had managed to save her earnings from her modelling, two hundred and fifty thousand Euros. This money was all of Annabella's life savings. After their marriage, there came a time when Ibrahim insisted she give up modelling altogether.

Ibrahim went into the restaurant business, but things were going badly. Annabella stepped in and gave him the two hundred and fifty thousand Euros to invest in a new restaurant. The investment was a success, and the business was doing well. They were not rich like Renee, but they lived in a beautiful home overlooking the rooftops with sea views and the outline of Spain in the distance.

Annabella never felt comfortable in Morocco, she was always left alone in that big house. The relationship between Annabella and Ibrahim's two sons from his previous marriage was strained at best, leaving Annabella with an immense feeling of loneliness.

After five years of feeling lonely, Annabella joined social media sites. One day while online, she met Santiago. Santiago was amazing! Annabella was intrigued by Santiago's incredible mind; he was also very charming, funny, philosophical, empathic, and understanding. He had a gentle soul and was incredibly romantic! Annabella fell madly in love with him. Santiago was not like the other men in her life; he was not wealthy, he was self-educated, happy, confident and content just the way he was.

Many women adored him, he was a writer, the kind of writer that shared his work, freely and never generated any money from his screenplays and documentaries; but Annabella adored him, and he adored her.

Every day they made contact with each other, sometimes speaking for hours on the phone through Wi-Fi or they would see each other through video calls on their computers. For a year they discussed everything under the sun. Both agreed they would meet in Paris when Annabella was scheduled to visit with friends. Annabella was there, but Santiago did not show up.

With her previous relationships, Annabella was able to distance herself, this was her plan with Santiago when she returned to Morocco.

As hard as it was, she had no choice; her heart broken, she could not allow this to devour her. Santiago wanted it to be like before, and it was never going to be like it was. Annabella tried to end it all but regardless of her responses to his emails over the past four years, Santiago is still writing to her.

Now and then she will respond to his email with very generic responses but nothing more.

Once more she comes back from thinking about all this, and she can feel the teardrops rolling down her cheeks. Annabella thinks to herself, "I have never had luck with any of them, every man has left me feeling disappointed and empty."

Still crying, she becomes angry with herself. Annabella gets up from her chair on the terrace and heads inside to her room. Once more she is exhausted.

That night she did not come out of her room when Ibrahim returned home. Annabella was not there to greet him, there was no meal waiting for him as she usually had done. Annabella could not tolerate the idea of seeing him or speaking to him. Ibrahim did not come looking for her to console her or ask her if she was alright. It was

25

best to avoid him. During the week Annabella made sure she was not in the same room with him, nor would she engage him in random conversation, her silence was her way of showing her indifference to this whole mess.

A few days later the maid Adilah, was at the house helping Annabella. Adilah is a short woman with a kind face and very intuitive.

She knew right away that something was wrong because she knew Annabella so well. Working for her for the past nine years she always saw her immaculately dressed and groomed, but this week she'd let herself go, a sign that something was seriously wrong. She did not ask. Being kind to Annabella was normal, but, knowing something was wrong, and not wanting to inflame the situation by asking.

Adilah made sure to be extra kind with the hopes that if Annabella wanted to tell her what was wrong, she would feel comfortable talking it over with her. So, Adilah encouraged Annabella to work beside her as they made their way through the house.

Annabella did not speak of what was wrong, only making small talk about the weather and asking how Adilah's court situation was.

Another week went by, and there was still no talking, between Annabella and Ibrahim. The bandage was now off of her finger, and the fingernail bed seemed to be healing well. Still, Annabella continued to stay out of his way and avoid him at all cost. While he was out Annabella would sit on the terrace and get some fresh air, and at night she remained in her room not coming out until after Ibrahim had gone to work.

Chapter Three

Life Goes On

On the third week, Annabella had a shower. The shower was relaxing, and afterwards, she dressed casually and put some powder and lipstick on her face. In the mirror, she could see her old self-emerging however, this was a different Annabella, one without feelings for the house or the life she'd been living.

The emptiness and the distant past seemed to control and combine to make her feel more and more despair.

Today she was committed to not letting that happen. Music was what she used to soothe herself, so, she flipped on classical music.

The music was playing and she was resting on her bed, lost in the beauty of the music. Annabella had ignored her phone for several days, not answering her texts or emails and wasn't concerned about any of it over the past two weeks. Suddenly, her very silent phone produced the all too familiar "Ping" sound which meant an email had arrived. Reluctantly, she went to her emails and found an email from Santiago. "Oh God!" Speaking to herself out loud, should I open this or delete it? Curiosity got the best of her again, and she opened and read his email.

"I am sad to see you do not reply to me. There was a part of our life that was magical and filled with love. There was a time we could not wait to speak to each other, I recall how happy we were when we did speak together, about life, our hopes, and dreams. Just let me know you are alright, and you are well. This is enough for me. I love you."

She looks at the email for a few seconds, exhales a large breath and hits the reply key and starts massaging "You are so goddamn stubborn! Don't you know when to give up? We were finished a long time ago, and it was your fault, it was you're doing! Find yourself another woman to love you! I'm sure there are plenty of women, who would grab the chance to be with you.

As for me, I don't have any feelings left. I don't trust any man anymore!"

Annabella thinks for a second and then she hits the send button. The email is on its way to Santiago.

At home, the tension is so thick that you could cut it with a knife. There were Good Morning and Good Night exchanges and few words in between Annabella and Ibrahim. Everything else was quiet. Annabella never knew where he went when he left for work, and she never asked questions when he came home after midnight. Annabella was all too happy for him, especially if there was another woman in his life!

Perhaps, them he would give her a divorce, but, somehow, she could not envision this happening and she resigned herself to the fact that her life was good as it was going to be, with no hope in sight.

She knew full well she was not happy. For years she has not been happy. After several hours of searching the web, she closed the laptop and went and sat on the terrace in her chair.

It was a warm spring day, as she closed her eyes and fell asleep in the warmth of the midday sun and a gentle breeze that soothed her fragmented heart.

Annabella began dreaming about her mother. As in her daydreams, they were back in the little house they used to rent in Paris. Annabella was about eight years old, watching her mother in the kitchen cooking. Mother looked tired often. It was as if all of her energy disappeared from her. Mother appeared much like a wounded angel. In another part of her dream, Annabella watched as her mother took a dress out of a box and placed it across Annabella's fragile body, Mother's smile was radiant. As the dream continued, Mother was holding Annabella's hand while walking down the streets of Paris that Annabella did not recognise.

It was not unusual for Annabella to dream of her mother; she had passed away the year before she met Ibrahim, twenty one years ago.

Once again, the scene changes in her dream. Annabella was standing in front of her mother facing away from her as she combed her long black hair. Glimmers of another time, Annabella was on her bed wide awake even though her mother put her there to sleep an hour before.

Annabella gets out of bed and walks into the living room late at night to find Mother fast asleep on the couch, she looks at her, and she wonders why her Mother always seems so sad and broken.

The room filled with a feeling of sorrow like an invisible mist that came out of the cold walls.

Annabella walks over to her and grabs her by the hand and says. "Mama, Mama!"

Annabella stirs awake, feeling a hand on her hand. Opening her eyes Annabella sees Ibrahim, standing over her.

It wasn't odd that Ibrahim would take a break from work, but, Annabella was a bit disoriented, her lips were dry, she needed to fully wake and get a glass of water or some tea. It's been two months since she and Ibrahim had spoken. Ibrahim releases her hand and stands to look at her; it was apparent to him that Annabella's dreams were causing her some distress.

In a sheepish voice, Ibrahim asks "Would you like me to book a table; we can have dinner at the restaurant tonight?"

Softly, Annabella replies "No, no thank you."

"I thought perhaps it might do us both good. We can go to the hilltop restaurant, where we used to take Fluffy. We can be together and talk." Ibrahim was apologetic; he turned and looked out across the rooftops to the sea in the distance. "I am sincerely sorry about what happened between us." He was still not looking at Annabella.

"It's two months too late for apologies Ibrahim."

"I have decided to go to Paris for a while."

"I see, when?"

"In a month's time." "I have become a stranger to myself, what with losing Fluffy and our argument, my nerves shattered. I am an emotional wreck."

Ibrahim replies "Perhaps you can see the doctor, maybe he can give you something to calm you down. You've always had these mood swings."

"Why don't you see the doctor?" Now Ibrahim was looking into Annabella's eyes; he was genuinely concerned.

"No doctor in the world can give me, what I need, and there is no medicine that can save me." Annabella's voice was quiet and sad.

Ibrahim looks at her in silence for a few seconds, then responds

"If you'll give me the dates, I will make the arrangements for your trip."

"No thank you, I've already made the arrangements." replied Annabella

"When were you going to tell me all this?" Ibrahim's tone had changed, he wasn't pleased.

"I have no strength left in me to argue with you. You have broken me Ibrahim."

"Do you think I wanted all this for us, to be like this? I am trying to keep everything together, the house, the business, it is not easy for me either Annabella."

Annabella stands up and strolls to Fluffy's grave. Standing over the grave, Annabella replies; "I'm heartbroken, and I miss Fluffy."

Ibrahim is searching for some sympathy and replies; "She was my baby too you know!"

"This is not about Fluffy, Ibrahim." she turns and faces Ibrahim and slowly starts walking back, stopping three feet away looking at him, "It's us! Everything is about us, and it is not about the house or the business or Fluffy, it is just about us!" Annabella could feel herself begin to tremble. Her voice audible, but oddly quiet at the same time.

"The restaurant is not doing too well. When you mentioned the money, you gave me for the business, I got upset, and then you attacked me.

I did not want that to happen. Breaking your nail was an accident. For two months you have not spoken to me, and I am the one who has come to you today to talk with you."

Annabella stands there listening without a reply.

Ibrahim continues, "You are my wife, and I try my best to take care of you, to keep a roof over our heads."

Annabella interjects: "You take care of me? We haven't slept in the same bed for ten years, we have not kissed each other good morning or a good night for ten years, not a hug for ten years! Now today, you've mentioned the restaurant, the house, and Fluffy.

Why not a word about me and my concerns? You are my husband. I only came to Morocco because I loved you. I gave you the money because you are my husband and I thought we could somehow work

31

as a team. I never wanted to be in the restaurant every day, but it would have been nice if you had made me feel a part of the business. As for the house, I have asked you, no, I have told you, many times that this house is far too big for us and it would be better to downsize.

I don't care about the money, and I don't care about the house. I cared about the fact that at seventy years old you're killing yourself by working day and night."

"I asked was what was going to happen to me if anything happened to you and you could not give me a simple answer.

After twenty years with you, it only seems appropriate that we could discuss the possibility of me being without you and what would happen.

Instead, you've avoided the conversation, and it's only natural that due to your silence that I would believe that you would give everything to your two sons. You've given them everything, and they show neither of us any respect."

Annabella continues; "Between the weddings and the houses, the cars, and the money, you've spent a fortune on those boys, and they've never even said "Thank you, Papa" Zero appreciation for you and the sacrifices you've made, and I have silently resented!

All the time away from you and I was spent making sure that those two kids were taken care of!"

Ibrahim loudly interjects; "I've told you not to speak about my son's they are none of your business! You've gone too far Annabella!"

Annabella responds with her voice raised; "Gone too far? Ha! Tell me here and now this minute, what is going to happen to me!"

"We will talk about this when you get back from Paris! We need time to calm down, but I don't want you to ever mention my sons to me again! As I've said a million times, they are none of your business!"

Now you are being a bully Ibrahim! Your sons have no character! They are cheap, entitled and lack the respect that so-called- men should have. They are both a disgrace!'

Ibrahim slaps Annabella across the face hard. Her head swings from the impact, her nose begins to bleed, her eyes water. Annabella is holding her face and begins to speak French as she glares at Ibrahim:

" Vous n'avez aucun caractère pour même commencer à comprendre ce qu'est un vrai gentleman, vous êtes une disgrâce au nom sacré du mariage, vous et vos fils, Ibrahim, pouvez tous aller en enfer, en ce qui me concerne"

Annabella is still glaring at Ibrahim; he begins to lift up his hand to slap her again but stops himself. Annabella storms off into the house. It was the first time in twenty years, Ibrahim had ever hit her, and he knew it was an unforgivable sin. Having identified the history, she had with Erol, and how he beat her, Ibrahim knew he'd crossed the line by losing his temper and laying hands on Annabella.

What she said in French was: "You have no character, even to begin to understand what a true gentleman is! You are a disgrace to the sacred name of marriage! You and your sons Ibrahim, can all go to hell as far as I'm concerned!"

Ibrahim is left standing there alone outside. He was wrong; he had no solutions. He sighs deeply, hands in his pockets he stares at the sea.

Annabella is in her bathroom, washing the blood that was flowing from her nose. Looking in the mirror she can see the slap mark on her face. Filling her hands with water she washes the blood from her face. Walking back into her bedroom, she sits on the bed and applies some facial cream to her   slapped red face.

Mind racing, she has the stark realisation that with that one slap, any hope of salvaging her marriage was over. Feeling lost and alone, she was reviewing all the reasons there was no hope for this marriage. Too much time alone without friends or family, her companion Fluffy is gone, there was nothing left to hang onto.

Yet, somehow she felt deep down inside that there was a light at the end of the tunnel that would one day shine for her.

Crying but not feeling desperate, she just wanted to rest. There were two choices, take the sleeping pills and pain pills and not wake up, or not. For some reason she felt a sense of hope, it was unexplainable but, taking her life was not an option. The bad things that were happening lead her to believe that it was now time for good things to happen. Lying on her bed, she closes her eyes, hoping to drift off to some distant magical place where she could escape the cruel realities that had just taken place.

All the recent dreams of her mother had her believing that there was a message amidst the ideas. Annabella had concluded that it was not the hard work that killed her mother's spirit, but rather the sensitivity of her soul and the suffering she endured by living in this cold and cruel world. Mother had been a gentle soul living in a cruel world; the similarities between mother and daughter were remarkable.

Annabella made up her mind that she would start a new life in Paris by leaving Morocco. There needed to be enough money to get her settled in Paris and pay her living expenses for the first six months while she searched for work.

"Work!" Annabella had not worked in years but, was willing to do any work even cleaning homes. She decided to leave at the beginning of August giving her four months to get everything in order without arousing suspicion from Ibrahim.

A list of thing she would have to do without began with not having Botox. The cost of Botox was the same amount as a flight to Paris.

Cancelling her gym membership, cutting back on clothes shopping and cosmetics would be significant savings! Doing the math, she included her personal savings account that held 4000 Euros. Annabella was making an escape plan.

A small apartment in Paris would be less than 1000 euros if she lived on the outskirts of Paris. The plan was taking shape, and any good idea had a backup plan so, she looked into her jewellery box.

Not including her expensive watches, she had roughly 40,000 Euros worth of diamonds, bracelets, rings, earrings etc.

With the list in mind, she would have enough to live for at least one year, by then she would ask Ibrahim for divorce. Hopefully, she would find full-time employment and could rely on herself after a year. Desperate for change now, something had to be done, her sanity was at stake.

Each day she was becoming unhappier and agitated, falling into a depression.

So, it was all settled. Committed to leaving, all she had to do now was play the game of a wife until August and then she would go and start a new life.

Chapter Four

A New Beginning

It was the middle of summer now and sweltering hot in Morocco. A luxury car stopped outside Annabella's house. In the passenger seat is a man named Gabriel Alexandre, from a law firm in Paris that deals in Real Estate.

Gabriel was a sharp dresser; he was apparently successful and perhaps, a bit arrogant. Wearing a black pinstripe suit with a starched white shirt and red tie and black Ferragamo Italian loafers he reeked of success. Gabriel told the driver "Wait for me, I think I will be back sooner than later." Gabriel then steps out of the car carrying a briefcase and walks towards the door of the big beautiful house.

Ringing the bell, he has a moment to look around the grounds; the property is pristine.

After fifteen seconds he rang the bell again.

Annabella opens the door; looking rather smashing. Her hair is brushed, she's wearing a designer outfit, and her makeup is perfect yet understated, showing her true beauty with no signs of injury.

The fingernail that was broken was replaced with a false nail to match her other nails; nothing is out of place.

"Mrs Anabella Amir?" inquired Gabriel with an official voice "Yes." replied Annabella in an uncertain voice.

"Well, at least I am at the right house, speaking with the right person." said Gabriel.

"Why do you want to see me? May I ask who you are?"

"Is it possible to speak inside Mrs Amir?" asked Gabriel politely

"No it's not, my husband is not home, and I do not invite strangers into my house. If wish to tell me something, you may tell me here; otherwise you may leave me your card. I will get my husband to call you, and you can arrange a meeting if it's important. If you are selling something, I am not interested so don't waste my time and your time."

"Mrs Amir, my name is Gabriel Alexandre. I am the founding partner of The Gabriel Law Firm in Paris. Here is my card. We deal in Real Estate. I am not here to sell you anything. I am here at the request of my client to offer you a job."

"A job what are you talking about? I don't have any qualifications for work, not unless its housework." Annabella replied

"Well, my client thinks otherwise," Gabriel smiles warmly

"Who is your client?" asked Annabella

"I'm not at liberty to say who my client is, but I can say this much, this is a legitimate visit on behalf of my client.

I have been instructed to offer you a job for three weeks designing the interior design of his newly acquired estate in the South of France" explained Gabriel. Opening his briefcase he produces the contract, and hands it to Annabella.

"You will be paid twenty-five thousand Euros for your three weeks work all you have to do is to arrange some furniture and where everything will go in the house." explained Gabriel

"Is this a joke?" asked Annabella glancing at the papers for a second.

"No, Mrs Amir, this is not a joke. Let me make things easier for both of us" he puts his hand inside his jacket pocket and produces a cheque book with his company name, and shows her. Next, he produces his wallet and credit cards with his name on them, she looks at them and hands them back. "I cannot show you my passport because it's at "The Desert Sun Hotel" that's where I'm staying. I will be leaving tomorrow night, and I hope that's enough time for you to think things through and give me an answer. It's been nice to meet you Mrs Amir have a beautiful day!"

Gabriel looks at her for a second, turns and leaves the front door, heading to the waiting car.

Annabella follows him with her eyes. Looking at his business card, and the contract, she then turns and closes the door behind her.

In the lounge, Annabella looks at the card, checking her cell phone to search the Internet for "The Desert Sun Hotel" for the phone number and address. Both appear on the website search. Annabella takes a breath and dials; she can hear the number ringing.

Then the receptionist picks up the phone and speaks. "The Desert Sun Hotel Yusuf Speaking, how may I help you?"

"Hello, this is an urgent call, I would like to speak with Gabriel Alexandre please could you please put me through to his room?" Annabella wanted to hear what the response was going to be.

"I'm sorry, but Mr. Alexandre left an hour ago with one of the hotel cars and the driver. Would you like to leave a message? I'd be happy to give it to him when he returns."

"Yes please tell him his secretary rang and ask him to ring me at the office. Thank you!" Annabella ends the call.

Ten minutes later Anabella has a cup of coffee in her hand, a dish of fruit, and her laptop nearby.

Opening her laptop, she searches the Internet for Gabriel Alexandre. A page opens up with over fifty million pages relating to the name from social media profiles, to poets, and writers, she clicked on the image button on the search bar, and a new page opened.

Scrolling down the images she found his picture. Clicking on the photo, a new page opened at "The Gabriel Law Firm Specializing in Real Estate in France Established: 1993." There are photos of Gabriel and his partners on his website as well as a list of all the legal services the firm offers.

A sudden look of realization falls on Annabella's face.

Annabella starts to think. Who is this mysterious person that wants to hire her as an interior designer? Picking up the contract she looks at it from top to bottom, it all seems real.

Thus far everything Gabriel Alexandre said, checks out. Annabella picks up Gabriel's card and dials his cell number.

The Desert Sun Hotel is a Five Star Luxury Hotel that caters to the wealthy and upper middle class who want a quiet break away from it all and to play a few rounds of golf, in the nearby Palms Golf Resort.

Annabella enters into the foyer. She is immaculately dressed in a long summer dress wearing high heels, carrying her handbag. Gabriel is waiting for her sitting in the lobby with his briefcase on the table and a cup of coffee in front of him. As Annabella approaches, Gabriel sees her, gets to his feet, and greets her.

"Thank you for agreeing to meet me, Mrs. Amir!"

The two shook hands. Gabriel waits for Annabella to take a seat, he holds the chair out for her, Annabella smiles and sits across from Gabriel. "Please call me Annabella."

Gabriel sits down, "Annabella is a beautiful name. May I offer you refreshment or perhaps some lunch, while we chat?"

"No thank you." replied Annabella

"Curious thing happened yesterday, my secretary rang me to ring her at the office. Gabriel was smiling as he looked at Annabella.

"Stop fencing with me Mr. Alexandre, you knew very well it was me."

"I know very well because my secretary has my cell number and would ring me directly." Gabriel continued "It is my job to research people so I know a bit about you.

You were born in Holland to a low-income family. Your father left when you were five years old. Your mother worked hard to raise you as a single parent.

You moved to Paris when you were seven years old and then when you were eighteen years old you became a fashion model… a very successful one if I may add. You met your first husband and got married. He was a wealthy businessman. You gave up modelling after you are married." As Gabriel was about to continue with Annabella's history, she interrupts him.

"I am aware of my history Mr. Alexandre. Can we get to the point, please?"

There a few seconds of silence while Gabriel composes himself.

"There is nothing to add, everything is in the contract."

Annabella gave Gabriel a suspicious look and replied; "You will not tell me who "The Mystery Employer" is and why he or she has chosen to employ me?"

Gabriel responded with a stern look on his face leaning forward towards Annabella;

"I can tell you this much in confidence, he, or she, is real, and he or she is a good person, with a great deal of wealth. I will also tell you this but, strictly off the record, you will get to meet him, or her before the three weeks are over and you can ask him or her all the questions you want. No doubt he or she will accommodate you with all the answers to all your questions. That's all I can say."

Gabriel leans back to his more comfortable position

"I will not be able to travel for at least a month." said Annabella with an undertone of urgency in her voice.

"That's not a problem." said Gabriel with a reassuring voice.

"And at the end of three weeks, I will be paid twenty-five thousand Euros? Is this correct?"

"No" replied Gabriel "You will be paid fifteen thousand Euros when you sign the contract, and the balance when the job is completed, in three weeks."

"I can explain the holiday to Paris to my husband, but how do I explain the twenty-five thousand Euros?" Gabriel leans forward and looks at her for a long moment.

"If you have a happy marriage, then go home and tell your husband you have found work for three weeks. If not, then don't tell him."

"My marriage is a mess really, and I am thinking of filing for divorce. I want to live in France again. Perhaps, in Paris in the future."

"My firm can assist you in your divorce if you decide that is what you wish." Gabriel opens his wallet and produces a credit card.

"Here, take this." Annabella looks at him as if to say, "What is this?"

"I have opened an account with fifteen thousand Euros in it. By the time your flight date arrives, you can withdraw the money.

I will give you the pin number when you leave the hotel feel free to look into it if it makes you comfortable."

Annabella takes the card and looks at it for a second. "What if I take the money and don't show up?"

Gabriel looks at her for a second and smiles.

"I believe that not only will you show up, but you will accomplish your commission. Further, your rewards might not be in the twenty-five thousand Euros you will be earning in the process.

Your reward and riches might come in the form of answers that you will get when this task is all over with." "Should you decide not to honour your end of the contract, I have been instructed to tell you to keep the money."

Handing her the contract, Gabriel continues, "If you read the contracts now, you'll see there is no mention of the fifteen thousand Euros, it only mentions ten thousand."

Annabella takes the contracts, Gabriel says. "You may examine them now if you wish."

Annabella quickly reads the first page and skips to the last which requires her signature. Gabriel hands her his pen and Annabella signs the contract.

Gabriel asks "Could you please give me your email address so that my secretary can handle your flight arrangements?" Annabella takes a piece of paper from her handbag writes down the email address and puts it on the contract and slides the contract over to Gabriel.

"Thank you, Annabella. I am leaving tonight for Paris. Tomorrow, I will instruct my secretary to book a flight for you for a month's time and a return to Morocco.

You will find your tickets in your email. Please print it off before your departure. Should you need anything, please don't hesitate to call me. I believe you have my cell number, it's on my business card."

Gabriel picks up the credit card from the table and hands it over to Annabella with a warm smile on his face. Annabella takes the card and places it in her wallet.

"Well, this concludes our meeting. I think a round of golf will help me kill a few hours and help me to relax before I return back to Paris. Golf always helps me think."

"Mr. Alexandre, I want to say Thank You, and I'd like to apologize for being rude to you when you arrived at my home.

My apology is sincere. I had no idea who you were. I thought that perhaps, you were somehow involved with my husband."

"Please, call me Gabriel. No need for an apology, you did not offend me. Oh, I almost forgot, I must give you the pin for the card."

Annabella watches as Gabriel jots down the code on a small piece of paper and hands it to her. Annabella places the piece of paper in her wallet next to the card.

"I'll see you in a month in Paris. If you'll excuse me, I have a golf round I need to get in before supper. Gabriel slides the contract into his briefcase, extending his hand to Annabella. They shake hands and smile at each other.

"Thank you, Gabriel; I will see you in Paris at your office, in a month."

With a smile on her face, Annabella walks towards the foyer of the hotel. Gabriel watches her as she leaves and he heads to the receptionist. Handing her the briefcase, he asks; "Could you please keep this safe for me?" The receptionist replied; "Yes Sir, I'd be happy to."

Chapter Five

Mysterious Journey

Annabella heads to a bank. Not her bank, but one where she is not known and waits in line at the ATM. Annabella removes the card from her wallet and approaches the machine. Sliding the card into the device, she puts the code in when prompted. The machine asks her what she'd like to do.

Her curiosity was evident; she needed to verify that there was money in the account. Annabella chooses a balance inquiry and indeed there on the screen was 15,000 Euros.

That was all the verification she needed. Withdrawing the card, she returned it to her wallet and left the bank.

One hour later, in her bedroom, Annabella takes the photo of her and Fluffy from the side table and opens the back of it placing the card flat behind the picture. Putting the back onto the frame, she sets the frame in its original spot.

Sitting on the bed, thinking to herself how much she wishes that her companion was still with her, she truly missed Fluffy.

Feeling emotional, after the day, and the past few months, her tears fell as she thought about how fragile she was, how tired she was of suffering.

Curling up on her bed, she thought about the day and her meeting with Gabriel. Everything was strangely serendipitous. Wondering whom the "Mystery Person" was, allowed her to shift gears in her head and the tears stopped. Maybe God was listening?

The next day, Annabella, and Adilah, were working together to clean the house.

Annabella's mind was in Paris. Keeping her phone next to her, at all times in anticipation of the incoming email from Gabriel's secretary.

While dusting her thoughts wandered again to the "Mystery Person" Who was this person? She knew many models in Paris when she was modelling, and some of them went on to marry influential people. Perhaps, it was one of them?

After considering the models, she ruled them out. It was possible that her first husband Renee was behind this. Maybe after all this time, his guilt caught up with him about leaving her with nothing and this was his way of making that up to her.

There were a half a dozen possibilities and people, but, one by one she crossed them off her mental list. Even a brief thought of Santiago, but no, an instant NO!

That night while in bed Annabella, started to think about her life. How she could have made the mistakes that she had made? How she could never find the kind of love she dreamt about, a love that fairy tales were made of. She longed for never-ending tenderness, a hero, a knight in shining armour.

Why hadn't she found someone who would take care of her emotionally, and make the little girl in her soul calmer while still respecting the woman she was?

Dreams, all dreams that did not come true. Annabella realized that she had been compromising and settling for people that would never fulfil her desires or share the same thoughts.

Thinking about the twenty-five thousand Euros, she envisioned it as her "ticket out" of her loveless marriage and back to Paris where she felt at home.

Was it possible this was a practical joke or a pack of lies created to defeat her and wound her further, or was this real and legitimate?

This must be real, or why would someone fly all the way from Paris with a contract that was legal and binding, give her access to a credit card and a bank account with money already in it?

Annabella has always thought so negatively about the possibility that her dreams could one day come true. Knowing she must change her thoughts and that, in and of itself was going to create some challenges for her.

Sleepy and tired of thinking so hard, questioning everything, she closed her eyes and went to sleep.

It was morning, and the ping from her phone woke Annabella. She opened her eyes gently and picked up the phone and went to her emails.

Located in the "Spam" folder was an email from Gabriel. Annabella sits up and opens the email.

"Gabriel" was in the subject heading along with; "Per our conversation, tickets and instructions as promised." There were attachments, which she quickly opened.

In the attachment were two tickets, one to Paris and the return to, Tangier Lbn Battouta Airport, named after "Lbn battouta" (1304-1368) a Moroccan traveller who was born in Tangier, To Paris Orly Airport. The body of the letter was from Gabriel's secretary.

"Dear Annabella,

It is my pleasure to introduce myself.

I am Severine. I will be your liaison between Mr. Alexandre, and yourself.

I do hope this message reaches you in good health and happy spirits!

In the attachments, you will find your two tickets, your departure from Morocco to Paris and your return to Morocco."

Please feel free to contact me if you have any questions. I am happy to assist you."

Sincerely,

Severine"

The law firms heading, telephone number and address in central Paris were included.

The departure ticket was dated for a month away. Annabella felt an uncertain excitement rush through her body as she continued to wonder who this "Mystery Man or Woman" could be that wants her to design the interior of their home. The question remains in her mind continuously.

She decided to keep the tickets in her email until it was the day before her departure.

There was no need to have to hide them from Ibrahim, nor did she want to discuss it with him with the volatility so high. No longer could she stand to be in the same room with him, to argue or suffer further interrogation.

Her mind was made up; she would not tell him until just before her departure.

The argument has caused a hard shell of resentment and Annabella was not about to let down her guard. It was clear that Ibrahim would never consider her feelings, nor would he be forthcoming about his intentions regarding her future should something happen to him.

If she was being honest with herself, she'd known it was over between them for years. Their life was a farce.

Annabella saves Severine's email address into her contact list.

Composing a letter was the next step in her new adventure, Annabella was excited to respond

"Dear Severine,

Thank you for the email. I'm happy to make your acquaintance!

If you would be so kind as to inform Gabriel, that I will be there on the arrival date we agreed upon, I would be very grateful.

It would be lovely to see photos of the house inside and out if you have them. I'd love to have an idea of what I will be working on so that I can put together some ideas before my arrival.

Kindest regards,

Annabella"

The email is then sent off to Severine.

Logging out of her email, Annabella becomes animated. Jumping out of bed, she heads to the bathroom, stopping by her closet to gather some clothing before getting into a quick shower.

In the mirror, she quickly brushes her teeth, moisturizes her face immediately, and quickly gets dressed. Everything has quickness about her after the email.

Taking her laptop into the kitchen, she makes some coffee.

Ibrahim had already gone to work. She is free to turn on her laptop while drinking her coffee. Searching the Internet, she begins searching houses for sale in the south of France that have interior photos.

Annabella is curious to see how they are decorated. Each property she looks at looks like something from a fairy tale. Such beautiful rooms and lush gardens and lush landscaping and fountains. Some of them had lavish swimming pools and Koi ponds.

Annabella is lost in a million thoughts and ideas, lost in the photos.

This was a beautiful escape from the emotional prison, she felt she'd lived her whole life.

A safe place for her to take her soul on a journey into what could be, "a future of freedom." A place to relax and energize, recharge her spiritual batteries and mend her broken heart.

Looking at all of these photos, Annabella asked herself if all of these lavish homes, extravagant decorations, expensive art and huge mortgages ever made anyone truly happy? This thought would follow her. Annabella had always questioned the idea that money was either; "The key to happiness," or "The root of all evil."

The following morning Annabella is walking towards the kitchen carrying her phone.

Still looking and feeling a bit dazed from the day before, she noticed her reflection in the hall mirror; no slap mark was evident. She continues walking until she reaches the kitchen. Time for some coffee and perhaps some toast for breakfast.

Picking up the remote control for the TV she switches it on, there is an inspirational program on called; "Think of Today" A woman is giving an inspirational talk from the studio of how important it is to look upon today.

TV announcer; "Look upon today as a day that knows all your secrets. Look upon today, like a flake of the thousand days that have come and gone in your life, that has broken your heart and spirit that brought you to your knees."

Annabella walks over, grabs the kettle, fills the kettle up, and switches it on while still listening to the presenter.

"Look upon today, as a fragment of the thousand days, that have nurtured you, healed you, protected you, loved you, and gave you hope and faith. Look upon today, as a memory bank where you can withdraw past dreams, happier times, treasured moments that have enriched your life."

Annabella prepares a cup, puts a teaspoon of coffee in, one sugar and she continues to watch TV.

"The loves that had come and gone in your life were a gift. Look upon today as a miracle. When you step outside of your house into the street, you are in an open space on a planet spinning in space, and you will not fall off into the great universe."

Annabella continues to listen

"Look upon today as a blessing that you share your feelings with every living person, every animal, and every plant on the planet that is constantly breaking and healing in life."

"What blessing is this woman talking about?" thinks Annabella

"Look upon this day, as your salvation, your forgiveness towards yourself, towards others, and realize that all you have and all that you will ever have, is your own life. How you treat others and what you contribute towards the human race is what matters. Look to this day, as a day that knows of your secrets."

Annabella looks disappointed she mutes the sound on the TV, just then her phone rings. Looking at the phone, she does not recognize the number but answers it.

"Hello"

"Hello, Annabella Amir?"

"Yes"

"This is Severine Mr. Alexandre's secretary calling from Paris."

"Oh Hi, how are you?" asked Annabella excitedly

"I'm very well, thank you Mrs. Amir.

I am just calling to inform you, that the pictures you have requested have been sent to your email, but I wanted to clarify one thing. Your work will not involve the main house. There is a barn close to the house that has been converted into a guest house. You will be designing that from scratch, the reason for this is that the house was bought as it was.

Our client has not decided to do the main house at the moment. All the details and pictures are in the email I have just sent you."

"I look forward to meeting you when you arrive in Paris if you need any other additional information, please don't hesitate to email me or call me."

"Thank you so much for your phone call Severine, I have not had time to check my emails.

I will look now. I look forward to meeting you in person when I arrive in Paris."

Annabella's voice was happy and excited at the same time.

"My pleasure Mrs. Amir, I look forward to seeing you too!

"Have a lovely day!"

"Same to you Severine!"

Annabella hung up the phone feeling lighter than she could remember for a very long time. It felt like she had a huge weight taken from her shoulders. With a smile on her face and a positive perspective, she opened her email to view the photos and read the property descriptions.

This was a good day!

The home was sold furnished. Central living accommodation had a vaulted salon, small kitchen, professional kitchen, large salon with fireplace, dining room, reception room, sauna, massage room, eight elegant bedroom suites, a large Penthouse apartment that has a living room with a fireplace, reception room, TV room, bedroom with bathroom and dressing room. The grounds are enchanting! There was a Caretakers cottage and forty-acre grounds. A terrace, patio, swimming pool, Jacuzzi, meadows, and pastures. One hundred ten acres non-adjoining land.

Outbuildings: Stables, Reception rooms, as well as eight-bedroom suites and a total of ten bathrooms.

Annabella now understood why she had only been hired for three weeks. If it had been the house, it would have taken a year!

A converted barn would be very manageable for Annabella and an opportunity to be back in France doing something she truly enjoyed while getting paid handsomely!

This was nothing short of a blessing from the Universe! Annabella was not just excited. She was giddy inside! A feeling long forgotten, but, very welcomed indeed!

Annabella forgot all about the incident the day before and was feeling energized after the phone call, the photos, and all of the positive things that could come from this journey.

The photos of the barn were rather beautiful. There were brown wooden beams in the ceiling of the living room with large chandeliers hanging from the beams.

The fireplace was white and about six-foot-high, big enough to stand in. There were three bedroom suites in total, one on the main floor, the other two were upstairs giving privacy for guests with a seating area between the upper suites.

Annabella begins to focus on converted barns for inspiration. Searching the Internet, she finds converted barns in France. All of the images of barns had one thing in common that she already knew they would, they all had wooden beams on the inside of the main room and upper part of the barn.

So many beautiful pictures and floor plans, so many types of furniture to choose from and fixtures for the lighting and bathrooms. The list was mounting in her   head.

She decided she would start a list and keep it on her phone or send the links to herself of the websites that she could go to once she knew what her budget would be for this project.

This was to be a way to show her talent in design. She had designed and decorated many friend's homes and apartments for free, but now she about to be paid for making a home feel comfortable and inviting.

None of the houses she made into homes for friends were beautiful or majestic as the main *chateau*. Annabella was going to apply all her knowledge into making the barn on the estate into a home for someone.

Thinking of France and the mountain air was so refreshing. It was as if, a "New Life" was waiting for her in France and the light inside of her was beginning to burn once more.

Lifting her head from her laptop, she notices the television is still on. There were two women and one man seated around a table.

The program was geared towards books and authors. The woman in the middle was holding a book entitled; "Emotional Rhapsody."

Un-muting the television Annabella hears,

"If you believe in the magic of love, if you believe in fairy-tale endings, here is a book that has sold one hundred million copies in three years. The book has been named as "The Greatest Love Story of The Twenty-First Century!" The true mystery about this book is who wrote it."

"The author is listed as Ivan Baranowski. Many of the experts believe that this is not the real name of the author.

Reports coming out of Hollywood are saying that there is a "Ten Million Dollar Deal" being negotiated to make this book into a "Fairy Tale Classic Love Story Film   for the big screen."

Annabella looks at the screen for a second. She is not remotely interested in what they are saying about the book; she takes the remote control and switches off the TV.

Chapter Six

Arriving in Paris

Pierre is standing near the arrivals, a tall man around forty years old, dressed in a smart black suit with white shirt and black tie, holding up a small board with the name Annabella Amir written on it.

He watches the sea of people coming through, some greeted by family and friends, pulling their suitcases behind them, at last Annabella comes through the arrivals, and after a few steps she stops to look around her.

There she sees Pierre, holding the board with her name on it. At the same time Pierre sees Annabella and knows it is her. They walk towards each other and meet

"Mrs. Amir my name is Pierre, he says with a smile, I am here to collect you and escort you to Gabriel's law firm."

Annabella responded with a half-smile; "Thank you Pierre."

"Please allow me," said Pierre taking, the handle of the suitcase from Annabella, they begin their way out of the airport toward the car.

After ten minutes, Annabella is seated in the back seat of a black Mercedes.

Classical music is playing on the radio that can hardly be heard, so as not to disturb Annabella, she is looking out the window at the buildings and houses as they are whisked by her leaving them behind the car as they travel along, a sense of calm has come over her.

Annabella was feeling like she was home now.

"Do you know Mr. Alexandre well?"

"You mean Gabriel? Yes, I know him very well and his wife Stephanie and their two children, as well as both sides of their family." said Pierre proudly.

"How did you meet him?" Annabella asked inquisitively.

"I met him under crazy circumstances. I was only twenty years old, I had married the girl of my dreams, and she became pregnant. I was without a job and had no money or prospects. I had to provide a roof over my wife and family. I was desperate. I borrowed some money, and bought two ounces of marijuana to sell to make some money.

As luck would have it, I got caught! I was in big trouble. I owed money to the dealer, and now I was in trouble with the law. I felt so ashamed, when I was charged with "Possession with Intent to Distribute!"

"I was devastated, I had no idea how it would turn out because it was my first offence, and I was a bit naïve. I was released, to appear in court on a specific day.

Gabriel's law firm was expanding into Criminal Defence and as luck would have it and I had an interview with him.

I told him everything. I felt so ashamed, and I felt I let my wife down and myself down.

I let my family and friends down. It was the lowest point of my life.

Gabriel assigned a new criminal lawyer from his office to me, but the real help and surprise would come at the trial.

I plead guilty to my crime and in my defence; the lawyer from Gabriel's firm came forward and stated I was working for him as a driver, effective immediately.

The judge showed me sympathy my first offence and all he did was asked me to do was to keep the peace for one year not to get into any more trouble.

When my wife and I came out of the court building, I sat on the stairs and I cried like a baby. My wife was smiling and crying at the same time."

Clearly Pierre was still emotional when he spoke about the generosity shown to him by Gabriel.

Annabella was very touched and replied;

"It's a beautiful story Pierre. Thank you for being so candid with me."

"Can you imagine how I felt in that courtroom, I thought I was going to prison, I wondered who would look after my wife and child."

I felt so blessed and fortunate, as though there was some "Divine Universal Intervention."

"It must have been hell for you." said Annabella, searching for a reply.

"Hell!" It was the closest thing to death that I had ever experienced in all my life. In that courtroom, I died spiritually, physically, mentally, only to be reborn a better person having come out of there.

How can you ever repay someone like Gabriel for what he has done for me?"

Pierre's face was showing signs of emotions that Annabella was not exposed to in the company of a man.

"Perhaps, one way of showing and paying him back, is showing him your worth, your loyalty your trust as a person." Replied Annabella

"My children call him Uncle Gabriel, his wife Stephanie is Auntie Stephanie, their children looks upon my two children like brothers.

He is an older brother to me and an inspiration to me and my family. Gabriel has never spoken about that incident to me, my wife, and children.

Never over the past twenty years that I've been working for him." There was so much pride and respect in Pierre's voice that it was obvious the two were as close as brothers with a mutual reciprocal respect.

A short silence and then with an upbeat voice Pierre announces: "We've arrived!"

Annabella looks out the window to the office building that is three stories high with beautiful big writing as a sign that reads, "The Gabriel et ses partenaires Cabinet d'avocats"

Annabella exits the car and enters the law firm with Pierre. The office is modern and many offices with big glass enclosures to serve as offices for the firm's partners.

At the reception desk Pierre addresses the woman behind the desk with a very familiar and warm, "Hello Severine!

Would you please inform Gabriel that Mrs. Amir has arrived?"

"It's a pleasure to meet you Mrs. Amir, please have a seat; Gabriel will be with you shortly. May I offer you a cup of tea or coffee, perhaps, a sparkling water?"

Annabella relies "No Thank you Severine, kind of you to ask."

Severine starts walking towards Gabriel office Annabella cannot help but notice her long beautiful legs, her rounded bottom, and her elegant walk. She opens the door slightly and informs Gabriel of Annabella's arrival. A moment later she was back at her desk looking at both Pierre and Annabella and states; "He will be with you in just a few moments."

As promised, Gabriel appears after a few seconds. Gabriel came out of his office, holding what looks like a book in a brown wrapping, he stops at Annabella and Pierre

"Welcome Annabella, I hope you had a pleasant flight."

"Yes, thank you!" replied Annabella, with a smile

Gabriel turns to Severine, "If anyone calls for me please tell them

I am out of the office for at most one hour."

"Annabella, would you please give your passport to Pierre he will check you into the hotel and bring your luggage to your room for you."

Annabella hands her passport to Pierre, and Pierre walks away leaving the building.

"Now it's time to meet "The Real Boss." said Gabriel is leaning towards Annabella as if he was sharing a secret.

"I thought you were the boss." said Annabella surprised. They walk towards the door to leave the building.

"If only I was "The Real Boss!" Anabella, you haven't spent a penny from the credit card I gave you."

"Have you been checking up on me, Mr. Alexandre?" asked Annabella

"It is my job. I check up on everybody. I am not just a lawyer you know; I am a great sleuth, a great detective like Hercule Poirot. I am sure he was French and he emigrated to Belgium." continued Gabriel, with a broad smile on his face as he opened the door for Annabella to leave the building.

Arriving at "The Boulevard de la Tour-Maubourg" five-star hotel

Gabriel and Annabella enter. The hotel is very to the Eiffel Tower, at the reception desk Pierre is checking Annabella into the hotel.

Gabriel and Annabella walk into the dining room that is on to the side of the reception area. Seated at one of the tables is Stephanie Gabriel wife. Gabriel introduces his wife to Annabella.

"Darling this is Annabella, Annabella, my darling wife Stephanie "The Real Boss" who takes care of my life, our sons, our home, and she is an accountant, a lawyer at the shops, and the judge that settles disputes among family and friends."

Annabella admires the love and the teasing that is going on between them.

"Nice to meet you Annabella please have a seat." said Stephanie warmly

"Nice to meet you Stephanie." Annabella replied, settling down on the seat across from her.

Gabriel kisses Stephanie on the cheek, then he hands her the book, wrapped up in paper. They are very much in love, you can't help but notice the way they touch each other and look at each other.

"Gabriel what have you done that you are furnishing my ego with so many compliments?"

"I have taken the liberty to organize a tour guide for the two of you for tonight Annabella." said Gabriel with a smile. Annabella looks at Gabriel, he looks at Annabella and then indicating with his eyes towards and down at Stephanie.

"I'll see you girls later! Have a great tour. Annabella, you're in great hands!" said Gabriel as he leans down he kisses Stephanie on the head. "Thank you darling" Stephanie replied with a deep loving smile.

Gabriel leaves the restaurant to go back to work.

Pierre approaches the table

"You are booked in Mrs. Amir. The porter took your luggage to your room and you can pick up the key at the reception desk when you are ready.

Are you two ladies enjoying your evening?" asked Pierre politely.

"Thank you Pierre" replied Annabella humbly.

"Stephanie, if you need me to shuttle you girls around on your tour this evening, call me please."

"We will be fine my darling."

Pierre bows his head slightly at Stephanie, then smiles at Annabella and leaves the table.

Stephanie and Annabella look   at each other for a second;

"Don't worry, it was my idea." explains Stephanie

"Thank You Stephanie. This is so very kind of you!" replied Annabella

"Last night, I heard Gabriel talking with a client on the phone, the client whoever he or she was, obviously concerned that you should not be left alone since you are in Paris.

Anyway, Gabriel assured the person he was talking with not to worry that you'd be safe and looked after if you needed anything!"

"That's when I realized that no woman should be left alone in a city. So, I offered to be a guide for a few hours." said Stephanie with a full heart and a warm and engaging smile.

"If you prefer to be alone, I totally understand and can leave after the meal." said Stephanie in the hopes that she did not make a mistake.

"Thank you, Stephanie, I'd love to spend a few hours with you on the town. I used to live here many years ago." said Annabella in a sad voice that was detected by Stephanie

Just then the waiter came to the table, Stephanie and the waiter knew one another.

"Would you like to see the menu Mrs. Alexandre?" asked Andrea the waiter

"I will have the usual Andrea please, but perhaps Annabella will like something from the menu. I am having a Caesar salad" said Stephanie looking at Annabella.

"I will have the same, please." replied Annabella looking at the Andrea.

"May I get you ladies a drink?" asked Andrea

"We are in Paris, France! Bring us a bottle of champagne please Andrea!" Stephanie said with a smile. Andrea nods to her and walks off.

"Champagne?" questioned Annabella

"A celebration that we met in life! It's only crushed grapes that have been left abandoned to be fermented several times. They then add a little sugar cane and brandy to get the desired taste and serve it to us as "Champagne." said Stephanie with a smile

"It sounds a little like my life, crushed and left aside and yet served as a living corpse to the world." replied Annabella dismally and philosophically explained.

"We are all crushed grapes, and crushed beautiful rose petals, in the streets of memories where once youth and hope wandered. Everything has a price in life, and the price we pay is either that we are happy or sad, that's the only currency life issues." Stephanie looks seriously at Annabella for a second "Yes" replied Annabella in sad broken voice

"Did you know in the early days of Champagne making, between twenty and ninety percent of the bottles exploded?" Stephanie said amusingly

"Oh my God! I hope no one was killed with all the explosions going off in the cellars!"

I hate to think that we are drinking this beautiful drink today at the expense of some innocent man who lost his life, trying to make a living to support his family."

"There is always that possibility, the workers adopted wearing iron face masks for protection, when walking through the Champagne cellars."

Andrea arrives at the table with a bottle of Champagne in a bucket and two glasses in his hand.

He places the bucket on the table, and he fills the glasses up and places them gently in front of the two ladies.

"Thank you, Andrea."

"My pleasure! Enjoy ladies!"

"What shall we drink to?"

"Friendship?"

"Friendship it is!" said Stephanie raising her glass and meeting Annabella's glass in mid-air across the table. They both take a sip and lower their glasses.

Stephanie looks at the brown wrapped object that looks like a book that Gabriel had given this package to Stephanie and Annabella had not forgotten it, nor did the thought leave her mind that it may have something to do with her.

Stephanie started to unravel the paper wrapping.

Finally, the book is revealed, Stephanie reads the title of the book aloud.

"Emotional Rhapsody" Written by Ivan Baranowski

"Have you read it?"

"No, I don't read much these days."

"Well, I recommend you read this when you get a chance. It is supposed to be, "One of the Greatest Love Story's" written in the past hundred years! So "they" claim. I will deliver my verdict when I have finished it!"

"I wonder where all that inspiration of love came from, to a man like Ivan Baranowski?" Annabella asked with a curiosity.

"I don't know, maybe he fell in love with someone and his heart was broken. Perhaps, an unrequited love? What we do know so far, is that no one knows who this man is!"

He is obviously Russian with a name like Ivan Baranowski; however, no one knows anything about him except that he has sold one hundred million copies of the book since it was published three years ago."

"Oh my god!" gasps Annabella "Can you imagine selling one hundred million copies of a book?"

"It's been translated into so many languages, and now there is talk of film rights being negotiated for millions of dollars, with a well-known Hollywood studio.

Apparently, they are talking about ten million dollars just for the rights of the film as well as a percentage of the film. Not only is he is a brilliant writer, but he is a shrewd businessman as well!"

"Maybe he is happily married and he wants to remain anonymous." Annabella, trying to sway Stephanie in another direction of thought.

"Who knows?" "It might not even be his real name, he might not even be a man, and it could be a woman using a man's name!"

Stephanie raises her eyebrow.

Andrea brings over the two plates of Caesar Salad and places them in front of them.

"Is there anything else I can get you?"

"No thank you, Andrea" said Stephanie politely.

Annabella, changing the subject as she picks up her fork to eat.

"May I ask you something?" she said in a more serious tone of voice

"Sure, of course!" replied Stephanie as she began her first bite of food.

"Did you know, or did you happen to hear, if it was a man or a woman talking with Gabriel?

"No, I only heard Gabriel's reply that you were here alone in Paris. I gathered that the person on the other end of the phone was concerned for your safety. Whoever it was, I could not hear their voice. Gabriel was standing on the other side of the room."

"Can I tell you something?" asked Annabella

"No, not unless you tell me a tragedy, that has a good blessed ending. If you tell me something, that is a tragedy that has no blessed ending then you are visiting the graveyard of broken dreams in your soul."

"What is this something you want to tell me?" asked Stephanie, sipping her champagne.

"I have been commissioned to do interior design in a converted barn part of an Estate in the South of France. I don't know who I am supposed to be working for, and I am trying to find out."

"Well, I cannot help you there.

I can assure you that after thirty years of marriage to Gabriel, I can say with full confidence he has given his word to this person that you should not know who he or she is. Gabriel will not break that oath, not even if it's me that is asking him."

"I wonder if this story of mine will have a blessed ending. I don't even know why I agreed to take on the commission not knowing who I am working for."

"Personally speaking, I think whoever employed you to design this converted barn, will let you know who they are when the time is right, but then again, they may not.

I have a feeling something beautiful is going to happen in your life." said Stephanie is looking, straight into Annabella eyes

"Why do you say that?"

"I don't say that, you say that, with the look in your eyes, and the tone of your voice, and the vibration of your soul." said Stephanie with confidence.

"Oh my god, what are you a psychic?" asked Annabella with astonishment

"No!" replied Stephanie. "I am a middle age woman having champagne and salad with a new friend I've just met." They both smile and continue eating.

Chapter Seven

Revisiting the Past

Annabella and Stephanie have left the restaurant and are walking along the River Seine. It is a warm Paris evening; the water reflects the lights along the walkway. The river boats are filled with tourists. The boats are also adorned in lights and give one the feeling of romance seeing Paris at night.

"What you said at the table earlier was true." said Annabella in a sad voice.

Stephanie looks at her for a second anticipating that she was about to hear something personal.

"I have been married for the past twenty years. In fact, we got married right here in Paris. We were happy here, and then we moved to Morocco." Annabella's tone of voice gave away an underlying truth.

"How long have you been unhappy Annabella?"

"My marriage ended ten years ago. The only thing that keeps it legal is a piece of paper and that does not serve either of us any longer I'm afraid."

"I am sorry to hear that."

"My definition of "emotional torture" is being married to someone for twenty years, living separate lives. The past ten years have been totally empty, no intimacy, separate rooms, very little conversation, not sharing dreams."

"We are strangers to each other that pass each other in the kitchen or on the terrace. When necessary, we attend social functions as a couple, but that ends at the end of each event. Thank God we no longer have to socialize as we did in the first ten years we were married.

I used to have a dog named Fluffy; she was my best friend and constant companion. I was devastated when she passed away six months ago."

"I am deeply sorry for you Annabella; I don't know what to say."

"There's nothing to say. Five years ago, I started talking with a guy on the internet. It was all rather harmless. His name is Santiago he lives in London. We grew closer the more we spoke, which was every day, sometimes for hours at a time. I fell madly in love with him and he fell in love with me."

"Santiago, is he still in love with you?" asked Stephanie in anticipation

"Yes! Madly in love with me. He is such a romantic, very tender hearted and loving. He's sent me such beautiful emails and text messages. He has Je ne sais quoi.

"I poured out my soul to him. I told him all about my life, my disappointments, my heartbreaks, my relationships, my philosophies about life, everything. He knew things about me that even my own husband does not know about me. For the first time in my life I felt complete as a woman.

I felt alive because he knew how to love me as I have always dreamt of being loved. It was dreamlike perfect while it lasted."

"Annabella, I am not known for patience when someone is telling me a love story so please don't keep me in suspense, what happened to you both?"

"Four years ago, in the middle of all this madness, after being in love with each other for a year I decided to come to Paris. Within one week I was on the plane, I asked him to meet me here. I was so excited and in love, but he never came to meet me. After that I gave up all hope on love." Annabella was clearly emotional.

"Did he give you an explanation as to why he never came to meet you in Paris? Sorry, I am a sucker for love stories." shrugging her shoulders, said Stephanie with a twinkle in her eye.

"He said, "It was too soon and it was impossible for him to be in Paris with me."

"What a cheap excuse! A whole year, and he says, 'It's too soon?" In my opinion, this qualifies him for "The Bum of the Decade Oscar!"

"No, I realized after it was too late, the real reason. I finished everything four years ago.

He writes to me now and then asking if I'm ok and telling me he wants to speak with me but I always scorn him."

"Well? What was the reason? Why didn't he come and meet you? Please don't tell me he is married?"

"No, he is not married. I came to the conclusion that he couldn't afford the trip to Paris to meet me."

"Annabella, what are you telling me?" asked Stephanie very perplexed

"I am saying that he is poor, he lives in a rented room, getting by from day to day." explained Annabella with reflections of the past distant days.

Stephanie stops walking and grabs Annabella by the arm they both stop they look at each other

"Annabella, I know you have lost your marriage, but have you lost your mind also?"

"What are you talking about?"

Stephanie explains with an emotional look in her eyes

"You had the richest men in the world in your life, and you say he was poor?"

"What are you talking about?" asked innocently Annabella

"To be in love, is to be alive with life. You said it yourself just now. To be in love is the magic of life; it is the discovery of the holy grail of life. It is the magic of being in love with a person that loves you in the same way as you love them, and if you have that, you have everything in life!"

"Maybe so, but it's too late now." insisted Annabella,

"Why is he dead?"

"No, he is not dead! It's been four years since I finished with him and he still writes to me.

I do not encourage him. Sometimes I write a few lines in reply, just to let him know I am still alive even without him! It's strange, because you are the first person I have told this part of my life too.

 The funny thing is I feel so much better having finally shared this with you!"

"Don't mention it; I have that effect on people! I'm not sure why people are so comfortable around me but, please know I will keep anything we share in confidence and that you can trust me."

"There is that certain, je ne sais quoi, I felt comfortable the first moment we met."

"I felt that certain, je ne sais quoi about you as well Annabella. I hope we can become good friends. I do not trust people easily, but those who have my trust, can rely on me. I will always stand by you, through thick and thin."

This was music to Annabella's ears.

"I am the same; I have one or two close friends. In Morocco, I have only acquaintances. The lifestyle and the mind-set are very different to mine."

"I can understand that! Now, I must ask the immortal question!" Annabella had no idea what an "immortal question" was.

"Are you still in love with Santiago?"

Stephanie was trying to be empathetic and she gave Annabella a few seconds to ponder the question before either of them continued.

"I can tell you this much, he kept all our conversations we had from the very start. Seriously, he kept all of our messages, everything. He sent them all to me in one folder.

 I kept the folder and sometimes I read them." Annabella appeared sad as she spoke about this.

Stephanie said nothing. After looking at her for a few seconds she turns her eyes away, looking around her as if to change the subject.

As they start to walk across the bridge Stephanie walks slowly, admiring the Eiffel tower.

Annabella asks in a gentle voice, "Will you tell me how you and Gabriel meet? He seems like such a good man."

"Are you sure you are ready to hear such a tragic story?" There was a mocking tone in Stephanie's voice.

"Oh, please don't tell me you are unhappy in your marriage like me!" replied Annabella in an alarmed voice.

"What happened between me and Gabriel, you will not find in romance books or films!" exclaimed Stephanie with a twinkle in her eyes.

"Is it that bad?"

"You will have to decide that when I have finished telling you. Gabriel is an incredibly intelligent man, but there is one single word that is missing from his vocabulary."

"What word is that?"

"The word, "No!"

I don't believe he understands the word No. Thirty years ago, I went for an interview at his office for a secretarial job. I felt an instant attraction to him; it was a really strange sensation. I had never felt it before. The feeling has never left me. I know it's madness, but, I still get the butterflies in my stomach when we are together!"

Annabella interjects, "That's fantastic!" What does the word, "No" have to do with all of this? How long did it take him to ask you on a date?"

"What? As soon as we had eye contact there was this magnetic force between us. We talked for what seemed like ages, and then he asked me if I had my CV. I looked at him in a strange way, and then he asked; "Do you have your resume, to explain what jobs skills you've had in the past?"

I don't know what came over me that moment as I rudely replied, "Do I need a resume to sit behind that old desk and answer your phone calls?"

"Oh my God! You must have been mortified waiting for a response!"

"I know, said Stephanie with the knowledge that she said something stupid.

I really needed the job and I thought right there and then I blew it, he looked at me and said; "You have the job! Can you start tomorrow morning at nine?" I said; Yes! I was shocked to say the least that I got the job!"

"No wonder he calls you, "The Real Boss" What happened next?"

"The next day, this makes me laugh even now, I showed up to work, Gabriel was standing there saying "Good morning" to me and looked me straight in the eye and said; "Stephanie", I said yes, he said; "I am going to marry you!"

I got scared, I thought, oh boy this guy has read too many law books! I am going to need a lawyer myself if this continues."

Annabella laughed out loud. This is the first time she has laughed in a long time.

"I haven't gotten to the funny parts yet!" Stephanie said "Every day for six months I would walk into the office, and I would find a single red rose, with a note, that said; "Will you have dinner with me?" I never answered him."

"Why?" asked Annabella innocently

"I was so in love with him that I was afraid I might disappoint him. Then, it got really strange!"

"How?" asked Annabella with a look of disbelief on her face.

"I was living with my parents, there was a knock at the door, and it was Gabriel with a dozen red roses for Mama and a bottle of brandy for Papa. He was invited into the front room.

I came downstairs and said hello to Gabriel there was this deafening silence in the room.

My father is a straight talker so, he asked him directly; 'What's the purpose of your visit son?"

Gabriel answered him directly; "Sir, I have come to tell you that I am going to marry your daughter."

My parents were dumbfounded, and so was I! My father turned to me and asked; "How long have you two been dating?"

I said; we are not dating!"

My mother said: "What? You have never been on a date together?"

I said; "No!" Gabriel stepped in and said; "We work together." I said; "He is my boss."

My mother said; "How romantic!"

My father said to Gabriel in a stern voice; "Young man, I was in the French Resistance during the war, and I believe you should know I have a gun in the house!"

Gabriel was shocked. He said: "Sir, we don't need a gun in this situation, what we need is collective calm heads. I give you my solemn word my intentions are honourable and noble towards Stephanie. I love her, sir, he said, but he said it in such a sincere way that I was so moved that I couldn't breathe.

Then, as if that whole scene had not taken place, Gabriel replies; "Nice meeting you both!" And he walked out the house.

"I was shaking inside, I wanted to run out in the street after him and shout from the top of my voice I was madly in love with him too but, I did not." Stephanie appeared disappointed with this moment that was lost to her at that precise time, her look was pensive.

"Oh my God, I have never heard such a romantic story!" "What happened next?"

The story of Stephanie and Gabriel was mesmerizing to Annabella as she had not had this instant connection with anyone one before. It was as if she was listening to a book, a romance novel.

"I think this is a good spot to sit," said Stephanie pointing to the public bench with the Eiffel tower behind the bench. They both sit down and Stephanie continues with her story.

"For the next two weeks the single roses continued with the same note; "Would you have dinner with me?" I could see he was really suffering emotionally.

The office was closed for business, it was late afternoon, and it was just the two of us in the building. I gathered my courage."

Walking into his office, I said to him; are you really in love with me?

He looked into my eyes and said; "Madly, from the first moment I saw you!" I asked him: Do you want to marry me? Gabriel replied: "I would marry you under a tree in rags and slippers."

"WAV" said Annabella in a low shocked voice Stephanie stops for a second and she breaks into a little smile as if she can still see the event right now like she was watching a movie.

"You said yes, right?" asked Annabelle, Stephanie was far away in her thoughts

"No! I thought I would tease him a little more!"

"Oh my God! It must have been hell for him!"

"I know, but I couldn't resist the temptation.

I told him that I was handing in my resignation and I wanted to leave." All the colour left his cheeks; I truly thought he was going to die there in his chair!

He looked at me with his tears in his eyes, he then asked; "Are you in love with someone?"

I said; "Yes madly, he said, choking on his words; "Are you going to marry him? I replied; yes, he's proposed and is waiting for my answer."

Total disbelief on his face, he replied; "Congratulations! Thank you for letting me know." His head lowered, he sat in front of me breaking into a million pieces of disappointment.

I lifted up his face with the palm of my hand and said to him; I am madly in love with you! I want to work for you as your wife. He cried.

I couldn't have predicted falling madly in love with anyone like I had with Gabriel.

A love like this only ever comes around once in life, I was not about to throw it away. Today, we are as madly in love as we were back then."

Annabella breaks down and her eyes fill up with tears.

"We have two grown kids, both married, and we are expecting our first grandchild in the next few months."

Stephanie nods her head gently with a tear in her eye, she turns, looks at Annabella; she is also crying wiping under her eyes.

Annabella is looking at Stephanie and remarks, "What? You're going to tell me all these beautiful things that have happened to you and I'm not supposed to cry? I wish something like this would happen to me, once, just once in my life."

"Maybe one day it will." Stephanie replied

"I have been waiting sixty-two years and it has not happened yet. I am afraid I have given up on the, "Holy Grail of Life," and "The Magic of Love." Her voice was riddled with happiness for Stephanie and Gabriel and a sadness that reflected what was missing from her own life.

"It took one look with me and Gabriel to fall madly in love! The most important thing I've learned in life is that anything can happen to anyone, even when they are not looking for it."

"Beautiful things happen to other people. When it comes to me, it always turns into regrets and disappointment."

"I'd like to take you somewhere, I want you to see something it will only take twenty minutes by taxi. Will you come?"

"Yes." Stephanie's curiosity was peaked. They both got up off the bench and began to walk.

Ten minutes later, both seated in the back of the taxi, Stephanie continues with her story.

"There is a sad part of our history. Do you wish to hear it?"

"Please don't tell me there is another woman involved!" said Annabella

"No, something more devastating than another woman involved. Five years ago, I was diagnosed with breast cancer."

A short moment of silence, and Annabella replies; "I am so sorry to hear that. Are you cancer free now?"

"Yes, but we were devastated… My left breast was removed."

"I am so sorry to hear this. I can't imagine how devastating this would be for you!"

"I lost my self-confidence, I didn't feel like a complete woman anymore, and I certainly did not feel attracted to Gabriel.

Of course, he was steadfast in his support of me, giving me my space when I needed it and so incredibly thoughtful.

Every day for six months, I received a red rose as a token of his undying love for me. I know how lucky I am to have him and his love."

Tears rolling down her cheeks, Annabella comforts Stephanie with a warm and consistent hug, and Stephanie continues her story.

"With a card that said; "For me there is only you! You are my life! I love you!"

"For six months I would not change in front of him.

I would not let him touch me. We never made love during that time. Then one night, we were in our bedroom, and things changed.

Typically, since the surgery, I would always turn off the light and change in the adjoining bathroom. I would then slip into bed next to him quietly."

"On this particular night as I came out of the bathroom the light was on. I was wearing my pyjamas as usual. Gabriel walked up to me and looked me in the eyes. No words, just both hands ripping off my top."

"I tried to resist. I cried out to him to stop. He did not hear me. Forcefully, he held me tight, taking off my bra; my tears of shame did not stop him. My mind raced as this was happening, the main thought was that he would not see me as the woman he fell in love with.

79

He continued despite my shame, burying his head against the empty spot on my chest where my breast used to be.

Right above my broken heart. Kissing me there in that empty spot. Crying and kissing me on my scars; he brought me back to life that night.

I wrapped my hands around him and we cried and hugged, kissing passionately we made love as it had never been before.

Total surrender on my part, unconditional love oozing from every orifice. This was love, this was life, and this was living. We were alive, deeply, completely alive!" Stephanie was crying softly with this beautiful memory spoken aloud.

"You're both so incredibly lucky to have each other." The tears were streaming down her face, a quiet reminder that love like this had never lived in her own life.

"You are the first person I have told this story to. I don't know why I shared this with you to be honest." Wiping her tears with a handkerchief of Gabriel's that she kept in her purse.

Softly smiling in the dimly lit cab, Annabella replies; "I have that effect on people. I myself have never been that lucky enough to have someone love me that intensely."

"You never know what tomorrow will bring." "Anything can happen to anyone, at any time in life." You may find the strength to give someone your heart, your trust, your love, and your life again!"

Surprised Annabella replies, "What? At my age?"

"You are in the prime of your life, and you are dying to be loved, like I was dying to be loved the night Gabriel and I shared after my surgery."

"To be totally candid with you Stephanie, I have given up on ever having that kind of love."

"May the power of the universe strike you down with "the madness of Love!" May you fall madly, deeply, fully in love with someone that neither of you will recover from the depths and the strengths that you will share. May you find your "Forever Love" Stephanie's voice was like what Annabella had imagined an Angel's voice would sound like, full of love and sincerity.

Annabella smiled at Stephanie and asked; "Was that a blessing or a curse?"

"Both!" replied Stephanie with a cheeky smile. Annabella began to feel as though she was with a very special and blessed woman, her mind was expanding.

"On a serious note; I am not surprised that Gabriel is a man of high virtue and standards.

When Pierre picked me up, he told me how he got his job as a driver for Gabriel. I was very touched by his story."

"It's amazing how a little kindness can change a person's life. The person can be a total stranger, yet kindness, kindness, can help that person achieve what seemed impossible to them. As long as they realize that there are good people in the world, they are then open to start anew. In the case of Pierre, he is not a driver he is family and his family is our family; and so, it goes!"

The taxi stops in a small side street. Stephanie tells the taxi driver to wait, and they both exit the taxi.

Annabella is standing and staring at the little old house that had been built a hundred years earlier to house the poor. Stephanie knew of these homes, but quietly waited for Annabella to explain why they were there.

Annabella speaks in a very melancholy voice, "This is where I used to live as a child."

It was as if she was there again as a child. Envisioning herself playing in front of the house, walking through the fog holding Mother's hand; both dressed in worn out clothes carrying a shopping basket made of cane.

Annabella's eyes welled up with tears, no longer able to contain herself. Annabella breaks down and cries aloud.

In her very special way, Stephanie whispers, "It's alright; everything is going to be alright." Hugging her gently as only Stephanie can, Annabella cries for a few more moments and then turns with Stephanie to head towards the waiting taxi.

CHAPTER EIGHT

ABOVE THE CLOUDS

The taxi stops outside the hotel that they had dinner at earlier and where Annabella is staying for the night. Gabriel is there waiting. He greets Stephanie with a soft kiss on the lips.

"Hello darling." Stephanie smiles tenderly at Gabriel; her thoughts had been about him all evening and she lingered in his loving eyes.

"Did you ladies have a good   time?"

Annabella replied; "Yes, we had a beautiful night. Thank you, Gabriel." Annabella had a new-found respect and understanding for Gabriel, he was indeed a "gentle man."

"The pleasure is all mine! Tomorrow morning Pierre will pick you up at 10:00 a.m. Will that give you enough time to get ready and have breakfast? After breakfast, he will transport you to the airport, to catch your flight to the South of France."

"Your arrival at the house should be about one o'clock. You will be greeted with a glass of homemade wine made by Roberto De la Mancha.

You will be in the best of care there as Roberto and his wife Maria are there at your disposal." Annabella leans forward and kisses Gabriel on the cheek softly.

"Madam, please I am a married man!" Gabriel was smiling a cheeky smile and holding Stephanie around the waist.

"Thank you both for everything!" Gabriel looks at Stephanie and says in a loving voice

"Have you been spreading rumours about me?" Stephanie smiles, hands over a personal business card to Annabella. "My number and email are on this card, promise to call me please." The two hug and look at each other for a moment. Promise to call me please!!"

"I promise! I will stalk you every day on the phone!" Her eyes glowing with admiration and a new-found friendship.

"I expect nothing less from you! Safe travels darling!"

"Thank you! You are both very lucky to have each other and the love you share so generously, it's such a beautiful life! Thank you for a lovely evening and such a warm and inviting welcome to Paris."

"Good night Annabella." "Good night to you both." replies Annabella.

Gabriel and Stephanie walk to his car parked in front of the hotel. Gabriel opens the passenger door for Stephanie, who turns and looks at Annabella indicating with her hand gesture to call her. Stephanie gets in the car; Gabriel shuts her door and gets in the driver's side. The car starts and they drive off. Annabella follows the car with her eyes for a few seconds, then turns and heads into the hotel. Her spirit is feeling more and more alive.

A few moments later, Annabella is in her room on the fifth floor. Taking a seat by the open window, she gazes out to the Eiffel Tower just a few streets away. Emotionally, she wonders again where her life is going. If only she had the same love that Gabriel and Stephanie shared; how different her life would have turned out before now. Sadly, she feels that it is too late for her, that her chance for a real and fulfilling love she could share was gone.

Thoughts of being broken beyond repair, feeling that nothing in the world was going to make her happy; she came to the conclusion that this was going to be what's left of her life.

At sixty-two years old, she is in a marriage with no future. Living a life of doubt, lack of self-esteem and confidence had become her "norm." Truly, she believed that there was no miracle waiting for her to mend her broken soul. This self-fulling destiny was killing her.

Opening her phone, she sends a message to Ibrahim. The message was simple and short.

"Just letting you know I arrived safely. I'm off to bed."

Stretching out on the big comfortable bed, she drifts in and out of past memories filled with disappointments. Opening her photos on her phone, she finds a favourite picture of her with Fluffy cuddled up together in Morocco.

There in the sunlight on the big chair on the terrace they were happy together. Looking at the picture for just a few seconds, she closes the phone.

No sooner than then she'd closed the phone than it suddenly began to ping loudly. Emails were coming through. Perhaps, it was Ibrahim, replying to her message; she was less than enthusiastic to read his response but she opened up her email.

The email is not from Ibrahim. It was from Santiago. There was a photo attached to it. Santiago had placed two photos in separate frames side by side. There were heart shapes in front of the pictures and the word "LOVE" between the two little hearts.

"My Darling Annabella,

I have not heard from you for a month. Every time I write to you, you scorn me, you rant and rave like a spoiled child. I get so mad sometimes. Why can't you be a little bit courteous to me? Why can't we return to the love we had between us?

Why can't we arrange to meet properly? You have been so unkind and angry with me for the past four years. I have been blocked from all social media that you are connected to. I can only email with the hopes you will respond, but you fail to respond most times and on the rare occasion that you do, you are scorning me. Please Annabella, let's arrange to speak properly on webcam so we can resolve all this, and clear the air.

My feelings have never changed for you.

Please, please, think about a proper communication and let me know.

Santiago X"

Annabella spends a few moments deeply reflecting on what and how to reply to Santiago.

Hitting the Reply key, she begins to write;

"I don't like this picture. It would be best if you deleted it on your end as I will do so on this end. Please delete all of my photos from your computer. As I told you before, we are finished and staying in contact by email is me being courteous.

There is nothing to discuss when it comes to you and me as I have told several times already. It is not like we will ever see each other so, what is the point of dragging up the past.

Please, find someone else to give your love to.

Look after yourself.

Wishing you all the best."

Annabella hit the send key. It was her hope to remove all doubt about her and Santiago of ever meeting, in this lifetime.

After looking at the picture for a few seconds she deletes the email and places her phone on the charger by the bed. Resting and reflecting on her life, with the calm breeze floating through the white curtains hanging on the window, with the Eiffel tower in the background with the flashing lights, Annabella drifts off to sleep.

In the morning as promised, Pierre collects Annabella from the hotel and they head to the airport. As usual, soft classical music is playing on the radio. Annabella looks out the window at the people on the street and the buildings, recalling her time with Stephanie and how enjoyable it was to be with a woman that understood her.

Soon they are out of Paris. The car passes a big signpost that says "Paris Orly Airport."

Annabella continues to reflect.

Wondering where and when all this mystery will end. Annabella begins to think about just how beautiful last night was with Stephanie. Their conversation over dinner, what she confided in Stephanie about her life and how Stephanie responded was more than she could have anticipated.

 It was as if they were two sisters confiding in one another without judgement and giving each other loving support. This was a very rare type of friendship that Annabella hoped would only continue to grow in the future.

Truly, Stephanie was a charming, kind, and gentle woman, whose dignity remained intact even after being ravaged by cancer.

The car approached the main terminal of the airport, Annabella thought this was where she would depart from, but Pierre continued driving.

 Annabella asks "Pierre, where are you taking me? Why are you passing the Main Departure Terminal?" Pierre looks in the mirror above his head and replies;

"Your departure is a little different. May I have your passport please?" Annabella produces her passport and hands it to Pierre; the car slows down and stops at a checkpoint for the airport that leads to a private jet.

Pierre hands over some documents along with Annabella's passport to the female controller at the gate. Looking at the passport the woman then leans in and looks at Annabella and hands it back to Pierre. "Merci, bon voyage Madame" said the woman with a smile. Pierre drives through. Stopping the car near a white Cessna Citation CJ2. Federico the captain, is around fifty years old, in his pilot's uniform is standing by waiting for them.

Pierre opens the trunk and removes the luggage handing it to Federico. The luggage is placed on board and everything is ready for departure. Annabella gets out the car and looks at the jet and then looks at Pierre.

Pierre has his phone in his hand and dials a number through to Gabriel. Gabriel answers. Pierre into the phone "we are here." Motioning to Annabella to take the phone; she speaks into the phone "Hello."

"Hello Annabella, I wanted to wish you a safe journey and tell you that the captain has a letter for you. Do you have any questions to ask me before you go?"

"Gabriel, I have never been on a private jet like this before, who is paying for all this? The five-star hotel and a private jet; this must be costing a fortune!"

"Don't worry, it's all been taken care of, relax and enjoy the experience! Call me when you arrive! Again, have a safe journey." Gabriel ends the call

Annabella is escorted by Pierre to the steps of the jet, "I will be here in three weeks to pick you up. Do have a safe journey Mrs. Amir!" " Thank you, Pierre."

Annabella went up the stairs and into the plane; she is shown to a seat with a small table in front of the seat by Captain Federico

"Mrs. Amir welcome aboard! My name is Federico; I am your captain for the day. We will be cruising at 41 thousand feet with the speed of 470 nautical miles per hour. We will land at Perpignan airport in approximately, one hour and twenty minutes. I have been instructed to give you this envelope."

Instead of opening the envelope right away, Annabella decides to wait until they are in the air.

Federico comments to Annabella, "Mrs Amir please put your seat belt on for the take off. Once we are airborne and at cruising altitude you can remove it. Right now, it's time for take-off."

Once in the cockpit, Federico closes the door behind him.

Annabella put on her seat belt and in mere moments the private jet starts to taxi its way towards the runway. "This is amazing" thought Annabella. Never in her last 20 years did she imagine being alone in a private jet, on her way to the South of France to meet a mystery man or woman. Today was another good day!

Within twenty minutes the plane was flying at forty-one thousand feet and it was incredibly peaceful. Annabella opens the letter which reads:

"Dear Mrs. Amir, Thank you, for accepting my request to decorate the newly renovated barn on the estate. All of the furniture is in storage right now, and will be delivered to the estate, in two weeks. I have contracted the two men who will deliver the furniture, to stay with you to help for two days. This should be handy as they will be happy to hang mirrors, paintings, light fixtures and anything else you may need done during that time. I am leaving you, my Skype ID so we can stay in contact. I do not do webcam, chat, or voice chat, but you're welcome to write to me. My Skype ID is: Theo31. In the meantime, enjoy your stay at the house.

Theo"

Annabella looks at the letter and then looks out the window at the white clouds that appear to be soft cotton puffs stretching for miles. Annabella closes her eyes, imagining herself totally relaxed and floating like the clouds high above the world. Just then, the cabin door opens and Federico steps out and stands in front of Annabella with a smile upon his face. Annabella's eyes open in shock and disbelief, "Wh, Whoooo, what…

What are you doing here?"

He looks down at her seat belt, it's still engaged. "Mrs. Amir it's alright to take your seat belt off now." She unbuckles the seat belt.

"I am sorry, I am so nervous I have never flown in a private jet before. It's so small and I'm not sure if it's safe or not. Actually, I feel claustrophobic, if I'm being totally honest with you."

Federico stretches out his hand for Annabella. "What are you doing?" Federico replies, "Please indulge me, I want to show you just how safe this plane is!"

Annabella takes his hand and he helps her out of her seat and they go into the cabin. "Please have a seat." Annabella slowly sits in the co-pilots seat, and Federico sit in the pilot seat. "You have just been promoted to co-pilot!" This was the first time that Annabella sat in a cockpit of a plane. There was so much to take in; her eyes went from left to right and up and down, so many buttons and gauges, nothing like a car. There was a sense of true freedom in this place above the clouds, she was excited and calm all at the same time.

Looking into the distance, beyond the gauges and buttons, was the sun. A red beautiful sun floating upon the clouds. "What an amazing sight!" she thought. "Have you ever seen anything so tranquil and so beautiful before?" asked Federico. Annabella felt like she was in a trance looking at this amazing view in front of her. "Never!"

"My wife adores flying."

"How long have you been married?"

"Twenty years. Can you imagine of all the places in the world to meet your wife, you meet her in the sky?"

"Are you serious?"

"Yes, I was a pilot in the navy, after my tour, I took a job on a commercial airline. Most fighter pilots become commercial pilots or private pilots."

"And your wife was a stewardess on the plane you were flying?"

"No, not quite. I was the first officer on a flight; the captain suffered a heart attack. I got on the speaker and asked if there was a doctor on board and notified the nearest airport that we need to make an emergency landing.

One of the stewardesses brought the doctor in; I'd never seen such a beautiful doctor before.

I had no idea she was going to be my future wife. She was so sharp and, on the ball. She asked me to change places with the captain.

The stewardess brought the medical box, she asked the captain to chew on an aspirin, and then she gave him a nitro-glycerine tablet under his tongue. An oxygen mask was placed on him and twenty minutes later we made our landing and he was taken by ambulance to the nearest medical facility.

He survived!"

"So, your wife is a medical doctor? In what field?"

"No, my wife is a flight instructor, that bit about being a doctor was a lie because no one was stepping up and she knew what to do and stay calm during a crisis."

"She's lucky; she never got arrested for "Impersonating a doctor.""

"Oh, don't worry about that, she was punished a lot worse than getting arrested for impersonating a doctor."

"Really, how? What happened?"

"The captain's wife was six months pregnant at the time. Together they decided to name their baby girl after her." Federico is now smiling while looking at the sun on the clouds.

"I hope you don't mind me asking, what's your wife's name?"

"Florentina" replied Federico lovingly

"Florentina, what a beautiful name." replied Annabella thoughtfully

"Are you enjoying your brief co-pilot experience Mrs. Amir?"

"Yes, very much, I have never seen the sun above the clouds like this before. Straight in front of us suspended in the air and yet we are flying, and it feels like we are not moving at all." Annabella was no longer claustrophobic nor stressed, she was content and relaxed.

"I have something to tell you Mrs. Amir but, if you repeat what I am about to tell you, and the wrong person hears it, I can get into great trouble." "Do you understand this must be confidential Mrs. Amir?"

"Yes! Might I assume you are going to tell me something that relates to me? As no one has told me anything so far."

"Yes"

"I promise you, whatever you tell me will be held in the strictest of confidence, and it will never be repeated to anyone!"

"You are an extremely lucky lady, Mrs. Amir."

"Interesting statement Federico, as I have never been lucky in my life. Why do you say that?"

"The person who chartered this plane, had specifically put into the contract, that you be brought in here, to witness all this beauty from inside the cockpit." explained Federico

"Oh my God! The funny thing is I don't know one person who would do this for me!"

"Whoever it is, wanted you to experience such beauty, and they know you, and you know them."

"That is impossible I tell you, I don't know anyone who would do this for me."

"I think it is a man, a man who is madly in love with you, whoever he is." Replied Federico

Providing an answer to the puzzle

"That's impossible I don't know anyone who has that kind of money to do something like this, except"... Annabella mind slowed down and she starts to think.

"Except whom?" Asked Federico

"Except Theo, but that's impossible," said Annabella adamantly

"Why is it impossible?" asked Federico eagerly

"Because I don't know anyone named Theo. I have never met him before; he is the man who commissioned me to do the interior design of a renovated barn on his estate."

Annabella was looking puzzled while gazing out at the red beautiful sun floating above the clouds in front of them. This was equally as mysterious as the questions to which she has no answers for.

CHAPTER NINE

SOUTH OF FRANCE

Perpignan Airport: The Cessna Citation CJ2 jet glides down towards the runway to land. After a short taxi, it comes to a complete stop. On the tarmac there was a black Range Rover.

The door of the vehicle opens at the same time that the plane door opens. Annabella steps out onto the tarmac while Federico gets her single bag. He carries it to the car and hands it to the driver. Annabella smiles and she shakes Federico's hand, saying, "Thank You."

"I'll see you in three weeks Mrs. Amir; you are booked for a return flight to Paris."

Federico opened the back door of the Range Rover for Annabella to get in.

"I look forward to seeing you in three weeks." replied Annabella with a smile

The driver of the Range Rover looked to be in his early thirties. He was smartly dressed in a black suit, black tie, and white shirt. After the luggage was in the back of the car, he returns to the driver's seat. Starting the car, they head to the exit. "My name is Pedro Mrs. Amir."

"Nice to meet you Pedro. Is the house far from here?"

"It's about thirty kilometres from here, but it's all mountains and valleys. The house is very close to the Spanish border, and not far from the Andorra ski resort."

"That's convenient! I can spend a day in Spain then, since it's that close"

Annabella looks out the window.

"You don't need to spend a day in Spain Mrs. Amir, this part of France was once part of

Catalonia is like being in Spain. Welcome to the most beautiful place in the world, where legends, myths and magic happen. Please relax and enjoy the beauty of this part of your journey. Pedro turns on the soft music for the ride.

"Thank you Pedro" replied Annabella. Sure enough a Spanish song begins to play on the radio with Matt Munro Alguien Canto. The music and the song seemed to soothe Anabella. Taking out her phone, she goes to "Skype" messenger application and opens the chat. Looking at the name Theo31 just below, is the name Santiago. Clicking on Theo31 the messenger box opens. Thinking for a few seconds she gathers her courage to write to Theo.

"Hello Theo, Just a brief message to let you know that I have arrived safely. I am in the car on the way to the house. I am curious to know if by chance, we've met before."

Pressing send, she waits to see if there is a response.

After a few moments, she closes the application and gazes out the window at the breath-taking scenery.

The roads were winding but they were not yet in the mountains. There are ruined fortresses on top of the peaks, forests on the other side, and in the distance on the high peaks of the mountain snow can be seen.

The clouds were like shrouds on the highest peaks of the mountain range. There were fields of grapevines, all in a straight line. The local grapes are made into local and international wines.

The Range Rover climbs the steep, winding road of the mountain trying to get to the other side. There at the top, the view is magnificent. The mountains stretch for as far as the eye can see, with small villages dotted around in some parts that can be seen clearly.

The Range Rover starts to descend on the other side. A river runs through the mountains and can be seen, as they pass farmhouses, cottages, and beautiful greenery. The road now becomes flat and well maintained.

Suddenly there is a ping on Annabella's phone. Quickly opening her phone, she looks at the messages. There is no message from Theo31. Next, she checks her emails; there is a message from Santiago.

Disappointment falls on Annabella's face and she thinks about deleting the message. Reluctantly, she opens the email.

"Hello Annabella,

Thank you for the email. I know what you are looking for in a man. You are looking for security, the security you never had. Regardless of the fact that you had been married to wealthy men who had everything, they never gave you emotional security. Sadly, it left you feeling empty inside and emotionally detached.

They left you with nothing but heartache, no money, no property, no sign of ever really loving you, or respecting you.

You need someone, who can give you the same kind of lifestyle as you had with your other relationships but, it should include the love you need and want so desperately.

I do not have what they have monetarily but, they will never have what I have, the capacity to love you unconditionally. I would rather keep what I have, than have all that money and be as cold and dead inside as they are.

I live for giving to others, to be an inspiration, to share knowledge, to be compassionate with words of comfort. I have always treated you with compassion and love.

I will no longer send you emails. Your replies have broken my heart into a million pieces each time I read them. It's hard to imagine that we were once madly in love with each other as I read your email responses. Your heart has changed and become hardened.

I will always be your friend. I will always reply to you if you write to me. I always wish beautiful things for you in your life, regardless of the outcome between us.

Stay blessed Annabella

Santiago X"

Annabella reflects on the email, she reads it again, decides not to respond to it. Instead of deleting it, she closes her email and again focuses her attention out the window.

CHAPTER TEN

THE CHATEAU

The road becomes a single lane road as Pedro begins the drive up the side of the mountain. Annabella is looking out the window into the distance and enjoying the beauty of nature.

There is sad emptiness in her eyes despite the beautiful scenery. The Range Rover climbs to the top of the mountain and turns right. Here the land is flat and there are agricultural fields on both sides. Ahead and to the right is the Chateau, and there before it is the big converted barn.

A few outbuildings, a chicken pen, adjoined by a fenced small building and land for the few goats. The stables are further to the left of the barn. In the pasture, there are three horses grazing peacefully.

A large greenhouse and a vegetable patch sit next to the "Caretakers Cottage." This was the home of Roberto and Maria. There is another old building that used as a garage. Everywhere she looks, Annabella see's nothing but peaceful beauty, a respite from all of her sorrow.

The Range Rover stops outside the Estate. It's magnificent! Waiting to greet Annabella is Roberto De La Mancha Sergio and his wife Maria.

Roberto is a man in his fifties. He is unshaven with a mixture of grey and black hair on his face. His appearance is that of a "man's man." Roberto's hands are slightly dirty from working the land but nevertheless he looks charming.

Maria a slim woman around the same age as her husband, in contrast, Maria has an angelic face, soft, kind and gentle, where Roberto looks primitive and fearless. Maria has blond hair with grey roots that are visible, and yet her beauty is so natural.

Annabella steps down from the Range Rover. Pedro has already retrieved the luggage from the back of the car and brings it and lays it near Roberto's feet. Turning, Pedro gets back in the car and starts it up and leaves. Annabella stands there looking at Roberto and Maria for a few seconds.

"You must be Annabella." Roberto states with a deep and thundering voice

"Yes" replied Annabella softly

"Mr. Alexande, called and said to expect you around about this time today." Roberto picked up the luggage and watched as Annabella became totally aware of the immense beauty of this place. Under her breath but loud enough for Roberto to hear, Annabella says. "It's beautiful here!"

"Welcome Annabella, my name is Maria and this is my husband Roberto."

"It's a pleasure to meet you both."

Roberto speaks; "Welcome! I am the gardener, the pool attendant, the keeper of the animals, the vegetable garden, the exterior of the house and the land surrounding the property.

My lovely wife Maria takes care of everything in the house.

I don't interfere with her work in the house, and she does not interfere with my work outdoors. We live in harmony, and there are no arguments. Please, let's do go inside now; Maria will get you settled in."

As they enter into the hallway, there is a beautiful dining table with a white cloth on it, as well as on the chairs. A beautiful staircase leads upstairs, to the left of the entrance into the hallway stands a small table with a bottle of wine and several small glasses upon it.

Roberto puts down the suitcase and wanders the few feet to the little table. Opening the bottle, he pours out three shots; one for each of them, he hands one to Maria and one to Annabella.

Roberto raises his glass and speaks, "My late boss used to do this." Roberto crosses himself with his right hand and then continues "With all new guests, when they came to the house for the first time as a blessing, and a welcome, you have to drink this in one gulp."

"Salute!" "Salute!" replies Annabella, and Maria raise her glass. Roberto downs his drink in one gulp without any problem, Maria drinks in the same fashion as though it was a soft drink.

Annabella drinks her drink down. Her facial expression changes to shock, she starts to cough and choke for a second. Seconds later Annabella says, "What is that stuff made of?" Maria is smiling, nearly breaking into a giggle.

"Like most drinks, it's made out of grapes. My special brew and the recipe are a secret, but, what is not a secret, is that, it will kill anything in your stomach that is not supposed to be there! And if your brain is toxic, it will clear that, but a second glass might kill you! No worries, we prefer to keep our guest alive, you'll not have another of these to concern yourself with!"

"You're not kidding! What is this stuff made of?"

"Come along now, never mind what this stuff is made of, Maria will take over now and show you, to your room. I have work to do in the great outdoors. I will see you girls at dinner later this evening." Roberto walks out the door.

Annabella and Maria are left standing looking at each other for a few seconds; there is a beautiful energy between them that Annabella is very aware of.

"I have prepared some food for you. I thought you might be hungry."

"As a matter of fact, I am famished. Thank you for being so thoughtful Maria!"

Maria leads Annabella into the kitchen at the end of the entrance hall. "Follow me, it's the small things that people do in life that matters the most!"

The kitchen is beautifully equipped with industrial high-end appliances.

In the middle of the kitchen is a huge square table with drawers on either side for cutleries and other small dishes and cups. The ceiling above has wooden beams from which all kinds of pots and pans are hung from a chain link oval shaped pot hanger. Annabella notices all the pots and pans are copper and are very clean and very expensive.

Annabella sits at the table, Maria serves up a wild boar steak, with cubes of potatoes, crushed garlic, rosemary, and thyme leaves, and it smells delicious!

"What is it if you don't mind me asking? The smells are delightful and the meal looks delicious! I must know what it is."

"It's wild boar steak and potatoes. Here, let me give you your silverware and a napkin so that you might enjoy eating it."

"Thank you, how long have you and Roberto worked here?"

"Thirty-five years. Before us, Roberto's mother and father used to work here. When they retired, Roberto and I took over. The man that Roberto's mother and father used to work for Philippe, died, six months after his wife died.

Philippe loved his wife very much, and after she was gone, he just gave up on life.

Philippe has a son; Enzo and he took over the estate around the same time Roberto and I started working. Enzo's wife died of cancer a year ago. Philippe never recovered and placed the estate up for sale."

"I am sorry to hear that." Placing another fork of food to her mouth, Annabella remarks, "This is so tasty!"

"May I ask what brings you here Annabella?"

Annabella thinks for a second "I am here to furnish and design the inside of the converted barn. I'll be here for three weeks. Forgive me please; I thought you would have known that."

"I see. So, you are an interior designer then? Have you worked on many big houses?"

Annabella stops chewing, "To tell you the truth, this is my first commission."

After finishing her meal, Maria shows Annabella to her suite. It was lovely, a double bed with red covers and red pillows dominate the room. The walls are painted cream, neutral and relaxing.

There is an alcove window with double doors opening outward onto small balcony outside. A mirror hangs in a frame on the side wall, below that a cream coloured arm chair surrounded by candles.

In the middle of the room on the wall across from the bed is an alcove half circle brick under that is a large wooden chest. A small writing table with a wooden chair is on the opposite side of the bed. There's a door that leads to the bathroom which is sizable with a big soaking tub and a shower.

Maria puts the suitcase at the foot of the bed on a bench. Looking at Annabella, she states

"I hope you will be comfortable here. If you need anything, please do not hesitate to ask."

"Is it ok to go and look around the barn? I mean is it open, or do I need a key?"

"No, it's open. First, let me show you around the rest of the house here so you know where everything is, it's a beautiful house and it has seen a lot of love in its history."

"Thank you, the house has great energy, I'd like that very much! You lead the way and I will follow" said Annabella

Maria walks around the house showing her the expansive beauty and tells her all of the history that the house has. First, she shows her the large salon with a fireplace, then the dining room, then the reception room. Annabella is taken aback at how lavishly the home is furnished and decorated.

Maria takes her to the sauna and massage room. Upstairs there are eight-bedroom suites. There is a vast penthouse apartment, with salon, a fireplace, reception room, TV room, bedroom with bathroom and dressing room. The bedroom suite is stunning and rather remarkable.

They arrive at the entrance of the big house. Maria was pointing to a cottage. "That's the caretaker's cottage where Roberto and I live. Beyond that, the stables where the horses are kept.

There is a chicken pen, a goat pen, and the greenhouse. As you can see we keep a vegetable patch as well. That over there, pointing to a medium size building, is Roberto's workshop, with all kinds of tools there to fix things around the house or on the grounds and next to that is another large building used as a garage." The tour was over and Maria excused herself heading to the cottage and Annabella went back inside.

Finding her way back to her room, Annabella walks over to the double doors, opens them, and steps out onto the balcony.

Her senses were awake! The fresh air smelled of mountains and trees. The rolling hills were a lush green that seemed to go on forever. Below her, she could see a swimming pool that was hidden for privacy by high shrubs and trees.

Standing there, she feels calm and relaxed but, her mind is full of wonder. What is this all about, why is she here? Removing her phone from her bag, she looks at the "Skype" application. There are still no response messages from Theo31. Setting her phone down, she opens her luggage and begins to place her clothing in the wardrobe.

A bit later Annabella has walked to the converted barn. Opening the doors, she steps inside. As it was in the photos, the fireplace was huge, white, and beautiful.

The high ceilings with the wooden beams were so much more complimentary in person than in the photos. Except for the two hanging chandeliers, the place was empty, like a clean slate. Annabella spots the door to the garden close to the fireplace. To the right is another door, which leads into the kitchen, utility room, and the downstairs half bathroom.

Annabella has a good look around downstairs, and then she takes the stairs to the right-hand side of the wall.

Climbing the stairs she continues to look around, as well as looking down from the balcony, trying to see if she can get a picture in her mind. Since the furniture is in storage, she will have to wait to see that she will have to work with.

Looking into the upstairs suites she notices a small window that overlooks the back garden and beyond. A perfect peaceful view, which any guest would delight in.

The master suite is located on the main floor. Located in the front of the barn it has a large window that opens out to the road leading to the estate.

Annabella can see far into the distance from there, what a place to create beautiful dreams.

Outside the door is a small wooden bridge with thick glass on both sides, she crosses over and opens the small door. To her surprise there was a shower, toilet, and wash basin.

After taking the entire tour of the barn, Annabella's mind is full of really "Country-French," or "Shabby Chic" types of décor. Again, she must wait for a view of what is in storage. Accessing the storage must be done as soon as possible, she only has three weeks.

Annabella comes out of the barn closes the door behind her a start walking towards the house.

Roberto is placing some straw and hay for the goats in the pen by the side of the road; she stops and looks waiting to catch Roberto's attention. After a moment he finally sees her and makes his way towards her.

"It's absolutely beautiful here!" said Annabella in a contented voice "Oh yes, it is!" replied Roberto looking far into the distance and around the mountains. "Mr. Surgio, may I ask you a question?"

"You may call me Roberto, you may call me De La Mancha, you may call me Surgio, but please; no title as Mr. I am a humble servant of nature. Now what is the question you wanted to ask me?"

"Can you tell me who the owner of this house is?"

Roberto's face turns serious, "No, but I can tell you, that when I found out what was going to happen, it frightened the life out of me."

"Why would the sale of the house frighten you?"

Roberto starts to explain the events that took place

"Maria my wife got a phone call to expect some people here on Tuesday. Monday, the day before the viewing was going to take place, I decided to go hunting as I often do with my horse Beauteous. On the way back from the hunt, there is an olive tree about five hectares below on the other side of the swimming pool. Beauteous always stops there for a rest before making the final journey up the hill to the house."

Annabella listens patiently to see where all this is going and what is the relation to the sale of the house. Roberto continues with the story

"Usually, I lie down in the shade of that small olive tree, the very same olive tree my father had planted years ago. I was resting my eyes with my shotgun next to me, dozing in and out but, I was conscious not to fall asleep. I heard this buzzing noise like a big bee flying over,

105

and then it seemed to stop. Next, the noise of the bee started slowly coming down towards me. I opened my eyes, and there about twenty feet above ground I saw this flying thing!

I was scared. I grabbed my gun pointed and fired but, I forgot there were no cartridges in the gun, so I started to load the gun, and this thing is flying away. I manage to get one shot off, but it was too far away by then."

Annabella is not amused; she thinks Roberto is making this up as a joke.

"Are you telling me Roberto, that you saw a flying saucer, and that you were about to be abducted by aliens? Or what do you think this was?"

"No, no, no! I jumped on Beauteous and hurried back to the house. When I got here outside were three men. I got off the horse and approached them, they were all looking at me on the laptop they had set up on a table outside. They used a drone to film that part of the land and I was on film, firing the shotgun in a panic.

They were all laughing! I can't say I blame them, I did look kind of funny. I didn't care, I was scared at the time and I took action, and it was then I met the lawyer Mr. Alexandre."

Mr. Alexandre seems to get around" replied Annabella

"Oh, you've met him, then?" asked Roberto

"Yes, I have met him."

"They took hundreds of pictures of the house I mean they took pictures of every single part of the house, the outbuildings, the barn, the animal enclosures, the land, everything! They were here for hours. A week later we were informed that the house had been sold and that our jobs were secure. That was a relief. They told us to carry on as usual. This was six   months ago.

We've not heard a thing from anyone, and no one has been here since.

A week ago, we got a phone call that you were coming to stay for three weeks to design the barn interior."

"Someone once told me that money has the power to do anything, even buy houses without ever seeing them." replied Annabella

 "quest'uomo deve avere le palle, come il toro, as they say in Italian,"

"What does that mean?" asked Annabella, never hearing the expression before, and not understanding Italian

"This man must have balls, like the bull, to buy a house for three million Euros without setting foot on the property."

"What makes you think it is a man?"

Roberto thinks for a second, shaking his head, in deep thought

"I don't know. Anyway, it's none of my business, I just work here with Maria."

"Have you ever heard of a man called Theo?" asked Annabella
Roberto turns and looks at her "No." he replied

"The day they were here taking pictures and frightening the life out of you, did they ever mention the name Theo?" asked Annabella thinking maybe she could jolt Roberto' memory

"No, never." replied Roberto as he turns and walks towards the goat house

Annabella lowers her eyes, she looks defeated. Theo? Perhaps, it is not his real name she thought to herself, and she turns and starts to walk towards the house.

As Annabella enters the living area of the house she starts walking towards the stairs, where Maria is coming down the stairs carrying some sheets and pillowcases to be washed. "Your phone was ringing earlier in your room." Thank you said, Annabella, as they both walk past each other.

Annabella picks up her phone in her room and looks at the calls. There is a missed call but, she does not know the number. She looks into "Skype" for messages; no message from Theo31. Scanning her emails, nothing. Taking out the charger for the phone from her bag, she places the phone on the charger and makes her way downstairs.

 Maria is in the utility room starting the washing machine; she turns and sees Annabella standing there.

"I wanted to ask you if it is ok for me to give you hand while I am waiting for the furniture to arrive from storage?" asked Annabella wanting to be helpful

"You don't have to do that and I wouldn't let you anyway. You are a guest here so, relax, and enjoy your stay!" said Maria assuring her that it was alright

"I did not want you to think badly of me being around the house and not doing anything." Annabella explained in a soft voice

"The thought never crossed my mind. Please Annabella, relax, and enjoy yourself! Make the most of your time here. It's an amazing place to be! Roberto and I would not swap this hill top for any other place in the world! We feed from the beauty, and the mystery of the land and nature." Annabella is now clearly aware of the effect this place has on Maria and Roberto and whoever it was that bought it sight unseen.

"It's an amazing place. I have never seen a place like this before." replied Annabella

"Enjoy and live in the moment, make beautiful memories. When you go back home, you can look upon the time you have spent here with a sense of wonder. You can live those moments twice! Come, let me show you the back of the house."

They walk into the garden area that slopes down the hill. The grass is immaculately cut. There are huge, planted pots made of pottery that houses several plants.

Maria turns and walks down the steps on the side of the garden, that opens up into the swimming pool area with a few reclining chairs on either side of the pool.

There is a BBQ area further back from the pool to the right side directly from the middle of the pool.

"You and Roberto are so lucky to live in a place like this" said Annabella,

"Yes, we have always felt like we were a part of the family here, we have the freedom to use everything in and out of the house after working hours" Maria reflects with love on the owners they used to work for before.

"Do you have children?"

"No, we decided long ago that life was too hard, and we did not see any logic in bringing children into this world, knowing that they will also suffer. As all people experience suffering in the world, we do not regret the decision."

"I do hope we can become dear friends for the three weeks that I'm here." said Annabella

"Thank you, I'd like that very much!" said Maria then she continued Roberto and I usually have breakfast, lunch, and evening meals at the cottage, but, under the circumstances I was thinking maybe you might like to join us so you won't feel alone. If you prefer to be alone, I can prepare your meals for you and you can have them at the house."

"I would love that. I will have breakfast here at the house and the evening meal at the cottage with you and Roberto. Thank you for being so thoughtful Maria, that's so very kind of you!"

CHAPTER ELEVEN

WISHING ON A STAR

That evening around eight p.m. the three of them are seated around the dinner table in the kitchen in the caretaker's cottage. Maria is serving up a stew. "Mm that smells delicious! What's in it?"

Maria looks at Roberto, who takes over the conversation. Pointing out the window and to a mountain not too far away that the outline can be seen as darkness intensifies and the night comes on

"Do you see that mountain over there? I go there and whatever moves, I shoot it, and it ends up in the pot." explained Roberto with a smile.

"Oh, stop teasing our guest will you! Don't take any notice of him Annabella! What we have here is venison stew with leeks, potatoes, and herbs." said Maria and then she sits down and they all began eating.

The conversation continues for two hours at the table with a few glasses of wine. Around ten p.m. Maria and Roberto walk Annabella to the front door of the house. The sky is full of brilliant shining stars.

"Thank you both for a wonderful evening, what time do you wake up in the morning?"

"The rooster is my alarm clock, and sometimes when I am in a middle of a beautiful dream, he starts crowing. I feel like shooting him!" said Roberto jokingly Annabella chuckles with a big smile in her eyes

"We don't lock doors here but, if you feel unsafe in the house alone, the key is behind the door. People often find it hard to find this place; they always miss the little road that turns to the house."

"Good night Annabella sleep well." said Maria politely with a warm smile.

"One more thing" interjected Roberto, "What?" replied Annabella, "Go onto the balcony in your room, and look at the sky. Make a wish, or say a prayer."

They turn and walk away from Annabella. Maria slides herself under Roberto's arm as they walk towards the cottage. Annabella looks at the beautiful love that she is witnessing between them, she turns and walks into the house closing the door behind her.

Upstairs in her room, Annabella wanders to the French doors and with both hands pulls them open. Stepping onto the balcony Annabella looks deeply into the sky. The night sky is glowing and sparkling with stars, she looks for a while in amazement, and then she softly speaks into the night.

"Please God, for once in my life, write a happy ending for me."

Eyes searching the sky as if she is following her own voice so that she can be heard among the stars, she is lost in the possibility that anything can happen.

Suddenly there is a pinging from her phone. It's a message of some sort. Turning back into the room, she turns on the main light and picks up her phone. It's Skype" with a message from Theo31. Annabella feels a sense of unexplainable excitement.

"Annabella,

I hope you are enjoying your stay so far and you that are comfortable. To answer your question from your earlier message, the answer is; No. We have never met in life or in person. I plan to visit the house hopefully the day before you leave. I'm trying to arrange my schedule to accommodate a visit but, I'm not certain yet. Tomorrow, you will receive two small guests at the house, please look after them. Good night."

Annabella thinks to herself blurting out the words "Two small guests!" Repeating the words again "Two small guests!" What the hell does that mean?"

While still holding the phone in her hand, it rings! Annabella yelps, dropping the phone onto the bed. It's still ringing; she decides to answer the call.

"Hello! It's Stephanie!

"Annabella, I tried calling you a few times to see if you got there alright."

Annabella was surprised, her voice changes to positive; welcoming the conversation

"How did you get my number?"

"I blackmailed Gabriel for it! I want to hear all about what has been happening out there. You know me, I love to gossip!" The two laughed out loud and continued.

"I think the person who owns the house is a man, his name is Theo. That's what it says on his Skype ID."

"Have you not called him to hear his voice, or to see him on webcam?"

"He made it clear in the note I received on the plane that he does not make phone calls or video cam. So, I wrote to him and asked if we'd ever met in real life."

"Did you get a reply?"

"Yes," he replied; "No, we have never met in life."

"Maybe we are reading this, all wrong! Maybe, someone recommended you to him to just to design the barn?"

"I think you might be right Stephanie. I got a strange message from him just a few minutes ago on Skype."

"What did he say?" asked Stephanie

"Let me read you the whole text ok?" Perhaps, that will give us a clue. I'm paraphrasing so you know."

"The message reads: "I hope you are enjoying your stay and that you are comfortable.

To answer your question in your message, you sent.

(That was me asking him if we ever met before)

The answer is No. We have never met in life.

I plan to visit the house, hopefully one day before you leave.

If I can arrange it, but not certain yet."

Tomorrow, you will receive, two small guests, at the house.

Please look after them, good night."

"Is that it?" asked Stephanie

"That's it! I have no idea who or what the two small guests are, or what it means.

I tried to think what they could be and the only thing I can think of being kids.

I quickly ruled that out as this Chateau is so beautiful, it's like a palace!

The scenery here is amazing! I've made two new friends, Roberto and Maria. They are the caretakers of the estate and the property.

Stephanie, I have to go. I have an email to reply to, and I have an early start in the morning. May we speak tomorrow?"

"Sure darling! Sweet dreams good night!"

"Thank you, sweet dreams to you and good night."

Annabella goes through her emails and opens the email she received from Santiago.

Mustering up her thoughts, she writes a reply.

"Hello Santiago,

I want to say a few things. You own your own life. I will not say that there was nothing between us.

Looking back now; it was a time of great feelings for us both. In reality, it's just part of a dream or wishful thinking. I could never leave my husband at this age because he's older. Your mind must be free to do this. You have your freedom. I do not.

I am a married woman and cannot just act upon my feelings as I wish. Honestly, our age is against us.

We both know what we are losing, but there is no way of predicting the future to say that we'd be   perfect for each other.

I need a man to care about me, to look after me in every way, not just financially. Emotionally, this is important to me, but you couldn't do it. I knew it wouldn't last more than a year.

I've wanted to tell you that no one is perfect, especially me, but you can't seem to see this. We could most probably be the worst thing for each other. I was thinking I'd like to get another dog, as I miss my Fluffy terribly. That pup was like my child.

I have to go now,

Take care and look after yourself.

Bye"

Hitting the "send" button, she places her phone on the nightstand she readies for bed.

The sky was still dark when the rooster started to crowing at the top of his lungs.

Annabella opens her eyes and looks out the window it is still dark and the rooster continues to crow. Looking at the time on her phone, its 4:30 a.m.

Dragging herself into the shower, she dresses and heads downstairs into the main kitchen makes herself some tea. Taking her tea, she heads back upstairs to her bedroom.

Checking her phone for messages she feels chilled and wraps herself in a blanket.

Opening the balcony doors, she heads outside to watch dawn break. Such a beautiful and majestic sight to see. The colours of the sky changing, the sun popping up on the eastern horizon, she has a spectacular view, like she did in the cockpit of the jet.

A sense of calm came over Annabella while watching the sunrise. It was a new day, a new adventure and possibly a chance at a new life. Today the "small guests" were arriving.

Annabella had no idea that forty-five minutes had passed as she watched the sunrise, she noticed Roberto was out feeding the horses, the hens, and the goats. Roberto collected the eggs from the hen house

Maria had cleaned their little cottage and was making her way over to the Chateau. It was time for Maria to begin her daily chores and cleaning. In her hand was a fresh bouquet of flowers from the garden. Annabella thought about how kind this was of Maria.

A message sounds on her phone. It was Theo.

"Good Morning. I hope you slept well." Thinking to herself, how does he know I'm awake?

Hitting reply, she writes: "How did you know I would be awake this time of the morning?"

Five minutes later; Theo responds. "The rooster, the morning sunrise, and expectation that you might receive a response from me."

Annabella thought carefully about how to respond.

"The two guests that you asked me to look after, are they your children?"

Theo replied: "Yes, they are my girls. Please make sure you take good care of them!

Speak later.

Have a great day!"

Annabella knew that no "sane person" would send their daughters to be looked after by someone they've never met. Smiling and setting aside her thoughts, she figured Theo was just teasing her.

Annabella was left at the mercy of time until they arrive so she headed downstairs to see Maria. Maria was placing the flowers in a vase on the table for Annabella.

Maria asks: "Would you like some breakfast?" Annabella replied: "No thank you Maria. I'm still full from last night's dinner! I think I'd like to take a walk around the grounds this morning."

The morning air was still cold. A brisk morning walk will do Annabella good. Heading towards the garden she could not help but notice the immaculately cut grass. The garden was lovely, and lead to a slope.

Looking down the slope, she could see the olive tree that Roberto told her about where he encountered the drone making the film of the property; as well as the dirt road that leads and joins the road that leads to the house. So much to see and take in here at this magical place.

CHAPTER TWELVE
NEW ARRIVALS

Looking into the distance she saw the beauty of the morning mist covering the mountains. The morning sun was slowly clearing the mist and burning beautifully in the sky. Looking at her watch, it was now just around 10:00 a.m.

On the dirt road that leads to the house, she saw a yellow car going past and disappearing behind the forest trees. Running up the hill in excitement, she'd forgotten how far it was from the Chateau. Annabella had to slow herself down to take a deep breath of mountain air. It was refreshing.

Slowly approaching the house, she did not see Maria who was also waiting with excitement. The taxi arrived and pulled up next to Roberto who was down the hill. Roberto points the driver up to the front of the house where Annabella is standing huffing and puffing, her hair a mess, her cheeks flushed from running, the taxi approaches.

"I have a delivery for Mrs. Amir"

"I am Mrs. Amir" replied Annabella. The driver exits the cab and heads to the back door.

He returns with a box that has air vents in it and places it on the ground, and then another box, which appears to be heavier. Roberto comes to the fence by the side of the road and looks across the road. Annabella leans down and gently opens the box to find two white Maltese puppies, with a little water next to them; she is gobsmacked.

"What do you have there?" asks Roberto

Annabella takes out each puppy and holds them in each hand, while kissing their heads. "They are little puppies!"

"Well make sure you don't lose them, or some fox will have them for dinner! There are a lot of wild animals around here!" Roberto returns to his work.

Maria steps out the house and sees Annabella holding the two puppies in both hands.

"Maria, we have just adopted these two babies!" Handing over one of them to Maria she takes the puppy and starts stroking the beautiful white coat on her back.

"I need a signature, please to say they have been delivered safe and sound." said the driver "Could you sign here?"

Annabella takes his pen and quickly signs the paperwork. The driver gets back in the cab and heads off the property. Suddenly Annabella is overcome with emotion remembering "Fluffy" whom she loved and adored so much. Looking at Maria, her eyes welled up in tears, Annabella speaks: "I used to have one of these pups, her name was Fluffy, my great companion, sadly, she passed away six months ago."

"Well, now God has blessed you with two! Let's take them in and make them comfortable!"

Moments later in the kitchen Annabella is reading, a leaflet that came in the second box about how often to feed them and the list of vaccinations they've both had.

There was a certificate that explained that they were pure bred Maltese along with their lineage.

The second box contained enough food for the two for some time.

Just then Roberto walks in and stands there looking at the little dogs

"They are cute proper lady dogs. They are definitely not hunting dogs! Do they have names?" Annabella looks at the pedigree certificate for the names.

"The one with the black spot on her cheek is called "Paris" the other one is called "Venus" both are female."

"Paris and Venus, nice names for girls. We had a hunting dog for fourteen years named Rebel. He passed away last year and we thought it was fitting to bury him by the waterfall, he loved it there."

"I am sorry to hear that Roberto. I was telling Maria that I lost my dog Fluffy six months ago. Such an incredibly painful loss."

"Yes, well, I have work to do." Roberto turns and walks out, leaving Annabella and Maria fussing over the two puppies.

Two hours later, Roberto returns back from the work shed with a wooden enclosure he'd built for the puppies. "This is so they don't wander and get lost in this big house." Annabella notices that on one half of the quarter, he has soft pillows for them to sleep and rest on, the rest is left bare, with two little bowls of food and some drinking water, and room for them to walk and wander. How precious of Roberto Annabella thinks to herself.

Annabella gets to work with her cell camera and begins taking pictures of the puppies in that sweet enclosure Roberto had built for them. Only five photos but, she wanted to send them to Stephanie to show her that what had arrived was not human at all but rather, two perfect little female puppies.

Annabella wanders outside to send Theo a message. It is a beautiful sunny day and she is feeling amazing!

"Theo, Thank you, for Paris and Venus! They have arrived safe and sound and are perfectly precious. We will guard them with our lives, until you arrive!"

Hitting the send button, she looks off into the distance to try and pinpoint the sound she was hearing. It was the NATO fighter jets flying through the valleys they often come to the area for pilot training.

Annabella's eyes are drawn to a large transport truck at the bottom of the hill. Could this be the furniture for the converted barn?

Making her way to the front of the house, she sees Maria outside with Roberto. Joining them Annabella watches as the driver gets out and says; "We have a delivery for you."

"What is it?" asked Roberto curiously "It is a car." "A car?" "Are you sure it is for us?" asked Roberto The driver looks at the delivery board, he has in his hand and then passes it onto Roberto

"Is this the address?" asked the driver "Yes" said Roberto as the back of the truck was lowered. Inside there is a beautiful white convertible Mercedes SL500 AMG.

The assistant gets into the truck rear entrance and starts up the car.

Slowly placing the car in reverse, he backs the car onto the driveway. Once on the drive, the assistant stands next to the truck and driver pushes the hydraulic lift into place and sates: "I need a signature please."

"You must be Roberto De La Mancha Surgio?" "Yes" replied Roberto and he began inspecting the car for any damages. Roberto found no damages and takes the clipboard, signs the receipt, and handed it back to the driver.

"Thank you! The assistant asks, "Which one of you ladies is Mrs. Amir?" Annabella looks at Maria and Roberto "I'm Mrs. Amir" replied Annabella "Mrs Amir, my name is Nicholas. I am part of the Mercedes Training Team that is sometimes assigned to teach the new owners about this car. Have you ever driven this model of Mercedes before?" "No never."

"I have been instructed to teach you everything there is to know about this car. This way you will know where everything is, and how everything works. Please let us begin." Opening the passenger door for her, Annabella enters the car.

"I don't understand why you are to teach me all there is to know about driving this car?"

"Obviously Mr. Amir, wants you to know what the car does is all about and how to drive it safely."

"There is one small problem."

"What's that?"

"I can assure you, that this vehicle is not from my husband."

"Mrs Amir, I don't know why I was assigned to teach you the workings of this car but, I would really appreciate it if you will help me to accomplish what I have been assigned to do here today. I am sure there is a valid reason for this but, we both don't seem to have the answer."

They both put their seat belts on; he starts up the car, and then turns to Annabella

"Mrs. Amir, I want you to do something. I want you to pull this lever back, until the roof is completely down.

Please don't release it till the retractable roof is safely down and locked."

Annabella pulls on the silver lever, following her instructions; they are now in a convertible car.

Roberto and Maria look on with raised eyebrows. The car starts to drive down the slope away from the house, Roberto looks at the driver of the truck. This does not seem to be upsetting to him.

Ten minutes along in the drive, the car is blazing along the mountain lanes. Annabella's hair is floating around her. Nicholas explains where everything is in the car, and what it does. There is a straight away on the road, Nicholas puts his foot down on the accelerator, and Annabella is pushed backwards virtually glued to the seat. Annabella thinks this is her opportunity to find out who the car belongs to after all, cars have to be registered to someone.

"Who is this car registered to?"

"I honestly don't know, but my girlfriend works in the registration department of "Mercedes France" where the car was bought. I can ring her and ask."

"Please! I would really appreciate the call."

Nicholas stops the car on the side of the road and makes the phone call to his girlfriend. In several minutes he gets all the information. Getting a notepad out of his pocket, he writes down all the information.

"The car is registered to a company called Theorem Ltd."

"Theorem Ltd?"

Nicholas gives her the piece of paper with the correct spelling Annabella.

Checking the internet on her phone, "Theorem Ltd" doesn't exist, but the dictionary version of meaning of Theorem explains the word as: "It's a noun: that means; a general proposition not self-evident but proved by a chain of reasoning; a truth established by means of accepted truths.

"Are you sure it's called Theorem Ltd? There's no such company on the internet?"

"Oh, I forgot to tell you, the money was transferred to the purchase of the car from Belize."

"Belize? I don't know anyone from Belize." Annabella was completely searching her mind for possibilities when Nicholas interrupts

"I think it's time for you to drive." "Annabella exits the passenger side and walks around the car getting into the driver's seat. Placing her seatbelt on she begins to drive slowly along the road.

After an hour of driving, Annabella pulls the car into the drive at the Chateau, closes the roof, and turns off the car. Annabella and Nicholas exchange handshakes once out of the car. Nicholas hurries to the transport truck where he and the driver begin down the driveway and off the Estate.

Annabella rushes to her room, she sits out on the balcony.

Opening her laptop, she begins to research

Belize. Belize is a tax haven, it's one of the countries that do not give out information about who owns companies there and who has bank accounts there. Reading further, she stumbles across information about drug dealers hiding money there as well as state leaders.

Could this be Erol her former lover from Turkey?

Erol was a drug dealer in France when they were together. They had been apart for over twenty-five years now and Annabella calculates that Erol's age would be around eighty-five or more years old now; that's if he were still alive. Erol made her life hell, just thinking about him, shook her up; she'd never go back to him.

Talk about over thinking; Annabella realized her mind was racing and she was getting ahead of herself. Soon enough she would find out, but for now she was tired from all the fresh air, the drive and oh yes, the new puppies. Annabella lay upon her bed and drifted off to sleep for about a half an hour. Her dreams were of the sea with a man she'd never met before, yet she was in love with him, madly in love. Out of the blue, came two loud pings. It was her phone.

Rushed out of her dream, now in the moment and awake, there were messages from Santiago and a Skype from Theo

Reading the message from Theo first

"Annabella,

The car that was delivered today, is fully insured for any driver.

Please feel free to use it. If you have any problems get in contact with Gabriel. He will sort it out. I hope your stay in the house is pleasant!

I hope my babies are doing well.

Theo"

She thinks for a few seconds, then gathers her courage and replies

"Theo,

Thank you for allowing me to use the car while I am here, it's rather lovely! The babies are doing well and had arrived safely. My stay is very pleasant!"

I do have a question for you; what line of work are you involved in?

Annabella"

She thinks for a second and then she hits the send key and the message goes to Theo. Annabella can see that he is writing a reply so she waits.

"Theo31

My work takes me all over the world. It all depends on what I have to deal with.

She is animated and she gets to writing right away

"So, are you some eccentric businessman that collects, houses and cars around the world?"

Message sent

Theo31

"The furniture will be delivered to decorate the barn beginning of next week."

Bye for now."

Annabella closes the Skype. Exhaling deeply looks at her emails to read the email from Santiago.

"Let no man in the world have

The gift from god or nature

To see the little girl living

In emotional poverty

Living in fear and insecurity

Living in a sixty-two-year-old woman

I have come to see and know

I love with all my heart

All that I have seen

All that I knew

All that I have given

All that I love with you

Is given from my soul

To furnish your soul

When the choices come

No material gifts

No emotional gifts

Will match the immortal love I have in me

That only lives to love you."

Santiago"

She reads the poem again and she drifts back in time to five years ago when she fell in love with him. It's been five years, yet her emotions go wild when she thinks of Santiago.

Annabella hides her emotions by self-depravation.

Knowing that he loves and adores her gives her the sense of energy and love that she has never felt before.

Santiago had given Annabella so much love that whenever she thinks of Santiago this love always comes alive in her no matter what her circumstances are at the time.

The past four years have been a testament to those feelings. Annabella did not respond to Santiago's email.

CHAPTER THIRTEEN
MAGICAL WATERFALL

Later that night, Annabella, Maria and Roberto are gathered at the kitchen table for supper in the little cottage.

"Tomorrow we are going to the small lake. Would you like to come with us?" asked Roberto

"What about Paris and Venus? We cannot leave them at home for a long period of time." replied Annabella

"We can put them in a basket and take them with us. We will bring their food and pillows, they will love the lake!" Maria's voice was kind and gentle

"Are you sure?"

"Sure, I'm sure!"

"We have to keep an eye on them though there are brown bears, wolves, wild boars, red deer, wildcats, mouflons, squirrels, lynx and lizards, as well as Raptors. Especially the royal eagles and eagle-owls. This is not Paris!

This is God's country!" explained Roberto with full knowledge of what he'd just spoken.

"Are we going by tractor?"

"No tractor can go down that pony path. We go with the horses. Have you ever been on a horse before?" asked Roberto

"No, never!"

"Well, there's nothing to it! You pull to the left, to go left; you pull to the right, to go right.

When you want to go forward you tap with both feet on the horse's side and when you want to stop you pull both reins back. It's simple, there's nothing to it!" said Roberto smiling.

"Don't worry Annabella the horses are old, and tame. They will be tied to each other in a line Roberto leading the way. We will not be galloping across the country.

The horses will be walking," said Maria calming Annabella

"Well, that's comforting to know! I better be going. Thank you both for a wonderful evening!" Annabella heads towards the door and outside.

Once outside, Roberto calls to her, "Annabella!" Annabella replies "Yes Roberto!"

"In the morning we leave at dawn, be ready!"

"Why so early?"

"You'll see!" Roberto returns to the cottage, Maria is at the door.

Maria Smiles "We are going to have breakfast by the lake, it's very beautiful there!"

"I look forward to it! Good Night Maria."

She looks at Annabella for a few seconds, then turns and walks into the cottage. Annabella walks past the white gleaming Mercedes that shines in the moonlight and goes into the house, thinking how extraordinary it was.

Annabella pets the puppies and heads up to her room. Once out on her balcony, she searches the stars and again speaks out loud; "Please

God, I am sixty-two years old, for once write a good ending for me in life. I don't have much time left."

Her phone starts ringing in the room. Four steps in, she grabs her phone, "Hello Stephanie, how are you? " I'm fine darling. How are you tonight, are you having a good time?"

"Everything is fine, we took a delivery of a convertible white Mercedes today that sounds like thunder and drives like lightning. Tomorrow, we are going to have breakfast by the lake. I will send you some pictures. Apart from that, so far everything is fine. Hey, I just had an idea! Why don't you come here to the house there is plenty of room!

"Hey, don't tempt me, I know how to tempt myself very well!" expressed Stephanie "I will think about it ok?"

"Ok, and in the meantime, I will ask Theo and let you know. I'm sure he won't say no."

"What makes you think he won't say no?" asked Stephanie

"I don't know! I get a good feeling about this man. I feel like he is protecting me. He is always direct and always polite. He's never met me in real life. I found out today, he paid for the Mercedes that was delivered here today with money transferred from a company in Belize.

"I hope he is not some drug lord."

"Don't be so ridiculous, you have such fertile imagination! Gabriel does not represent such people; he has a sixth sense like radar. If there was something not right about this guy, he would have picked up on it, and dropped him no matter how much money he had!" Stephanie exclaimed.

"I guess you're right. Please give my regards to Gabriel. May we speak tomorrow? I am going to get some sleep now as I have to

leave at dawn with Maria and Roberto." Sweet dreams! Good night"
"Goodnight Annabella, sweet dreams." Stephanie hung up.
Annabella heads into the bathroom to take a shower and brush her teeth. The shower would feel great and help her relax.

Annabella slips into her pyjamas and into bed. In moments she was fast asleep.

The large window open, white sheer curtains, floating gently in the morning breeze; her peaceful sleep was rudely disturbed by the crowing of the rooster!

It could not be morning already! The roster continues! Cock-a-doodle-doo, cock-a-doodle-doo, cock-a-doodle-doo.

Reluctantly, Annabella opens her eyes to and steps out of bed half asleep, making her way across the room to the bathroom, she blurts out "Roberto shoot that rooster!"

After twenty minutes Annabella walks out the big house and makes her way across the road with a cup of coffee in her hand. Roberto has already saddled up the horses and is securing them to each other with ropes.

"Good morning Roberto, it's too early to be going out this time of the morning." said Annabella is trying to keep herself warm and watching Roberto skilfully securing the saddle on his horse Beauteous.

"There is a reason for everything in life, and there is a season for everything in life, if you are lucky to combine both together at the same time, then something magical happens." Maria comes out of the cottage with a warm winter coat and a scarf for Annabella, Maria is already dressed to go with a warm coat on and scarf.

"Here put these on before you freeze to death in the morning dew!"

"Thank you, Maria; I never realized just how cold it is." Annabella takes the coat and scarf and puts them on.

"Is this a random adventure we are going on, because I am here?" asked Annabella, looking across the distant mountains with mysterious clouds covering their peaks

"This is no random adventure to impress you. This is a weekly ritual for us that we have been doing this for the past thirty years." explained Roberto as he checks the shotgun that it is fully loaded and slides it down the side of the saddle into the leather holster he'd made for the gun.

Annabella and Maria walk inside the cottage and bring out food from the house for the picnic, and a straw basket that is for, Paris and Venus. Roberto distributes all the sacks of food and blankets as well as the straw basket to all three horses so they have equal weight to carry.

Two horses are tied to Beauteous Roberto's horse. He pulls her along and all the horses move off in a line towards the middle of the road between the big house and the cottage.

Annabella and Maria go into the house bring out Venus and Paris and some food for them. Roberto puts them gently into the straw basket.

Turning to Annabella, Roberto says; "Here, let me help you." "Ok, grab the saddle put your right foot here and pull on the saddle and I will help from here and then cock your leg over the saddle, don't hesitate just do it in one motion." requested Roberto kindly.

Annabella grabs the saddle and puts her right foot in Roberto's hands and she pulls, Roberto pushes her up, she cock's her leg and she is over the saddle. Annabella holds onto the saddle in front of her like she is holding on for dear life.

"Relax, we will make a country girl out of you yet!" said Maria with a smile as she mounted her horse smoothly. Roberto gets on his horse and gave it a little nudge with both feet and makes a funny noise with his tongue between his teeth "tutu."

The horse starts to pull away tagging Annabella's and Maria's horses. They are tied to each other like a chain, Annabella on the middle horse, Maria on the last horse, Roberto in the lead. Dawn is just breaking and the rooster continues his song from the top of his voice "cock-a-doodle-doo."

The silhouette of the horses slowly disappears down the slope on the other side. The horses follow a narrow path that is just big enough for single file horses.

The path had been carved out from years of travel down the path on horseback. It was Roberto's father that had carved this path many years ago when he would take Roberto to the picnic grounds each week.

Annabella watches Roberto skilfully guide his horse along the winding path.

The misty mountains surround them remind Annabella of a horror movie; dark and haunting. Roberto is pointing with his finger and talking to Annabella, "You see that mountain over there? That's where we are going!" Annabella figures the mountain is about a half a mile away, but it's joined by other mountains and Annabella replies, "The landscape all looks the same to me!"

"You are a city girl, what would you know about this kind of land?" Forty minutes of winding track the horses finally come to the side of the mountain that Roberto was pointing at. They continue. Just as they get to the other side of the mountain, Roberto stops the horses. All they can see is another beautiful mountain that is joined on with a horse track leading there. The top of the mountain is covered in mist.

In and through the clouds, water comes gushing out. It looks like the water is falling out of the sky. It's a beautiful waterfall! At the bottom of the fall is a small lake that is about thirty feet across and round and the lake turn into a small river on the opposite side of the waterfall that gently flows down the winding mountain river.

It's so serene, nearly surreal. Annabella takes out her phone and start taking pictures.

There are two majestic red deer, drinking from the lake, she takes pictures of them, and then she takes the larger picture of the waterfalls falling into the lake below.

Soon the deer sense a presence. There is movement in the mountains, as the horses start to move towards the lake slowly, they run away around the mountain into the clouds that surround it.

Annabella is mesmerised by the spectacle. "It is beautiful!" said Annabella with a voice that expressed such surprise and joy.

"Welcome to the Waterfall Restaurant! This is where we will have breakfast!" said Roberto proudly

Soon they were at the edge of the small lake and the waterfall; they all dismount from the horses. Roberto ties his horse Beauteous to a broken dry tree trunk that has been there for years, there was plenty of grass, green grass, to graze on for all the horses.

Annabella starts taking deep breaths filling her lungs with fresh mountain air. Roberto walks over to a pile of small stones that make a little mountain like structure and picks up a stone the size of his hand and adds it to the stack. Maria does the same.

At the bottom of the little pile of stones that make a little mountain on a flat stone is carved, Franco Surgeo, and under that his wife's name, Valentina Surgeo, and under that is Roberto De la Mancha Surgeo, and Maria Surgeo.

Annabella keeps with tradition, picks up a stone and lays top of the pile, then stands back and reads the names. "Your parents, Roberto?" asked Annabella "Yes, " replied Roberto with a sad voice; making the sign of the cross upon his chest with his right hand. "It was my parents that introduced me to this place when I was a boy. Both requested that their ashes be spread into this lake so that the waters that flow below these mountains can take them travelling through the mountains they had loved so much.

Both myself, and Maria have the same wish when we depart, but we don't know who to ask to perform that task."

He walks over to another little pile of stones that has wild oregano and rosemary bushes growing around it. This is our beloved dog Rebel that died last year.

We want to get another dog but, Rebel is still with us and my soul says to wait until he lets go.

We must wait until he has transitioned into the mystical realms of the universe where he will play with other dogs and animals, and then we will get another dog."

The horses all take a drink from the lake, Roberto starts to take down the food from the saddles and the shotgun, which he puts next to the baskets of food and Paris and Venus, who are still in the basket. Opening the basket, he looks at the two of them, such beautiful furry white pups.

Annabella looks and sees a dark spot where a fire has been lit many times in the past that is surrounded by big stones making it into a permanent cooking place. Maria opens a thick woollen blanket and spreads it on the ground close to the circled fire place. Roberto starts gathering dry wood and bringing them and dumping them into the circle of stones. After ten minutes all the food is out on the blankets and in the small straw baskets.

The sun starts to break through the mountains. Roberto picks up his double barrel shotgun and puts it near the blanket. Standing up and carefully looking at the mountain on the other side of the valley Roberto speaks. "Hello, my old friend, you've came out to say good morning to us!"

Annabella looks across but she cannot see anything. Looking even closer, focusing her eyes, she still cannot see anything. Finally, she asks "Is there something there on that mountain?" "Yes over there!"

Roberto as pointing with his finger, Annabella focuses her eyes, she still cannot see anything.

"Over there!" Maria said, pointing her finger. "I can't see a thing!"

Roberto lights the bundle of dried woods in the circle, and then walks over to his horse, and gets the binoculars and hands them to Annabella

" Here, try these" handing them to her, she puts them to her eyes and looks and then finally, she sees a brown bear walking slowly across the mountain range. "This is the first time I have ever seen a bear in the wild!" said Annabella When she finally lowers the binoculars down from her eyes, Roberto looks at her

"For six hundred thousand years the brown bear roamed these mountains, within one hundred years, bear hunting, and protection of farming livestock killed them all off, until the nineteen nineties. The French government stepped in. They introduced new brown bears to the Pyrenees. Now there is around twenty brown bears roaming the mountains, and they have a conservation order on them. We are lucky to see one today!"

Annabella was still looking up at the mountain to see if she could see the bear with her naked eyes as Roberto did, but she could not locate it, and after a few more seconds of looking she turned to Roberto, he is stripped down to his boxer shorts. "What are you doing?" asked

Annabella with a shocked voice "I am going for a swim" replied Roberto

"The first time I tried to swim across this lake I was fifteen years old I nearly died.

I had to come out of there the water is freezing, but my father (making the sign of the cross on his chest again) God rest his soul, he would swim across each week. After a while I got used it. Now, I look forward to it each week as it wakes up the senses!"

Roberto then walks into the lake with a grin on his face and starts to swim; Maria puts the shotgun close to her.

"There are royal eagles here and they are huge, their wingspan can be between five to seven feet long their claws are razor sharp. They've carried off a small mountain goats, rabbits, and small dogs, it's better to be safe than sorry!"

Maria puts long sausages onto a skewer for the morning BBQ, she also throws into the fire several potatoes that will be roasted, and then she starts cutting up tomatoes, cucumbers, and a large piece of cheese for the breakfast. Annabella gives some food and water to Paris and Venus.

"Maria, are you happy with your life?"

"How can anybody not be happy, living the life we live? Look around you, it's beautiful, and it's magical!" said Maria, looking at Annabella with searching eyes knowing that something was missing in her life.

"Perhaps, you haven't found what you are looking for in life Annabella."

"The problem is I don't really know myself what I am looking for, or what I want in life."

"I hope that one day you find what you are looking for Annabella. I hope you will come back and visit us here in the future. We have room for you in the cottage just like we have room in our hearts for you." said Maria lovingly

"Thank you! Being here feels like a life changing experience for me."

"It's the air! It takes away all the stress, and the beauty of looking at all this, soothes the soul. How many people in the world or a dog for that matter, can claim to have a backyard as beautiful as this?"

"It's a fairy tale! It's beautiful! Maria, I promise you, I will come back here again!"

"I believe you will."

One hour later, Roberto is fully dressed after his swim and breakfast is being served on plates around the fire.

Paris and Venus are between Annabella and Maria, looking cosy in their protective basket.

"When we started off so early in the morning I had no idea that we would end up in such a beautiful place!

With it being so cold this morning I never imagined how lovely and peaceful this place would turn out to be, this is how I envision heaven!"

"Well, speaking of heaven I said earlier, this is where Maria and I have decided to have our ashes placed when that day comes." said Roberto philosophically, as they all sat around the fire eating their breakfast.

About an hour later, they were all packed and mounted and they were heading back to the house. At the top of the hill before going around the mountain to leave the waterfall behind them, there is a little lay-by there, Roberto engineers his horse Beauteous around so they can all take one last look at the waterfall before going around the mountain.

As the horses turn and stop, they look down into the waterfall, Annabella's eyes open wide. Speechless, and wanting to look at this for a very long time, there is a beautiful rainbow that goes across the waterfall above the lake. Annabella takes her phone and clicks a few pictures, then looks at the beauty of this place. In all of her life, nothing had ever been so perfectly beautiful. Annabella's eyes lingered in the moment, freeze framing her surroundings in her mind for all time.

Roberto nudges the horse with his feet, the horses start moving along, and they leave the rainbow, the waterfall, and lake behind them as they head around the mountain, leading home.

That afternoon Annabella sat outside on a sun lounge chair, while Paris and Venus are let free to play by her feet.

Roberto was on the tractor cutting the grass going up and down the garden that slopes downwards and stretches for about a hectare. On one side cypress trees, on the other side as borders are large trees.

Annabella thought about Maria and Roberto and how happy they are living in the middle of nowhere and yet, Annabella in her modelling days, lived in a Château similar in size and amenities, with a pool, a sauna, etc. but she was not happy then. She had an "A-Lister lifestyle" with Erol but never the joy that Roberto and Maria had.

They mingled with celebrities, and famous people, in nightclubs and private parties, but this bored Annabella as she was far happier alone at home.

Annabella checks her phone, no messages. Checking her photos, she took earlier at the waterfall, she selects four pictures and she sends them to Stephanie, with the caption "Garden of Eden." Looking at her Skype, there are no messages from Theo. Annabella decides to take the initiative and write a message.

"Theo,

"Good afternoon. I wanted to ask you if you are alright with me inviting a friend to visit for a few days. The guest in question is Gabriel's wife, Stephanie. I thought it only proper to ask your permission, as it is your home.

Stephanie is such a sweet soul; I'd love to have her opinion on my decorating ideas while she is here. Please be kind enough to let me know if this is permissible.

Annabella"

Hitting the send button, she sets the phone down and turns her attention to Paris and Venus. These two little babies were adorable as she played chase with them, scoops them up and kisses their faces, Annabella can't help but be reminded of Fluffy as a puppy. Annabella grabs the two and takes them inside, places some food and water in their pen and pets them gently as they whine for her attention.

Annabella walks into the main living room where Maria is dusting some statues and clocks. Annabella grabs Maria by the hands and drags her outside and they stand next to the white Mercedes, Maria is staring at Annabella.

"No, no way, what if something happens? What if you scratch it?" said Maria

"Nothing is going to happen, we are insured! Come on, get in!"

Maria looks at herself up and down at her clothing, Annabella feels guilty that she did not think of this first; Annabella says: "You have twenty minutes, GO!"

Annabella smiled, as Maria darts towards the cottage.

In the meantime, Annabella, turned the car around, lowered the roof, and the convertible was waiting for Maria when she came out of the cottage.

Maria exits the cottages and runs to the car. Wearing a beautiful soft cheese cloth summer dress, her hair brushed, and an ever-so- soft light lip colour, brightened her lips, she looks stunning.

"This is the best I could do." blurted Maria "Your best is beautiful!" Maria gets into the car. Annabella put's her foot down on the accelerator and the car speeds away making a thundering noise from the huge engine.

At the bottom of the hill as they are going past below the garden; Maria reaches out and beeps the horn. Roberto sees them and Maria encourages Annabella to slow down so they can both wave at Roberto! Maria says loudly, "We will be gone for a while!" Roberto waves and responds; "God help all men!"

Two kilometres into the drive on a winding road, there are two jeeps with four young men in one, and three in the other. One of the young guys looks behind him and sees Annabella and Maria in the Mercedes. He nudges his friend.

The boys begin to tease Annabella and Maria, saying things, like; "Hey baby, I love your car, do you want to swap? "How about you take my number… The cat-calling continues, then Annabella says; "Let's go!"

 Slowing the car down almost to a stop, then she hits the gas! This car is supercharged and the two women fly past the jeeps as though they are standing still!

 Maria moves her fingers as if to say bye, she looks in front of her just as they are passing the first jeep.

There is a car coming at them. Maria, let's out that familiar, "Ahhhhhh!" and Annabella calmly steers the car into her lane and they disappear down the winding road.

As they are going through the valleys, Annabella states: "I have decided to start living Maria!" Maria gives her an odd look.

Annabella hesitates for a reply

"We are on the last chapter of our lives, make sure the living you make is the best. Make up for the lost time. I have no regrets about my life!"

"Do you want some of mine, I have loads of regrets! Honestly, the number of mistakes I have made, you could write a book about them!" Annabella replied.

"Roberto used to have this great saying, that he used to love reciting, but nowadays he does not say it any longer."

"What did he used to say?"

"He used to say that, "Every day is a new life to a wise man." He has this philosophy that every day we wake up, and we are born new."

"You can tell he is a wise old soul when you hear things like that." responded Annabella with respect.

"We have had our own share of problems. Who doesn't?"

"You want to talk about it? I have no wax in my ears and I hear every word you say!"

"When Roberto's father passed away Roberto was devastated!

When he had to release his father's ashes into the lake, he walked in as far as he could. Standing there he said; "We used to come here to swim, have BBQ's talk about philosophy and life. Today I stand here physically and you are in the spirit world. I return you to the earth, the place you loved so much!"

"I'm doing what you wished for me to do for you when you left. I am setting you free upon the waters that travel by day and night, in the sunshine and under the moonlit sky. You were a great friend, a great philosopher and above all else, a great father and teacher."

"I love you, Rest in Peace." Slowly he emptied the urn into the water and watched as the river carried the ashes away."

Maria turns and looks at Annabella; She is wiping her eyes

"Are you crying?"

"I am! I am known as, "Annabella the cry baby." I think the reason I cry is that I can relate to people and their sufferings. My emotional vibrations are very high and sensitive. I call this syndrome; My Empathic Syndrome."

Twenty-five minutes later, they are about to enter the high street of Andorra.

Maria says: "Welcome to Andorra la Vella." Everywhere they turn; all eyes are on the car. People are staring as if to ask; "who is driving and who is the passenger?"

After a few moments of this, Anabella, says; "Maria, do you have a driver's license?"

"Yes, Why?" Asked Maria "It is about to come in handy!" Annabella stopped the car and got out heading to the passenger door. Opening the door, she pleads with Maria; "Yes, Yes, please drive!" Maria is positive this is madness, but she gets into the driver's seat and fastens her seatbelt.

Annabella put's her seatbelt on. Maria puts the Mercedes into drive and slowly takes off down the street. All kinds of shopping offers were displayed in the shop windows as they whisked past on their way home.

The weather is beautiful and the high street is filled with shoppers and tourists. After ten minutes, they are on the road back to the house.

The road is straight with are no cars up ahead of them "Shall we blow some cobwebs out of this super machine?" inquired Maria to Annabella, who smiles and says; "Yes, go for it!"

Maria puts her foot down on the accelerator and the car takes off down the road like a missile.

Annabella looks at the speedometer Maria is doing a hundred and thirty kilometres per hour. Maria then slows down, there are cars ahead.

"Mercedes SL, 55 AMG, hand built with a supercharged V8 engine. Top speed, three hundred and thirty-five kilometres an hour, electronically limited to, two hundred and fifty kilometres an hour. Above all, the greatest quality is that it has is class, elegance, and muscle when your foot decides to hit the floor!" Maria floored Annabella with her knowledge of this car, and never taking her eyes off the road.

Maria turns the car to the side road and drives on going towards the house. Outside the house, Roberto had just finished collecting eggs from the chicken coup.

Approaching the road, the car comes whizzing up the drive, Roberto cannot decide if he should stay where he is or go ahead and cross the road.

It's too late; Maria puts on the brakes and the car tire's lock. They slide along the gravel stopping one foot away from Roberto, who drops one single egg onto the ground. Maria and Annabella just starred at each other with smiles on their faces.

"I'm insured but, I am not going to benefit if I die! You should stick to driving tractors!" Roberto was looking at the one egg on the ground.

"She has a face of an angel, but the heart of lion!" Roberto said to Annabella as he walks away into the big house.

Maria presses the button to put the convertible roof on the car. The roof glides over the car and locks itself down again. Maria turns off the engine.

"Where did you learn to drive like that Maria?" asked Annabella, getting her breath back

"My father was a rally driver, and my uncles were all mechanics. They were a great team! They won many rally races. Growing up with them gave me the knowledge of cars and engines. You could safely call me a qualified mechanic without a certificate.

My head was always under the hood of a car, fixing engines. I was even a co-driver in a few rallies with my late father and uncles. That's all in the past. These days I drive a hoover around the house, but I have a real Lamborghini!" Maria is looking at Annabella for a reaction. Annabella believes Maria is joking.

"No! Come on now, I'm not falling for that!"

"What? You don't believe that I have Lamborghini?"

"No, I don't believe you!"

"Ok! Come with me!"

Maria walks towards the building near the cottage that is joined with Roberto's workshop. The building has two huge wooden doors,

Maria swings open one of the doors, and in the middle of the building is a great big tractor.

"This is Lamborghini Mach VRT 250 tractor!"

Walking around the tractor Annabella states: This looks like something on steroids! I didn't know Lamborghini started making tractors!"

"They were making tractors long before they ever made cars."

"Really? I thought you were joking!"

"It all started by accident really. Ferruccio Lamborghini bought a Ferrari 250GT, from Enzo Ferrari; the clutch was stiff, and so he took it apart and learned that the clutch was the same clutch he was using on his tractors. Ferruccio asked Enzo for replacement clutch. Enzo said to him: "What do you know about sports cars you are a silly tractor manufacturer?" Lamborghini took that as a dare and as a challenge and he started building the Lamborghini sports cars."

"Do you actually drive this yourself?"

"Yes!"

They walk out of the garage; Maria closes the door behind her.

"You have the looks of a movie star, or a model on some glossy magazine cover."

"I was a model. When I got married, that all went out the window. Now, every part of my body has grown softer, rounder, and sagging. My hair is a whole other thing! I have to colour my roots every few weeks. I never thought my body would ache in the morning and when it's damp and cold.

When I was in my twenties, I never thought I'd look like this now. I was a beautiful young woman, time has a way of changing that, and I've noticed my confidence is lacking now."

"Who doesn't have confidence in their twenties? They haven't even learned to ask what life is all about at that age!"

"The Parisian Lights" have gone out of me, Maria."

"Yeah, well forget about "Parisian Lights." You should start worrying when the light in your soul starts to go out!

Maybe, the "Parisian Lights" have gone out for you but, the world lights, well they have just come on for you!

You are mature, beautiful, and sensitive with a beautiful soul. You are in the prime of your life, don't think about the past or you will miss the present moment"

Maria said philosophically with a smile, Annabella hugs her.

"Thank you, Maria."

"I guess it's time to get the hoover out and slow down a little now" said Maria walking into the house

Annabella thinks for a second and then she follows her into the house

Annabella walks into the kitchen to check on Paris and Venus. Roberto has the little dogs, one in each hand and he kisses them on their heads and then gently put them down into the wooden pen.

"I suppose, she told you about her great days as a rally driver." said Roberto, knowing that the subject must have come up somewhere along the line.

"Yes and from what I hear, she was pretty good at it too!"

"That she was! Come here, I want to show you something." Roberto and Annabella go outside into the garden area and stand outside the door, looking down the slope of the large garden.

"I thought I would make her day by letting her cut the grass with the lawn tractor one day twenty years ago. She went up and down this garden like she was in a rally car. Every time she went near the trees on either side of the garden I'd cringe. Every time she went near the large ornate pots, I cringed.

 I was looking behind me, praying that my old boss would not come out from the house and find her whizzing around like she was.

Eventually she finished and stopped the tractor right there at the edge of the garden. When she turned off the engine, I hear a voice behind me saying; "Now that's how the grass in the garden should be cut!" For a moment, I thought God was speaking to me. (He makes the sign of the cross again) I looked around me; my boss was standing on the balcony upstairs watching her." Roberto was smiling a kind of cheeky grin.

"Maria had a great time in the car today. Maybe, you should let her cut the garden more often. After all, the tractor is a lot slower than that Mercedes out in front!"

"Not possible! There's an embargo and sanctions on her, she is never allowed to use the tractor again; that's my job!"

"Don't you think that's a little selfish Roberto? Asked Annabella. Roberto's face turns soft

"It has nothing to do with her abilities or skills; she is more than capable and has demonstrated her capabilities throughout our marriage. I worry that something might happen to her.

I have spent nearly forty years with that amazing woman. Not a single day apart. We have never gone to bed with an argument, never gone to sleep or awoken without a kiss. The selfish part of me is that I don't know what I'd do without her if anything happened to her." Roberto shared this with love in his eyes

"I understand. Thank you for sharing this with me." "My pleasure!" said Roberto and turned to walk into the kitchen then stops and turns to look at Annabella

"She likes you, you know?" Annabella turns and looks at Roberto "I like her too very much! As the expression goes; "She is the salt of the earth." said Annabella with a smile

"I like you too!" said Roberto honestly. "Thank you, Roberto, I never had a brother, but, if I did, I would want him to be just like you; strong, wise, and a gentleman."

Annabella's words struck a chord in Roberto's heart and he looks at Annabella for a few seconds and then says, "Thank You." "You can always adopt me if you like!" Roberto leaves the kitchen with Annabella wearing a great big smile.

Annabella felt she was home. Finally feeling like felt she belonged somewhere now. Even though she was only here for three weeks, she was happy like a happy she has not felt for many years, if ever.

Annabella walks into her room carrying her phone, she looks at the messages. There is a message from Theo

"Annabella,

Of course, your guest can come and stay. There is plenty of room there for you and your guest! I hope you are having a good day so far!"

Annabella replies to the message:

"Theo,

"I am having a blast of a day so far! I do hope your day, or morning, depending on where you are in the world; is going well. I want to say Thank You for all your kindness, my stay here so far has been more than memorable."

Warmest regards, Annabella

The message is sent to Theo

Thinking for a few seconds and she rings Stephanie on her cell.

After a few rings Stephanie picks up the phone, she is clearly in a middle of crying

"Stephanie, why are you crying? What's wrong? What happened?" Stephanie still sobbing and crying at the other end of the phone like a baby.

"I've been crying for an hour, I think I have lost 3 pounds since I began crying."

Annabella grows more concerned, it's in her voice

"Has anything happened to Gabriel, or the children?" "No." "Is it a health problem?" "No."

"If it's not family related and it's not health, what is it?"

"The verdict has been delivered, and I am so happy at the conclusion, " said Stephanie still crying trying to compose herself.

"Stephanie! For God's Sake! What are you talking about?"

"It's the book that Gabriel gave me; you know the one, when we met at the hotel."

"Oh, that verdict Yes!" Annabella was relieved. I do remember a book at the hotel when we met."

"I have just finished it. The ending is so sad, that it will penetrate and break even the coldest of hearts into a pool of tears." Stephanie was sobbing.

"Ok, wipe your tears! I have some good news for you!"

"You know who he is? "No!" You spoke with him on the phone? "No!" Have you met him? "No!"

"What is that you are suffering from; No Syndrome?" Well, what kind of good news are you talking about? Please Annabella, get to the point!"

"He said "Yes!" there is silence for a second, "He said yes to what?"

"Will you get to the point I have been crying. I don't want to keep crying. There will be nothing left of me! Well?"

"How would you like to spend a week with me at the house starting on Sunday?"

"Are you serious?"

"Yes! I wrote and asked if it was ok with him, he replied "of course"! You can help me, with the barn, it will give you something to do instead of sitting on your ass reading romance novels and crying alone." Annabella said bursting into a giggle

"I will be there on Sunday for lunch!" What About Gabriel?" asked Annabella?

"Well, What about Gabriel? He can manage a week without me."

"Alright then, I will ask Maria to make up the room next door to me!"

Who is Maria?"

"She is the housekeeper here. I have told you about her before both her and her husband Roberto are very gentle, down to earth, wonderful people, you will love them both!"

"Ok, first things first, I have to find my lingerie!" "What are you going to do with lingerie here, there's nothing but mountains and rolling hills, with gardens and waterfalls."

"Not for their silly! For here! I have to convince Gabriel, that the whole topic of me coming there for a week to keep you company, was his idea!"

"You are so devious!" they both start to giggle.

"See you Sunday Darling! I'm thrilled to be joining you! Good night! "Good night Stephanie, I can't wait to see you!"

Annabella comes out of the house and wanders across the road and goes to the vegetable patch that's near the chicken coup and stables. Maria has her cane basket with her and is uprooting some onions and garlic along with some herbs and other veggies to make a salad with. Annabella notices that Maria is not wearing any shoes and is barefoot.

"Do you like gardening?"

"I used to love gardening, but I have lost interest in the past few years. We used to grow lots of fruits, not so many vegetables, or salads. I'm more of a flower person and I have all kinds of flowers in the garden as well as fruit trees. The weather is good in Morocco so, most things grow."

"I am more veggies and salads, there is nothing like growing your own and picking them when the time is right. You go from ground to mouth in twenty minutes. It's all organic. Most of the things we eat around are very healthy either organic or wild as nature provides everything we need here."

"There is something magical about this place! I could live here and be happy!"

"The air is pure and clean, we are constantly at nature's mercy and power, and we use both as a blessing."

"Is there any reason why you are barefoot in the garden?"

"Yes, when a person steps on the earth without shoes, the earth takes away all the negative energy from your body!"

"Is that really true?"

Yes! It's called; "Grounding" or "Earthing" When you walk on the ground, placing your feet directly on the ground without shoes or socks, the earth has an intense negative charge. This charge is rich in electrons the scientists say. The earth and its soil are full of antioxidants and free radical destroying electrons. By walking barefoot, one allows the earth to protect them against chronic stress, inflammation, pain, poor sleep, blood sugar, and many common health disorders, including cardiovascular disease." "It is believed that all disease begins with inflammation. This is easy, and comfortable way of fighting off the illness associated with age, weight, and stress. Kick off your shoes sometimes, it's very calming."

"Maybe I should do some grounding stuff, I am always emotionally charged!'

"Try it and see! The only way to know if it's working is to do it!"

Maria puts all the things she has collected in the straw basket and she starts to walk towards the house.

"Maria, we have a guest arriving on Sunday. Another lady, she is just like us in spirit and I know you're going to love her!"

"If she is anything like you that won't be hard to do! I will get the room next door to yours ready   for her for when she arrives."

"Thank you, Maria, her name is Stephanie and she will here by lunch on Sunday."

"What are you thanking me for? It is my job." They walk to the cottage and go inside.

CHAPTER FOURTEEN

LOVE AND NATURES REMEDY

In the little kitchen, Maria empties all the items she collected from the vegetable patch, into the sink and turns on the water to wash them. She is multi-tasking as she takes out a pan and puts it on the stove, she turns and turns off the tap and takes out a salad bowl.

"Do you want to help me cook?"

"Yes! Maria, what do you think about love? Is it all that it's cracked up to be?"

"Now that is a question that a fifteen-year-old would ask when they fall in love for the first time. Are you in love?"

"Who me? No! I just wanted to know what all the fuss is about."

"That is a question for your heart to answer. As far as I know, there are only three kinds of love."

Annabella responds: "What do you mean? Nature, family, and romantic love?"

"No! I mean there is a negative, positive, and then there is crazy. In what order do you want them   explained?"

"How about in the order you have mentioned them?"

"Ok. Negative love is when, someone loves you, but you have no feelings for them. The person in love with you is affected, they suffer dream and hope, but you are not affected emotionally.

"Positive love is, when two people are madly in love with each other, and they give the same love to each other. Tenderness, love, respect and friendship. This is the kind of love where one without the other; in life is half a person, they live but, they are only going through the motions unfortunately this is when one of them dies. The other dies spiritually. This is the strongest love, if you find it, and you have it, you don't need anything else!

Finally, there's crazy love. This is when you are in love with a person and they do not love you. It's also called unrequited love.

Jealousy is a component and is one of the worst of them, longing, desire, this crazy love is the same as negative love I mentioned earlier. The other way around, when you are in love and you are rejected, this can have a profound effect on your self-confidence, your emotions, creating instability and some people take to drinking, some to drugs, some even commit suicide when they feel rejected."

"After hearing all this; I wish I'd never asked now."

"The reality of life is cold and unforgiving. We spend all our life, trying to stay warm, alive, and loved. The last things that dies with us is, hope. Hope most of the time is hanging by a fragile string, yet if we let go of hope, there is no future."

"No wonder I am an emotional wreck."

"The problem with you is that you are too sensitive, and you need someone who understands you, someone who has a great deal of Savoir-faire."

"I have never been lucky in love. Now at sixty-two years old, everything is falling apart. Where am I going to find Mr. Savoir-faire? Knowing my luck, I will end up finding a man and we will end in a sad-affair, instead of a man who has, Savoir-faire."

"Annabella!"

"What?"

"You are polluting the cottage with negative energy! Change your thoughts for God's sake, or we are going to be poisoned with this meal tonight!"

"Don't worry Roberto's special brew, will kill any poison! What does he put in that stuff to make it so strong?"

"He won't tell anybody, not even me. He keeps it as a closely guarded secret, let me show you something.

Opening the top cupboard Maria pulls out a shopping bag filled with dried stuff, she opens it and shows it to Annabella, and she looks in and smells it.

"It stinks! Is this what he puts in there making the drink?"

"No, this is Marijuana. Hush! He uses this for his arthritis and it helps him, he grows it here on the mountain. It's better to hear it from him, and I'm sure he will mention this to you at some point."

"Jesus! I am stuck on top of a mountain, with two crazy people, who are actively involved in manufacturing moonshine, and growing Marijuana!"

They both start giggling

"You have lived a sheltered life Annabella!"

"Thank God I was sheltered!"

They break into full laughter in the kitchen.

That evening they all sat around the table eating the food that Maria and Annabella cooked. There are a couple of bottles of red wine on the table. They are drinking with the evening meal, Maria looks at Roberto and states

"We have a guest coming to the house on Sunday."

"That's good! The more, the merrier! Who is it?"

"Her name is Stephanie. A friend of Annabella's and the wife of Mr Alexandre."

"Oh, him! The man with the flying machine! I am sure she is a fine lady, even though I have not forgiven him yet for the flying machine drama. Did you fix a room for her?"

"Roberto De La Mancha Surgeo! Do I tell you how to do your work outside the house?"

"No."

"Then don't tell me how to do my work in the house."

"Sorry. More wine ladies?"

Roberto pours another glass for everyone. The cottage has become a home for Annabella and she has really taken to Maria and Roberto. She loves watching them interact with each other and she adores Roberto.

Roberto is like a small child sometimes, especially a cheeky and a mischievous one, and yet she adores his strength, his wisdom, and in that gentle soul of his; lives a giant fearless bear. He is definitely not easily impressed, he lives by his own rules in life, and this suits him perfectly as well as complimenting his relationship with Maria.

"Any friend of Annabella's is a friend of ours! She will be welcomed and respected, just like Annabella."

"Is this your "Adopt me as your younger brother" speech?"

"Would you prefer to adopt me as your nephew?"

"I beg your pardon!"

"Roberto De La Muncha Surgeo, she is not that old! Look at her, she is beautiful, and she looks fifty years old!"

"That doesn't change night into day; she is still older than me!"

"Are you saying that you would not like me as your older sister?"

"God of all the things you have given this good man, why you couldn't give him a little Savoir-faire!?"

"Never mind about Savoir-faire now, I have high standards. I am not like most men who proclaimed to be knights in shining armour, while wearing tin foil to mask their characters!

"I am incorruptible, my word is my integrity, my justice, my manners, my moral code my philosophy, my principles this is what my word stands for, and this is my life. You should be honoured to have a giant of a man like me to call your younger brother!"

"Roberto, I'd love to adopt you as my younger brother!"

"What about me?"

"Well, if I have a younger brother, and you are his wife, then you are my sister in- law!"

"Then, my dear sister in law, you two go outside, I will perform the ceremony outside I will be with you in a few seconds."

"Ceremony!? What ceremony?"

"I don't know, I have never been adopted before."

Roberto and Annabella go outside of the little cottage. The sky is filled with stars and the white moon hangs like a glowing lamp just above the mountains.

Roberto still hanging onto his glass of wine, Maria walks out of the cottage with a small plastic container that has a little water and a teaspoon in the other hand. Maria kneels down and takes a teaspoon of earth and puts it in the container. Stirring slowly, the mixture becomes a paste consistency. Handing over the plastic container to Annabella, she looks inside and raises an eyebrow.

Maria is on her knees again, this time she takes a handful of soil and gets to her feet. "Roberto give me your right hand," (he stretches his hand out) she turns his hand so that the palm facing the sky she places the handful of soil into Roberto's hand. Taking Annabella's right hand and she places it on top of the earth in Roberto's hand, they both gently clasp the handshake with the soil in their palms.

The ceremony is about to begin when a shooting star streaks across the night sky. Maria looks up, smiles, and is sure this is a sign that the Universe has given her permission to perform the ceremony.

"Religion tells us, that we are all from one God, and when we pray, we pray to one God. We say Thank you to God for our daily bread and the food that comes from nature and the soil.

We Thank God for our rivers, our streams, our oceans, and the food and beauty that is provided from water. Dear God, in your infinite wisdom, the essence and presence, by the laws of nature, and universal etiquette; we ask with grateful hearts for your grace, that you will be our witness here tonight as we stand before you."

"The soil that everything grows from, that takes away the negativity in the body, holding earth in the joined hands, will purify the heart and soul and the friendship, between brother and sister. By the great powers of the universe; I, Maria De Le Mancha Surgeo, declare that my husband, Roberto De Le Muncha Surgeo is officially adopted as a younger brother to Annabella Amir."

Maria dabs her thumb into the paste made of soil and she presses it onto Annabella's forehead, she turns and does the same for Roberto. Finishing, she says, Amen.

Roberto and Annabella look at each other for a few seconds, then they embrace, then they tip the earth out of their hands.

"Thank you, Annabella; I am honoured to have you as my older sister."

"And don't forget who is older! Please don't remind me too often ok?"

"Ok! Time for more wine! Come on girls we are family now!"

Heading towards the cottage door, Annabella put her arm around Maria's shoulder.

"I am blessed to have a sister in-law like you!"

Another shooting star race's across the sky. This is a magical place at night when all the stars are shinning so bright. Such a beautiful place to make wishes and dreams to materialize in the future.

Annabella finishes her wine and leaves the cottage escorted by Roberto and Maria. Three silhouettes walking across the lawn under the night stars and the white glowing moon, such a fantastic end to a beautiful day!

Halfway to the house, another white shooting star goes across the dark sky like someone was drawing a white blurred line across a dark canvas of stars. As they approach the door, they all stop and embrace. Saying Goodnight to each other, Roberto and Maria walk hand in hand back towards the cottage. Annabella goes inside the house.

Annabella like a good mother, she heads into the kitchen to say goodnight to Paris and Venus. They are both curled up asleep together in the wooden enclosure. Annabella looks at them and then leaves without disturbing them. Upstairs in her room, Annabella is finally feeling connected to the earth, the sky, the stars, the water, but more importantly to her new family, Roberto and Maria.

Annabella selects the song "Ave Maria" from her phone. Laying the phone on the table just inside the balcony so that she can hear the music while star gazing. Walking out onto the balcony, the stars illuminating the sky; she is still wearing the finger print of earth on her forehead from the ceremony that took place at the little cottage. Roberto is now her little brother and Maria, her beautiful sister-in law. Annabella clasps her hands together and begins to pray while the music plays in the background.

"Thank You God for bringing such beautiful people into my life. Thank You for bringing me to such a beautiful place. Thank You for my new brother and sister in-law. God, if you are not too busy and you have the patience; please look after that "Stupido Santiago" where ever he may be, and whatever he may be doing.

"You have given Santiago plenty of (je ne sais quoi) but not enough sense. He is a dreamer, please help him. God, can you look after Ibrahim, give him good health, even though we don't have a marriage

161

he is still my husband. Thank you so much for bringing Paris and Venus into my life. Amen."

Annabella walks back into her room and enters the bathroom to brush her teeth, glances in the mirror and sees her face with the fingerprint of earth on her forehead. Placing her hands together, she bows her head saying; "Namaste." Turning on the water, she washes her face and brushes her teeth, then turns on the shower.

After her shower, she dresses in her usual long T shirt and ties her hair up into a bun. One more check for messages from Theo but there is nothing. Annabella checks her emails, nothing, no voicemail either. Placing her phone on the charger, she closes her eyes and falls off to sleep. With another wonderful day behind her, perhaps her dreams will allow her to have a perfect night's sleep.

In the morning, Maria takes Annabella, the straw basket with Venus and Paris along with the Lamborghini tractor to a picnic place by the river. They are at the foot of the hill near the main road that leads to the Chateau. This piece of land belongs to Maria and Roberto. Settling down to have a picnic, Annabella let's Paris and Venus out of their basket. They are curious, but stay close to Annabella. Maria is fishing in the river.

"Have you never wished to live somewhere else?"

"Are you kidding? Look at this place! We went to Paris for two days many years ago. I thought I'd die from the poisoning car fumes! People everywhere, bumping into each other and having to apologize. There is always a present danger in the city, rape, robbery, muggings, shootings, and stabbings.

The stars are not as bright in the city as they are here; the air is polluted, not fresh, and clean. No space to roam and be quiet. Buildings everywhere no open space. Would you leave here if that is what is out there as a choice?"

"When you woke up this morning did you happen to bump your head anywhere?"

"Sixty-two years, no brother, or sister. I go for an evening meal in a cottage on top of a hill, three glasses of wine later; I leave with a brother and a sister in-law!"

"Count your blessings; we don't make friends with anybody. Oh! I think I have a fish!"

Maria reels in a brown trout, unhooks it, and puts it on the grass behind her in the field. Paris and Venus are curious when they see the fish jumping around in the grass, they in turn jump backwards, they have no clue what a fish is. Annabella sees the fish suffering on the grass.

Maria looks at her face and she can see she is also suffering while watching the fish; Maria grabs the fish and gently puts it back in the river.

"You can thank Annabella Amir for your second chance in life, and I hope your second chance gives you many years of life."

"Why did you do that Maria?"

"The fish was suffering, you were suffering. The dogs are jumping around going crazy. By the time you'd come up with an excuse to throw him back, he would have been dead by then."

"I'm sorry; I can't stand to see animals suffer!"

"Nature provides for us, but sometimes we have to kill in order to survive. We never kill for the sake of killing like some people do. All those trophy killers. All plants are alive. Anything that grows from the ground up from inside out is alive. Pick tomatoes from the plant it's alive."

"Well, what are we supposed   to live on, thin air?"

163

"Anything that grows is alive; this is the law of nature, we are part of that law. Most break that law by ruining the very land that provides for us, they spray everything with chemical pesticides. Is it any wonder that the world has seen a big increase in cancer in people over the past forty years?"

That's why we love our veggie patch, everything is organic, the eggs from the chickens, organic, the milk from the goats, organic. Nothing we ingest is covered in dangerous pesticides, just God's love and grace."

CHAPTER FIFTEEN

NEW FOUND SISTERS

Sunday mid-afternoon, Roberto, Annabella, and Maria, are outside the big house waiting. Stephanie called from the airport, she said she would be there any minute.

The taxi drives up and stops close to them. Stephanie steps out and, Annabella rushes to her, hugging her, giggling like a school girls.

"Yeeesss! We are going to have a great time! Come, let me introduce you. This is my younger brother Roberto. He is in charge of everything outside the house.

"Nice to meet you Roberto!"

"Nice to meet you Mrs. Alexandre!"

"Oh please, call me Stephanie!"

"Stephanie! Ok"

"This is my sister in-law, Maria, she is in charge of everything inside the house."

"Nice to meet you Maria!"

"Nice to meet you Stephanie! I have organized a room for you, next to Annabella. I hope you'll be comfortable there."

"Thank you, Maria; I'm sure I'll be perfectly comfortable."

The cab driver leaves the suitcase closest to them, tips his hat as to say goodbye, and off he goes down the drive.

"Well, let's get you settled, shall we?" Roberto picks up the big suitcase and marches towards the door followed by Maria. Stephanie turns to Annabella walking very slowly

"Your younger brother?"

"Yes."

"Since when?"

"Since Friday night. I have adopted him as my younger brother. Don't worry, by nature's law, it's all legal."

"Oh boy, I think you have had too much fresh air!"

"Come, I want to show you something."

Annabella leads Stephanie into the house and straight into the kitchen to see Paris and Venus.

"Oh my god they are adorable!" Stephanie picks up Paris and hugs her; Annabella picks up Venus, and hugs her.

"This is Venus and Paris!"

"What beautiful names for such gorgeous babies!"

Annabella is distracted with the pups. Through open door in the kitchen, Roberto enters with a small glass in his hand and a special drink he brews.

Roberto is waiting for them to come join him so he can welcome Stephanie properly. Placing Venus back in the pen, she takes Paris from Stephanie, now both pups are safe in their pen.

"Roberto is waiting to give you a proper welcome to the house.(Annabella says under her breath) For God's sake don't drink it in one gulp!"

They move into the large hallway, Stephanie walks over to Roberto, he has two little glasses filled in his hands, he hands one to Stephanie.

"As a Custodian of this magnificent property, one of my duties it to welcome you properly with a toast, but you must drink it down in one gulp Ok?" Roberto was smiling.

"Why not?" Stephanie replies taking the small tumbler with the white liquid, she looks at Annabella, who tells her with the movement of her lips and eyes

"Be careful!" "Salute!" Stephanie winks and knocks back the drink in one gulp, instantly spraying Roberto's face with the drink! Annabella closes her eyes and turns head away.

Roberto is flicking the drink of his eyelids and then gently wipes it away with his hand.

"What the hell is this?" asked Stephanie, she shakes her head and looks at Roberto.

"Oh, I am so sorry!" she says to Roberto.

Annabella covers her eyes with her hand, trying not to giggle out loud, but she cannot contain herself and she starts to laugh with Maria at the foot of the stairs. Roberto looks at her wiping his face with the palm of his right hand.

"Well! That didn't go down too well. Never mind." said Roberto who is being a good sport about the whole thing. Roberto downs his drink in one gulp, then begins to carry the suitcase to Stephanie's room upstairs. Roberto stops and looks at Annabella and Maria, who by now have toned down the laughter and are trying to look serious but laughter is underlying look on their faces.

"Are you two finished?" Annabella and Maria nod their heads Roberto starts to walk upstairs, Stephanie comes near Annabella

"Of all the places around you, you had to pick his face to spray?"

"I heard that!" Roberto says without breaking his rhythm of his walk up the stairs.

Ten minutes later, Stephanie walks out onto the balcony with her phone in her hand. Annabella has made a pot of tea and put it on the small table with two chairs on either side. Stephanie stops and looks around, the mountains and the vast panoramic view fill her eyes from right to left slowly taking in all the beauty of nature at its best.

"This is paradise!" said Stephanie as she sits down at the little table putting her phone down.

"Wait until you see it at night." Annabella said smiling.

"I can imagine it! It has that, Je ne se qui, an amazing energy. This feels like a place where one's nervous system can be restored." said Stephanie "I know this because when me and Gabriel were at our lowest, regarding my health, we went to a place in the French Alps. It was just like this, apart from the snow. The place was designed to bring back positive energy for nervous wrecks like me who had lost their way in life.

"Well, that's all in the past now and you are in good health, right?" asked Annabella, wanting some reassurance

"Everything is beautiful now! I am in the clear but, I know Gabriel constantly worries about it and   me."

"I could live in a place like this. I have been so happy ever since I arrived. I haven't even messaged my husband, Ibrahim except a brief text letting him know I had arrived, to which there was no response."

"Well, according to you, your marriage has been over for years. So, why pretend?"

"I know, but he is still my husband."

"Look, if you love your husband and you can save your marriage; save it if it's worth saving!"

"Sadly, the salvage portion of my marriage is way past gone. My marriage lies in ruins, in a place called Morocco." Annabella lowers her eyes for a second looking defeated, and then looks at Stephanie and smiles. Just then, the conversation is interrupted with Stephanie's phone ringing and buzzing on the table, she picks it up and looks at it.

"It's Gabriel on face time SHHHH!" Stephanie indicates with her finger for Annabella to stay quiet. Stephanie picks up the phone and clicks receive and Gabriel appears on video.

"Hello darling did you have a good flight? Is everything ok?"

"The flight was wonderful and I got here safe and sound! Everything is wonderful! I am just settling in now darling. I was a little concerned about you this morning, though; you were not too steady on your legs when you walked in to have breakfast." Stephanie is obviously teasing. Annabella opens her eyes in shock!

"Well, my legs were a little unsteady after last night, but I have to add, it was great, performances from both of us!" Annabella could see Gabriel as he smiled Gabriel with a twinkle in his eyes, he had no idea she was in the room at the moment.

"Ohhh yes! You still have it baby! Someone wants to say hello to you." Stephanie quickly hands the phone over to Annabella who is trying not to blush; Gabriel can be seen closing his eyes and opening them again knowing he has been tricked by Stephanie.

"Hello Annabella, please don't mention anything about last night's performance, or wobbly legs this morning." Annabella chuckles with Stephanie

"Thank you for your kindness Gabriel for letting Stephanie stay here with me for a few days. In return, I promise to keep an eye on her so she does not get into any wild mischief. So, you won't have any surprises in the future. Gabriel, I won't mention what happened downstairs earlier." Stephanie step in and nudges Annabella

"Will you behave?!"

"The only surprise or shock if I may say is I haven't managed to have to defend her in court.

With regards to her being there with you, well, there is a good reason for that, but the angel next to you has no idea as to why I agreed to send her there in the first place."

Stephanie snatches the phone from Annabella's hand and looks into the phone

"I know your secretary Severine has long legs that go all the way to heaven, and I know she has a great ass, you better answer me and you better think carefully what you say mister, or you will be served divorce papers before you can say "your honour" to the judge."

"Do you fancy her?"

"Yes."

Annabella opens her mouth in shock

"Have you flirted with her?"

"Yes."

"Have you been out with her?"

"Yes."

Annabella rolls her eyes to one side in shock

"Do you desire her?"

"Yes."

"Do you love her?"

"Yes."

"Do you want to make passionate love with her?"

"Yes!"

"Are you going to leave me for her?"

"Yes."

"Are you going to divorce me?"

"Yes."

"Are you going to marry her?"

"Yes."

Annabella does not know where to put her face, she bites her index finger

"Do you love me?" there is deafening silence as Annabella waits for the answer she holds her breath.

"Madly!"

Annabella exhales the large breath that she was holding onto

"I didn't tell you, I will be there on Friday. I have some loose ends to finalize on the sale of the house."

"Did you know about this before last night?" asked Stephanie with a cheeky grin

"Yes! Your performance last night made my brain numb; therefore I forgot to tell you. What can I say? I have to go, love; I have a meeting with a client who is waiting to see me.

"I love you! Bye!" "I LOVE YOU TOO!" Stephanie ends the call.

"For a second I thought about rushing downstairs and drinking one of those drinks in one gulp. I thought you two were serious about all that stuff!"

"Severine, is like a daughter to us. Gabriel has always developed a "Yes syndrome" when I start talking silly about other women. It's his way of reassuring me that he adores me and I have nothing to fear, but the reaction on your face was worth it! I tried to keep a straight face so you wouldn't suspect we were playing."

"Ha-ha, very funny! What the hell did you think the first time he did this to you?"

"I don't know why but, I just giggled through the whole thing. The first time he was telling me all this yes stuff, then when he was finished with the yes, stuff, with a serious look in his eyes, he said to me; "I would die without you, everything that I value, everything that constitutes riches in my life, in my heart and soul is you!"

"May God bless you both that you might grow old like this?"

"Well, we are not getting any younger and you better start getting your life in order or you will be alone in your old age, not that you're old?" "It's the small things, like what took place on the phone just now, that keeps our marriage alive, and keeps us safe and reassured.

The playing is what helps us live in that magic we call, "love." The truth is, I would die without him! Now the big question is how am I going to face Roberto after what happened downstairs?"

"Roberto my younger brother is larger than life. He has already forgotten about it I'm sure.

My sister in-law Maria, is such a tender soul. You will adore her; you will adore Roberto also when you get to know him a little better." Annabella's face was filled with a softness and love as she spoke to Stephanie about both Maria and Roberto. Stephanie could see the change in Annabella.

CHAPTER SIXTEEN

MYSTICAL THOUGHTS

Its early evening and Annabella and Stephanie are in the garden watching Paris and Venus playfully enjoying themselves by running around.

Annabella's eyes search the distance. Secretly she is hoping a romance like that between Gabriel and Stephanie was one that she might have one day. If only time could stop in this magical place…

"You know, I could live here, it is like a dream, a déjà vu. It's like I've lived here before in the past. There is a feeling in me that everything that has happened in my life, was to bring me here now, to experience this bliss now, it's uncanny how comfortable I have become here.

"Are you talking mythological, psychologically, philosophically, or just plain nuts?"

"I don't know, maybe all of them! The word "Inevitable" comes to mind when I think about how I ended up here at this time in my life, like it was preordained!"

"Well, I've been here for two hours and I already managed to spit in your adopted younger brother's face. I have a friend who is not here next to me; she is in the land of mystics, esoterica's, and sages. Much like the two little dogs that are playing and enjoying themselves, I am oblivious to what "reality" is and what constitutes "normal.""

"I have come to realize, that there is no such thing as "normal" in life, it is like everything is made up, it's like people make up life, as they go along."

"Well, we have to have something to do in life. I'm quoting something I read once; "A man said to a wise sage sitting by the road; why don't you teach all others to have enlightenment, so they can be a sage guru like you? The sage replied; how can I teach anyone anything when nothing in the world is real." … and that stuck with me."

"You see… that's what I am talking about!"

"What?"

"What you just said, that nothing in life is real, but, then again, what if everything in life is real but it's called, "experience?"

I watched an amazing documentary once about Nikola Tesla and he said:

"Everything is energy, and if your frequency is the same, you can become friends much easier, and if you are attracted to another person they would end up like you and Gabriel, married.

"All you need is the same frequency. You and Gabriel have that, but in truth, I have never had that before with anyone. Except…"

"Except!?"

"I was going to say Santiago for a second, but; I doubt anyone knows what frequency he operates on. Sometimes I think he is from another dimension."

"You spent a year talking with him, your words not mine! You said you spent hours and hours talking with him. I think your frequencies match.

I think yours and mine match because I've never felt as comfortable as when we met. The things I shared with you, I've never told anyone before."

"I felt that energy about you also. Recently I've found myself forgiving Santiago, after four years."

"What are you forgiving him for? What has he done to you? The poor man, all he did was love you."

"He broke my heart."

"Annabella, are you having a good time right now?"

"I am having the best time."

"Well, if you are having the best time, then no forgiveness is required for Santiago."

"Why do you say that?"

"You said, he broke your heart, and yet you said a prayer for him the other night."

"When I asked you if you are having a good time, you said "best time."

Santiago was in our conversation."

"And your point is?"

"I don't know. I think the point I was trying to make was, maybe your frequencies actually match, and maybe it is the same?"

"I don't think so. The man is a dreamer. I don't know, maybe I never got over the fact that he never came to Paris to meet me."

"Sometimes unexpected things happen to us and we think we are cursed or that we've done something wrong. Later we discover that what had actually happened to us was a blessing in disguise."

"You know, if he came to Paris, I don't think I would be sitting on this mountain top with you right now. I would have left my husband for him."

"Personally speaking, I am glad he never came to meet you."

"Why? Don't you want me to be happy?"

"Of course I do! I just meant that we would not have met, had you gone with Santiago."

"It would not have worked out between us. Living in a single room without an income, he is a dreamer, and all he wants to do is to dream. I need security and love not a bunch of impossible dreams.

"Dreams are the seeds of a better tomorrow; dreams are the seeds of advancement in the world of inventions. Dreams are the seeds of a distant goal that your soul knows you can achieve if you have the patience, the hope that lives deep within your soul. This single principle should above all be applied to love."

"Where did you get all that from?"

"Mr Baranowski, in his book "Emotional Rhapsody." It's not an exact quote, I improvised a bit but, you understand the main idea. "It's a love story, but it contains so much wisdom. I read the book as if he was speaking directly to my heart. I read it as if it was written especially for me.

Many comments about this book say the same thing. The book was written about the person reading it, as though it was individually written. I brought it with me. I thought you might like to read it."

Maybe, after I have finished with the barn."

After their chat, the girls join Maria and Roberto at the table in the kitchen at the cottage. Roberto pours out the wine for everyone, and then sits down. Maria brings a hot pot dish to the table and takes the top off. Steam comes floating out and the smell fills the room. Stephanie responds; "Mm… That smells lovely what is are you cooking?" Roberto interjects quickly, "You see that mountain over there?" Maria cuts him short, "Roberto!" He looks at her and with a defeated voice and says "Never mind." Maria in turns serves the food to each plate and then sits down herself at the head of the table, Roberto is across from her. "I am so sorry for what happened earlier in the house with the drink" said Stephanie apologetically

"No offence was taken." Roberto then takes a swig of wine

"I think you have already met my husband, he was here six months ago taking pictures of the house, for his client. His name is Gabriel."

"Oh! How could I ever forget him and his friends and their flying toys? How is Mr Alexandre?"

"He is fine. Thank you for asking. He is busy in Paris but, he will be here on Friday to conclude some business. Personally speaking, I think he is just going to come here to look over the barn once to see that everything is in order, he never misses a detail."

"Well, the furniture will be here tomorrow, and Theo said he has hired two men to help with all the fixtures and fittings. So, we should be finished by Wednesday evening, hopefully with a bit of luck!"

"This fellow Theo, is he the one who owns the house?" asked Roberto Annabella looks at Stephanie and then Maria

"Yes, I think so, but I cannot be certain. I have never met him."

"If you've never met him, then how do you know his name is Theo?" asked Roberto. Silence falls onto the table everyone starts looking at each other, without saying a word.

"That's ok. Maria and I have been working for him for six months, and we've never met him either."

"It's all mysterious of you ask me!" All eyes turn to Maria as she continues. "I mean, he buys a house without visiting here, he has all these people running around for him who have never met him, in my opinion that qualifies as "strange and mysterious!""

"I am certain my husband had met him or her."

"Well, that's another problem he could be a she."

"But we can be sure of one thing," said Stephanie "Every mystery has an ending and I am sure we will find out in the end who this mystery person is!"

All eyes still on Stephanie, in silence, looking at her. "Well, it stands to reason, I read a lot of mystery books and always in the end, the mystery is revealed."

"I think the whole mystery is about me."

"What makes you think it is about you?"

"I don't know I just have that feeling in my stomach."

"Well, I hope it has a good ending!" said Stephanie

"I've never had a good ending to anything in my life. Now my intuition tells me, this won't have a good ending either."

Annabella's eyes were welling up with tears "Please excuse me" Annabella gets up from the table and leaves the cottage.

"It's ok, I've got this. Thank you for your wonderful hospitality, everything is impeccable. Roberto stood up to escort Stephanie out and she replied, "I will see myself out."

Stephanie walks out of the cottage looking for Annabella who is half-way across to the big house. Calling out to Annabella "Annabella," she slows down and Stephanie catches up to her.

"Hey, it's ok. It's all going to be ok!" Stephanie hugs Annabella and then looks at her; she has tears in her eyes

"I think the problem is me Stephanie."

"What are you talking about? Let's go in the house and then we can talk." Annabella nods her head and they move towards the house.

Annabella sits outside on the balcony of her bedroom, Stephanie brings in two little glasses of the white drink that Roberto had left out for the guests who come to the house, and gently she hands the little glass to Annabella.

"Here, drink this down." Annabella takes the small glass and takes a sip. It really hits her and she shakes as the drink is emptied from the glass.

Stephanie looks at the drink in her hand, says, "To hell with it! Salute!" In one gulp she drinks the drink down. Stephanie starts breathing heavily, trying to calm herself down and then she finally lets out a big breath and then sits down across from Annabella.

"I am sure they use this stuff in winter to defrost the ice on cars!" Annabella looks at her and smiles, Stephanie smiles back at her.

"What did you mean, when you said; you think the problem is you Annabella?

"When I was eight years old, my mother used to work so hard to keep a roof over my head. After watching her pass out after supper each night, I decided one to help her.

I thought if I cleaned the house, she would look around and say, "Thank you Annabella, well done!" I thought she'd hug me and be very proud of me, but, she did not even notice that I had worked so hard to bring her joy. That night, I went to bed and cried most of the night in silence. I still have dreams about that night sometimes. It seems that since that time, I have this self-destructive behaviour thing.

I say that because if anybody, lets me down, even just the once, I internalise it and make it about me being a failure or less than worthy."

"It never matters how close they are to me, I am never the same with that person again. The older I get, the more I understand that I am in some way sabotaging my relationships due to lack of the people in my life not acknowledging me. My marriages ended due to this same issue!" Why I am such a failure in life? Silence fell like clouds onto the balcony.

"Life is not perfect; it gives and takes away Annabella! Without forgiveness, we are nothing in the world. Without giving a person another chance to make it up   to us, we are nothing in life!"

179

"The problem is, my life should be in ship shape, but instead it's in shit shape! I have no security, which leads me to believe I have no future. When I look back on my history, it's nothing but failed marriages, and relationships. It's a battlefield of memories with broken dreams and lost hope. I don't know if I'm strong enough to take another rejection in life. I should tell you I have decided to file for divorce when I return to Morocco."

"Out of chaos comes order. Out of a bad situation, something good happens. After rain come's sunshine and rainbows. If you find a single weak string; even that has hope, hold onto it with all your strength.

In life, miracles happen every day to ordinary people like you and me.

Also, there's no age limit to this gift of life as long as we keep alive the hope that live within us. Look what happened to me. I went for a job and ended up with a husband. Your life can change in an instant, at any time, in any place." Stephanie was so full of empathy that Annabella could hear the sincerity in her voice and felt a tinge of hope.

"You're right. I've never had a fairy tale come true, as I dreamed it, as I saw it." Stephanie is listening and thinking she must have an example somewhere…

"Give me a second I want to read something to you." Stephanie dashes into her room next door and she takes from her suitcase the book "Emotional Rhapsody" Stephanie returns to Annabella's balcony and sits across from Annabella.

"Oh, the book that makes woman cry!"

"Ivan Baranowski based this whole book of four hundred pages, on a few lines.

Keep in mind the story is based on today's times in life, and yet this is what he wrote before he started the book, it reads as follows:

"This book was inspired by these words."

"The young man was a blacksmith in the village, a magnificent white charger horse was brought to him, he was ordered to put iron shoes on the horse's hooves. After doing this he took the horse for a ride in the open field, and thereby a brook he met a fair maiden. He fell madly in love with her instantly.

He claimed that he was a decorated knight, but, she could see he was poor, and was a blacksmith. His black working hands betrayed him, but she never mentioned this to the young man.

After talking for about fifteen minutes, in perfect harmony and calm, their meeting was broken up when two ladies approached the maiden."

"The maiden took out her handkerchief and gave it to him; he took it without taking his eyes off of her. The maiden dashed off running towards the two women, assuring them that she was alright.

That evening a guard came from the castle, took the white charger with the new horseshoes and left. The dashing young man got to work instantly. Making himself a beautiful sword like no other. He then made himself silver shining armour, as beautiful as any knights."

The young man made wooden replicas of men in battle, and he would practice for hours, finding new ways of defeating the enemy. All of this because of a chance meeting in a field, and the handkerchief he kept pressed against his chest. Danger was looming and there was talk of an invasion, from another country. To preserve the dignity and the honour of the village and the castle that employed all the villagers, the king asked for volunteers for the impending battle.

181

"The blacksmith went to the castle as one of the volunteers. He showed up on an old brown horse that would not be able to stand the first charge in battle.

Proudly he was dressed in his silver knight's armour, holding his handmade sword. One of the guards came and took away his horse. The young man looked on sadly as others around the courtyard mocked him. Another guard approached him with the white charger that he nailed the shoes to his hooves; "This will be your steed." the guard said and he helped him onto the horse. There was silence around the forecourt; he turned rode with the knights out to meet the enemy."

"After five hours of battle, they had secured a brave victory. The young man had performed above and beyond the call of his duty.

He was chosen to be knighted. As he entered the great hall in the castle, there were people on both sides of the hall.

Waiting patiently to perform the ceremony was none other than the king himself, and next to him, his young daughter. A princess, the princess he met by chance in a field. After the ceremony, the princess stepped forward and said, "Thank you for bringing my horse back to me." The young woman who overlooked his poverty, gave him her white horse, and encouraged him with giving him her handkerchief, by speaking to him in a field with kindness, her father the king was rewarded with a knight of chivalry and virtue."

Because of an accidental meeting and events that followed, encouragement was given to someone who was ready to chase their dreams. This young man was ready to step forth, and take control of his dreams, as impossible, as they seemed at the time."

Stephanie leaves the book open on her lap and she leans back in her chair.

"I'd love to be loved just once in my life, the way I dream and desire to be loved."

Gabriel rings Stephanie on video chat to say good night, as they start to talk, Annabella, looks at her Skype, there is a message from Theo.

"Annabella,"

"I hope your friend has arrived and is comfortable. Wishing you both a pleasant evening.

"Good night"

Annabella responds:

"Theo,

"Thank you! Yes, my friend had arrived safely, and is very comfortable. I hope you are well and having a good evening.

"Good night."

Annabella sends the message and in that moment Stephanie has finished her call with Gabriel. The two join each other on the balcony to look at the night sky. What a perfect view of the Milky Way. All the stars seemed brighter and more beautiful in this perfect heaven like place, which fills the mind and soul with beauty and a sense of peace. The two stood in silence for a few moments just taking in the stunning view.

"No matter where I've lived, I have always loved looking at the stars at night." Annabelle expressed with a soft comforting voice. Stephanie was star gazing.

"We are so tiny in the universe. I'm going to get some sleep." Stephanie got up from her chair and lovingly hugged Annabella.

"Me too!" We have a very loud alarm clock that goes off around four thirty in the morning! I am so happy that you are here

Stephanie! Good night and Sweet dreams!" Annabella lingered in her sisterly embrace for a few seconds; this was a very special woman and friend. Annabella could feel her heart opening to the love that the people around her were showing her. A strange, yet beautiful sensation was welling up inside her and Annabella was embracing this marvellous beautiful new feeling.

CHAPTER SEVENTEEN

INTRUDERS IN THE NIGHT

Two o'clock in the morning Annabella was sound asleep in her bed, next door Stephanie is also sleeping soundly in her bed. Downstairs Paris and Venus are fast asleep, curled up in the pen. Suddenly the silence of the night is shattered by a single gunshot. Annabella sits straight up in bed, and under her voice she says "Gunshot!" Outside Annabella can hear Roberto shouting, "Hands up where I can see them!" Annabella jumps out of bed and rushes to Stephanie's room. The bed is empty.

Annabella starts looking outside the balcony, she is not there, and she looks into the bathroom no sign of her. Turning from the bathroom under her voice she says angrily "Stephanie where the hell are you?" A hand waves from under the bed. Annabella leans down "Will you get out from under there?" "I heard a gunshot!" "Stephanie for God's sake pull yourself together!"

Stephanie crawls out from under the bed and they both dash out of the room and downstairs. Finally out of the house, they stand near the white Mercedes.

Maria comes running out of the cottage. Roberto is pointing the gun at two men who are standing in front of a huge moving truck with the lights on.

"Did you come to rob the place?" demanded Roberto with a menacing voice. "We have come to deliver some furniture." Jimmy explained.

"What?! At two o'clock in the morning! Liar!" he shouted

Steve speaks up, "He's telling you the truth, we were supposed to arrive in the morning, and we arrived earlier than anticipated." Roberto was still angry and replied;

"Well, its tomorrow morning, and you are here two o'clock in the morning, open the back of the truck, I want to see if what you are telling me is true!"

He nudges the shotgun forward for them to walk back to the truck. The two men walk slowly to the back of the truck. Annabella and Stephanie catch up to Roberto and tag behind him.

"Roberto, please be careful with that gun for God's sake!" remonstrated Annabella. Maria has joined them on the walk to the back of the truck where Steve opens the doors.

The truck is filled to the brim with furniture, paintings, mirrors and everything else that belongs in a house or a barn. "See?" said Steve.

They all stand looking at the furniture in the back of the truck. Maria steps in speaking Italian

"Roberto, per l'amor di Dio, metti giù quella pistola, prima che tu spari per errore qualcuno" Everyone looks at each other; no one understood what she said. Translated from Italian it means "Roberto, for God's sake, put that gun down before you accidentally shoot someone!" He lowers the gun down, Maria continues

"Are you two gentlemen hungry?"

"As a matter of fact, I could eat something and a cup of tea." said Steve

Maria with a tender voice, "Follow me" Steve closes the back of the truck, locks it and they head towards the house following Maria. Annabella leans towards Roberto and asks

"What did you actually shoot at when you fired the gun?"

"I shot towards the sky, to frighten them." "I'm feeling shameful for waking everyone."

"Have you ever shot anybody?" Roberto lets out a grunt. Placing the shotgun on his shoulder and they walk towards the house.

Four thirty in the morning the rooster starts crowing. Annabella grabs the pillow and puts it over her head. Next door, Stephanie is oblivious to the sound of the rooster, she is fast asleep, her face half buried in the pillow. Downstairs Steve and Jimmy are sleeping in the same room, in two single beds. Outside in the chicken coup the rooster continues to crow!

The stars are fading from sight and dawn is approaching. The mountains in the distance are covered in morning mist waiting for the sun to shine and clear the mist away.

It was seven thirty in the morning and Roberto had been awake for three hours, feeding the animals and tending to chores. Maria was already in the main kitchen at the Chateau preparing breakfast for everyone. Roberto was always a man of action and a decisive decision maker when it came to things to be done; there was no nonsense with him in this regard. Opening the door to the bedroom where Steve and Jimmy had been sleeping, Roberto said; "Come on men, breakfast is served in a half hour on the patio and work begins directly after breakfast!"

Steve lifted his head off the pillow

"What time is it?"

"It's time to wash your face, have breakfast, and get to work. Come on, let's go!" Jimmy groans "Oh man!"

"Never mind "Oh man" "Men get your asses out of bed!" With that, Roberto closed the door behind him as he left the room. Jimmy and Steve sit up in bed and sit facing each other; Jimmy scratched his head and yawns.

Upstairs Roberto knocks on Annabella's door, and from outside, he calls her, "Annabella!" with a sleepy voice from her bed, Annabella answers

"Yes, what is it, Roberto?" "Breakfast is served in half an hour out on the patio." "Thank you, I'll be there." Stephanie heard the conversation next door, as Roberto was about to knock on the door it swings open, taking Roberto by surprise, he leans back in shock. Stephanie looks at Roberto

"Don't you ever sleep?"

"Not when there's work to be done, not when everyone needs organizing, and definitely not when that damn rooster starts crowing, breakfast in half an hour out on the patio!"

"I heard you!" Stephanie turns and closes the door, as Roberto heads downstairs to help Maria in the kitchen.

Sure enough, in half an hour, breakfast was on the patio. Everyone had only had time to wash their faces and brush their teeth and hair; the men had taken cold short showers.

Everyone was gathered around the table, there was all kinds of things to choose from that began with local cheeses, local olives, and tomatoes from the greenhouse.

Everything was fresh. Cucumbers, tomatoes, and fresh eggs, which were hard and soft, boiled. To drink there was fresh squeezed orange juice, coffee, tea, and water. There was homemade bread and toast with jam as well. A breakfast feast for everyone.

"No prayers are required (Roberto crosses himself) but, Lord, we thank you for this good food we find on our table this morning, from your Garden of Eden." Roberto takes the hot coffee pot to pour out some coffee for him.

 Annabella says "Amen" Stephanie looks at her with an expression that says why not and she, in turn, says "Amen" Roberto looks directly at Annabella

"I hope you don't mind Annabella, that I have taken charge of the situation this morning."

"No Roberto, not at all, it's fine. You are always so organized and efficient and I was told that Jimmy and Steve would be with us for two days to assist me with whatever I need in the barn.

"Two days should be enough to put everything together!"

Steve steps into the conversation, "We should be finished unloading the truck by lunchtime and in the afternoon.

We can start assembling the beds and putting things in their rightful place where ever that might be."

Roberto continued, "Well, there are six of us so it should make things easy."

Maria steps in swiftly

"Roberto some people at this table are guests here they did not come here to work, just because Mr. De La Mancha says so." Stephanie looks at Maria and then Roberto

"Well, don't look at me! I am good to go, count me in!" said Stephanie enthusiastically Annabella looks at Roberto and Maria

"Roberto and Maria, you don't have to do this, you have enough things to do around here."

"Good then it is settled! You're right, we have a lot of things to do around here, but for the next two days, Maria and I will help you with the barn. Once the truck is unloaded you can tell us where you'd like things." Stephanie shakes her head with a smile; she adores Roberto's macho approach to making decisions and his larger than life character. Jimmy recalls last night and he is eager to ask a question, to Roberto

"Regarding last night, if we did not cooperate with you, would you have shot us," There is pregnant silence

Roberto leans towards Steve and Jimmy who are sitting next to each other, across from Roberto. "I wouldn't shoot you where your vital organs are, I might end up killing you, but I wouldn't have any qualms about shooting you in the ass."

"It's there that you have plenty of padding and the survival rate is much higher!"

Roberto smiled. Both Steve and Jimmy lean back in their chair in solidarity of shock.

Twenty minutes later, the back of the huge truck is open, as are the two front doors of the barn. They all walk in Roberto is first in. "Annabella, I am handing present authority to you, you're in charge now." Everyone is waiting for your instructions."

"I think we need some expert advice here." Turning and looking at Steve and Jimmy, Steve takes a step forward, "The easiest way to do this, is to take all the furniture that belongs upstairs and set it aside, but close to the stairs making sure we have enough room to use the stairs freely." "Jimmy is this right?"

"Ok, tables, chairs, mirrors, chest of draws, settees, pictures, all on that side close to the wall. The far side, all rugs, and carpets, in front of the fireplace, there are large vases, mirrors, pictures in glass frames and fragile things on the truck; let's try not to break anything."

"We will put a plank of wood on this step inside the door so it will act as a smooth ramp for us to wheel things downstairs into the house. As you've seen we also have a tail lift on the back of the truck that will make our work that much easier."

"The greatest blessing in all this is the fact that there is no small stuff, like boxes of cutlery, plates, and cups and so forth, this is just house furniture." Roberto steps in again

"I have a few more things to say, and then we can start. Once we finish unloading the truck, we will stop for a light lunch, and then we will come back and do much as we can.

Later we have evening dinner, and after last night's sleep deprivation, I am sure we can all use an early night's rest. That will be more than welcome speaking for me that is. Does anyone else have anything to say? Good, then let us get to work!" Roberto rubs his hands and walks out of the barn.

Steve turns to Annabella; she's holding a clipboard with papers attached to it. "This is the inventory of everything in the truck." said Steve, "Thank you Steve." Annabella begins looking at the list of furniture.

Three hours later, the truck is empty and all the furniture was moved down into the barn. Maria had left one hour before to prepare lunch.

Everyone was joined around the table under the beautiful warm sun and had lunch together.

Annabella checked the Skype on her phone for messages. There was a message from Theo. Theo asked if everything was alright, and had asked if the furniture had arrived, and if she liked the furniture, he closed the message with the words. "Speak soon."

Annabella replied:

"Theo,

Everything is beautiful; I adore the furniture that was selected. I'm hopeful that you'll like the barn fully furnished." Speak soon,

Annabella"

After lunch, Steve and Jimmy were entertaining Roberto, and Stephanie. Telling stories about funny things that had happened in the past on the job. Roberto enjoys the stories, letting out a hearty laugh while Stephanie giggles uncontrollably.

Maria, ever efficient in her work, cleared the table.

Annabella in the kitchen kneels down next to Paris and Venus, who look up at her, wagging their tails in happiness. They feel safe and loved. She takes them out of the enclosure, grabbing each one, in each hand, and she brings them to her face and she hugs them.

Stephanie is outside and looks into the kitchen. Seeing Annabella holding the pups to her face and hugging them, she wondered how someone with so much love, tenderness, and beauty is not loved; a sudden sadness falls on her.

When they all returned back to the barn, Jimmy, Steve, and Roberto, took the beds upstairs. There is a four-poster bed for the master bedroom suite, which is on the main floor.

The two single beds, to the bedroom directly across from sitting area upstairs in one bedroom. The double bed went into the bedroom that had the windows looking   out onto the driveway.

With all the mattresses leaning on the walls near the landing, Steve and Jimmy, began to put the beds together, a process they had repeated so many times before.

Downstairs, Annabella, Stephanie, and Maria, had already positioned the long table with eight chairs on the large carpet covering a big chunk of the wooden floor. They had placed the beautiful golden covered settee that can seat four comfortably, directly in front of the large fireplace. On either side of the hearth, they placed the golden covered armchairs. Looking around Stephanie said "It is going to be beautiful!"

In one hour they managed to put together the four-poster bed. Roberto had managed to put the two mattresses on the two single beds in the smaller room.

They moved to the third bedroom, they put the double bed together, threw the mattress on it, and it was all done upstairs. They all are aware that tomorrow is when the real work begins, having to put the big impressive gold-framed mirrors upon the walls and paintings.

Annabella went from room to room taking pictures of the progress they have made so far regarding the furniture and fittings, and then sent them all to Theo from her cell.

It had been a short night, and a long day. At five o'clock, they all decided it was enough for the day. They headed back to the house.

Tomorrow was going to be the real test putting up the six huge mirrors that were five feet in height and three feet across, they must take great care in this process.

Roberto brought out four bottles of red wine, that he had produced himself from the three hectares of grapes, which grow on the south-facing side of the estate. It was a welcome sight for everyone, and after a few glasses of the red wine everyone was relaxed.

Maria served up the evening meal, with the help of Annabella and Stephanie. The three had chatted during the dinner preparation and conclude that; "all men are little boys, and they should be treated as such." They also agreed that when it came to Roberto, "he was like having five naughty boys all rolled into one but with panache strength and wisdom of a real man."

Around ten o'clock the sky was dark and filled with stars. Everyone had turned in for a good night's sleep after the long day. Annabella and Stephanie sat on the balcony with a glass of wine each relaxing and looking at the stars.

"I often wondered what Beethoven was thinking when he wrote

"*Moonlight Sonata*." Stephanie was tired but enjoying the stars and her friend, she thought about beautiful music.

"Where does such beautiful inspiration come from? The music captivates the listener after centuries have passed and brings on different dreams and visions each time, to anyone who listens to it?"

"I don't know, and I am sure we will never know." replied Annabella keeping her gaze at the stars. Stephanie continues the realms of genius.

"How does someone like Van Gogh who taught himself to paint come to the conclusion in his mind and write such words to his brother?" Van Gogh said in a message, "Our work has come so far that it will survive through a catastrophe." How did he know?

How did he understand that he was that good? That he would put himself among the greatest painters when he only sold one picture, "The Red Vineyard" He was the least known of all the painters when he was alive, and yet in death, he is immortalized as one of the most beloved painters of history." Annabella turns to Stephanie

"I always cry when I watch the film Wuthering Heights, especially the balcony scene.

In that scene, Heathcliff tells Cathy, "If he loved you with all the power of his soul for a whole lifetime, he couldn't love you, as much as I love you in a single day."

"Those words, always pierce my heart and soul, and bring me to a flood of tears." explained Annabella with a soft sad look in her eyes.

"They have left beauty for us in, music, paintings, and words, to move us emotionally to create in us, wonder, dreams, and aspirations.

Yet, I think they were all tortured souls, to produce such beautiful works as they did. They all spoke to our souls and they still do, but for now it's time to sleep. We have a marathon of a job tomorrow." Stephanie said quietly.

"It will all be finished tomorrow. I don't even know why he even hired me to do something that anyone could have done!"

"Maybe he wanted you to do it! Good night." Stephanie heads to her room, Annabella looks at the stars, takes the last sip of her wine, she looks at her phone and reads a message from Theo.

"Annabella,

Thank you for the pictures of the barn, and the progress being made. Good night, Sweet Dreams." Looking at her phone and goes inside the room brushes her teeth and then slides into bed, closing her eyes, she passes out.

Chapter Eighteen

Boys Day Out

Nature's alarm clock began to sound "cock-a-doodle-doo cock-a-doodle-doo cock-a-doodle-doo! Steve and Jimmy woke up, knowing that today was the last day for them, and they wanted to finish the job.

The two men made their way down to the barn. They begin by taking the wardrobes in the bedrooms. They took up two wardrobes and placed the largest in the master suite on the main floor. They also took up, chests of draws for each bedroom, and a small desk for each bedroom that had been separated and allocated to be taken upstairs, the day before.

In the house, breakfast was being served when Jimmy and Steve got there at eight o'clock. Annabella and Stephanie were spoiling Paris and Venus, with tender hugs and soft words. They were so adorable. Stephanie was teasing Paris "I am going to put you in my bag and take you to see the real Paris! They will adore you there, yes they will!"

Outside, at the big table, Jimmy and Steve sat down for breakfast, Roberto is already halfway through with his breakfast. "I saw you men going to the barn this morning." "You saw us?" asked Steve "Yes, I see everything around here, it is my job." said Roberto pouring himself another cup of coffee.

"We managed to take the chests of draws upstairs, and the wardrobes, you know, to get them out of the way. All we have left now is the big mirrors to hang on the walls, and we are done."

"If we finish early enough, we might be able to get away this afternoon and head back home."

"Why don't you boys slow down after you finished for the day? Stay and enjoy the beautiful tranquillity and the scenery." Roberto suggested. Jimmy and Steve look at each other for a second, Steve starts to explain

"The thing is Roberto; we have been awake since about five this morning and we don't want to be driving at night when we are tired, anything can happen on the roads."

"Who said anything about driving at night? You would stay the night, wake up early, when the rooster alarm goes off, and then you start on the road. You will have a few hours head start also being that early in the morning."

"Would you allow us to do that?" Asked Jimmy humbly

"I wouldn't suggest it if I was going to say no, would I now?" said Roberto with a grin.

"Thank you, that's very kind of you!" said Steve with a look of gratitude on his face.

Roberto brought the little enclosure for Paris and Venus to the barn, Annabella and Stephanie carried the little pups and gently placed them in the enclosure.

"You will be our source of inspiration for the day!" said Stephanie lovingly.

"And you will be my source of anger if you decide to use the pen as a spot to do your business!"

There were seven large mirrors to be hung. Annabella instructed Steve and Jimmy that two of them were to go on the wall in the master bedroom, directly across from the four-poster bed.

Two of the mirrors go on the wall soon as you walk into the barn on the right-hand side wall between the front door and the stairs going up. One was to go upstairs on the wall between the two bedrooms and the last mirror was to go onto the wall on the other side of the big living room area downstairs in the middle of the room.

Jimmy asked which mirrors were for upstairs. Annabella pointed to the four mirrors she had chosen for the upstairs. Jimmy, Steve, and Roberto started taking the mirrors upstairs, and laying them against the walls.

Stephanie was standing near the pups looking down at them smiling. Annabella was looking around the large room.

"Have you noticed something missing?" Stephanie looks around the room, but she does not know what she is supposed to be looking for.

"I don't see anything missing. It might help if I knew what I was looking for."

"There are no bed linens, no sheets, no pillows, no pillow cases, no pots, and pans for the kitchen. Also, there are no TV's!"

"I don't know, maybe Maria is going to sort all that out. Maybe she will bring a few things from the house." Stephanie didn't seem concerned with these missing details.

"I wonder who is going to live here. Perhaps, guests when they come for a visit?"

"There are ten bedrooms in the big house; it is not like there is a shortage of rooms now is there?"

"Imagine the power this man has to buy all of this, and he hasn't even been here! Imagine the house he must be living in right now!" said Annabella

"Maybe he's living in a castle! Who knows? You might get commissioned to sort out a few more properties for him if he likes this one!"

"I like this house! My first husband had a Château and one of the outbuildings was just like this barn. I begged him to let me have it in the divorce settlement and even said to him; I don't want any money, just the barn. He refused. I ended up getting no money and no barn!

I loved that part of the country; it was about forty kilometres from Paris."

"There is a saying for people like that, some people die at twenty-five, and they are not buried, till they are seventy-five." said Stephanie is looking at Annabella who has a sad expression

"How can you offer someone the world when you love them and everything is good and when the time comes to separate and divorce, they leave them on the streets?"

"Some people are like that."

"In my book, that is not a man! Courage, compassion, understanding, and the gift of giving during both the beautiful times and the bad times shared between two people. Now that is how a man should be.

All other men should aspire to be like that! Most of them who have wealth, not all of them but, most of them are so cheap in their character, that no amount of money in the world is going to correct that defect!" Stephanie sounded angry.

"You would make a great politician!" Annabella said jokingly

"If I was a politician, I would bring in laws that protect woman such as yourself, for what you had to endure!" Stephanie adamantly makes her point.

Lunch was served outside in the garden area at the same table on the patio where they had breakfast.

Annabella, Stephanie, and Maria are eating their lunch quietly, wild roast pheasant served with roast potatoes salad and bread, along with wine.

"Do you men fish?" asked Roberto looking across the table Steve and Jimmy

"We practically live on the pier where we live in Hastings." said Jimmy with a smile

"We have a couple of telescopic fishing rods in the cabin of the truck with some hooks and line all ready to go!" Steve said with a big grin.

"We don't have any bait though. Otherwise, we would stink up the cabin." said Jimmy, looking at Roberto wondering where this conversation was going.

"How long, before you finish with the mirrors in the barn?" asked Roberto?

"Not more than one hour." replied Steve with a smile.

"I have fish bait. However, where we're going we cannot go by car. Do you know how to ride a horse?" asked Roberto, looking at each of them in return.

"I have skills that are outstanding when it comes to a crash course in learning new things and so does Steve." said Jimmy sealing the deal.

"Good! I will get the horses ready. As soon as you are finished, we can be on our way. It will take us forty-five minutes on horseback to get there, that should leave us a good three hours of fishing and then we can be back here in plenty of time for the evening meal."

Jimmy and Steve, start eating their lunch quickly in order to get back to work sooner so they can leave sooner to go fishing. Stephanie noticed how they were eating their food, then leans forward and asked Maria in a whisper

"What is it with this fishing trip?"

"It is a form of sickness that usually affects the male species. Ninety percent more than the female species." Maria said in a voice that everyone at the table heard.

"I'll see if I can pop a few pheasants and rabbits for the house. If we are really lucky, I might even bring back a boar or a deer!"

"Do you have a licence for shooting game?" asked Steve with a concerned look on his face.

"The mountains and rivers are my home. I don't need a licence to shoot game and fish on my own home."

"Is he always like this?"

"Sometimes he is worse! He is still a little boy at heart."

One hour later, Roberto has the horses ready all tied together to Beauteous. Jimmy and Steve bring their fishing rods and hooks and join Roberto who is finishing sliding his double barrel shotgun into the side-saddle. He gets on his horse proudly, "Come on men let's get going!" Jimmy and Steve get on their horses respectively, and Roberto give a gentle nudge with his feet and Beauteous starts down the road, off the mountain that all the cars come up, passing the barn on the way.

"Hopefully, we will get a few brown trout, or maybe even rainbow trout."

"Don't we need fly-fishing rods for this?" Jimmy asked.

"Why do you always follow rules and regulations? We will bend a few rules and ignore a few more! Hopefully we will end up with a few trout." said Roberto

The three men and horse slowly starts disappearing from view going down the road that dips and winds.

Early evening as the sun starts to make the sky red in colour in the distance, Stephanie is on video chatting with Gabriel, showing him, Paris and Venus, playing freely on the grass.

"What time will you be here on Friday?" Stephanie asked Gabriel in a loving tone.

"I will be there before lunch to conclude my business and then we can all come back together on the private jet." replied Gabriel.

"What is this business, you have to conclude? Is this something outside of the sale of the house?" asked Stephanie inquisitively.

"It has everything to do with the sale of the house. You will find out soon enough when I get there on Friday morning. In the meantime, I'm going to go into the kitchen and see if I can find something to eat." Stephanie cuts in

"Oh, stop being such a wuss, you're such a baby sometimes!"

"I am a lawyer what do you expect? Anyway, we will speak tomorrow night. Say hello to Annabella and everyone there. I love you! Bye!" "I love you too!" Stephanie turns off her phone.

Annabella comes out of her bathroom wearing a loose white summer dress with a rainbow printed on it. Annabella is checking her phone for messages from Theo.

There is a reply to the ten pictures she sent earlier showing how the barn looks now, with all the furniture there.

Theo writes:

"Annabella,

The barn looks amazing! You've done a fantastic job! Thank You so much! I am sorry to inform you, but I will not be able to make the trip this time. I am busy with other engagements. I have a big favour to ask you if it's possible. Let me know if it's ok to ask the favour.

Theo

Annabella replies.

"Theo,

I am disappointed that we will not get the chance to meet in person. Please feel free to ask the favour you wanted to ask me and if I can, I will do it!

Annabella"

Annabella hits the send button and begins to towel dry her hair. She looks in the mirror and admires herself for a second and then she pulls her tongue out in vomiting gesture then smiles to herself.

Being honest, she really looks into the mirror and she likes the person looking back at her. Suddenly her phone pings, picking up her phone, it's another message from Theo.

"Annabella,

Thank you for giving me the opportunity to ask this personal favour. My best friend that I have known all my life is coming to the house on Thursday morning. He will stay for one night and then he will pick up the Mercedes and bring it to me. I wanted to ask you if it would it be too much to ask if you were to spend a day with him.

You can take the car and go to the local places, for lunch and sightseeing. In return I promise you, you can ask him anything you want to learn about me, and he will tell you the truth.

Best wishes Theo"

Annabella replies

"Theo,

I look forward to meeting your best friend! I have a lot of questions I will be asking him about you! Good night!"

Annabella sends the message, closing her phone, she walks out into the garden where Stephanie is playing with the pups.

Stephanie looks at Annabella with concern

"What's wrong? What happened?"

"Theo just informed me that he will not be able to make the trip. Apparently, he has business engagements. Then he asked for a personal favour which is to spend Thursday, with his best friend.

From his message, his friend will be coming to pick up the car so that he can take it to Theo. The best friend will be here for one day and night. Theo has requested that I take him sightseeing and what not. So, I agreed to be a babysitter for him."

"That's not so bad! You can become a detective with his best friend find out things about Theo!" Stephanie said with a twinkle in her eye.

"That's what he said!" Annabella sits on a chair at the table; she looks far into the distance down the garden and to the mountains where the sun is glowing red.

Roberto, Jimmy, and Steve are on the horses returning home.

They stop outside the big house; Roberto managed to bag three mountain hares, and four pheasants. Jimmy and Steve managed to catch five brown trout between them. They looked rather proud as they dismounted from the horses. Roberto gives the hare and the pheasants to them to take into the house, along with their five-brown trout. Roberto then leads Beauteous away with the other two tied horses to her and they head into the barn to be fed and watered. Jimmy and Steve are head to the house.

Jimmy and Steve bring in the fish, fouls and the rabbit and lay it on the table in the kitchen. Maria looks at them. "Well, you have all done very well on your hunting trip!"

"I envy you and Roberto for living in such a beautiful place as this. The trip was amazing and the countryside seen on a horse is a lot different than seeing it as you pass by in a truck." said Jimmy honestly

"Would you like me to prepare the fish for you to take home with you tomorrow?" asked Maria

"No! Please, they are our small gift for you, for your wonderful hospitality over the past few days."

"Thank you, I will put them in a plastic container and salt them and put them in the freezer, it keeps them fresh, and bacteria free."

"Maybe that's what we should do when we get a lot of mackerels in the future!" Steve, and Jimmy head to their room.

Outside in the garden Stephanie hands Paris to Annabella and holding on to Venus.

"I have a good feeling about this." Stephanie said with a smile on her face.

"What are you talking about?"

"About Theo's best friend." Annabella looks at her in disbelief.

"Don't be ridiculous! Good God woman! Do you think I go for anyone who wears a pair of trousers?" Stephanie leans towards Annabella's face to make a point

"Let me tell you something big sister! This man that is Theo's best friend, must have class, and must have style. Have you heard of the saying; "Show me your friends, and I will tell you who you are?"

"For all we know little sister, they could both be eighty years old! Not to mention, there is also a possibility that he might be married, or worse, he might be on a rebound! Even worse, he might even be gay, knowing my luck! Not that I have anything against gay people."

"Sit down will you! You are getting ahead of yourself here with all this negative stuff." Stephanie is trying to calm Annabella.

"I am not ready for anything. To be honest with you, I thought I was. I was so tempted five years ago, but that died in Paris with me crying alone in a hotel room. I need to get a divorce, be on my own for a while, and then go from there. I might even move to Paris."

"Now you're talking! I can help you if you decide to move back to Paris. You can come and stay with me and Gabriel. I'm sure he won't mind until you get yourself a little place. It will be fantastic! We would have the most amazing times together! I can introduce you to some of Gabriel's friends. I've met some of them and they are rather handsome!"

"First thing's, first. I will go back to Morocco file for divorce, and then take it from there. I'd love to come to Paris and be close to you and Gabriel!" Annabella hugs Stephanie with a smile of happiness. Roberto comes out and sits at the table, he looks tired and beat. Looking at both of them in turn.

"It's an early night for me tonight. I wanted to say to you girls that we will be having a BBQ by the swimming pool tomorrow night. Prepare yourself for lots of drinks and especially cake, that's it. I am off! Good night!"

"Roberto, what about evening dinner, you're not eating with us?" ask Annabella.

"No, I'm exhausted. I will have a big breakfast in the morning," and with a smile he leaves and heads towards the cottage.

The evening dinner was none eventful. They all ate without Roberto. After the meal and a few glasses of wine, Annabella and Stephanie helped Maria clean the table and wash the dishes.

Steve and Jimmy thanked Maria for their hospitality and kindness and said goodbye. They will be leaving at the crack of dawn and don't wish to disturb anyone. The two men head to the house to go to bed for their early departure in the morning.

Maria left the house and went back to the cottage. Annabella and Stephanie each took a cup of tea upstairs went and sat on the balcony outside of Annabella's bedroom. The stars were all out and were sending magic spells to all the eyes that would look up at them. The quiet reflection was broken when Annabella's phone began to ping. It was Theo.

"Annabella,

Thank you. Good night.

Theo"

Annabella replies

"Theo,

It's my pleasure! By the way, what is your friend's name? I forgot to ask you.

Good night"

Annabella"

She sends off the message and closes the phone and lays it on the table.

"Theo?" asked Stephanie "Yes, he just wanted to say Good Night." "It's so peaceful here I actually look forward to this part of the night, sitting here looking at the stars."

"It's very beautiful and calm." Stephanie remarked softly "It's so strange" said Annabella with mysterious look. Stephanie asks: "What's so strange?" "It's the first time in my life, that I have stayed at a house, where I never met the owner."

"Who knows, maybe one day you'll meet him, you never know! Besides, you have his Skype, and again, maybe he will commission you to decorate another property. Perhaps, he will turn up in Morocco and out of the blue to ask meet you for a meal!"

"I feel old and broken. I don't think I can ever be fixed." "It will come to pass, everything in life passes, and so will this feeling you have right now." "I am going to get a good night's sleep I need it. Tomorrow we can take it easy. Good night sister." "Good night little sister."

Annabella picks up her phone, walks into the room, and places it on the side table of the bed. Opening the little drawer, she takes out a pair of headphones and leaves them by the phone.

Taking a white T-shirt out of her chest of drawers, she heads to the bathroom to wash her face and brush her teeth. T-shirt comes on, she slips into bed and plugs the earphones into the phone and selects the song by Barry White, *Stone   Gone.*

207

It's romantic and slow and listening to the song she reflects upon her life thus far. Always searching for answers as to why things have forever gone wrong. Finally, she slips off to sleep while the music plays on.

It was four thirty a.m. when suddenly the silence of the mountains was broken by the rooster crowing at the top of his lungs. A half an hour later, the front door opens and out steps Steve and Jimmy with their overnight bags. Across the road they see Roberto with a box in his hand coming towards them.

They all exchange "Good morning" wishes to each other. "This is for you two. Share it on your journey." Roberto hands over the box to Jimmy. Steve responds: "What is it Roberto?" There are six bottles of wine, special wine, that I brewed myself. Also, a packed lunch for you both made with love by Maria. There is goat cheese, two dozen free range eggs, and several jars of jam that we make here, along with honey from the bees we keep."

The men reach the truck, Steve and Jimmy both shook Roberto's hand and thanked him profusely for the wonderful hospitality and the day of fishing and hunting. Both men see Maria and begin to wave goodbye. Jimmy looks down from the truck at Roberto "If you visit this part of the world again, you're both welcome here!" Steve smiles and nods his head to say yes.

Starting the trucks he slowly turns the truck around, and heads down the drive. Roberto stands there outside the barn watching until the tail lights disappeared. Roberto turns and starts to walk towards Maria, who is still outside looking at him as he gets close to her

"You want some breakfast my love?"

"Big breakfast! On one of those big plates! I will go and feed animals and be back here in half an hour." Roberto was off to his chores.

Chapter Nineteen

Unforgettable Beauty

After breakfast Annabella and Stephanie decided to spend a few hours in the barn to go over how the place looks and to see if they need to adjust anything. Roberto brought the wooden pen along with Paris and Venus and made them comfortable in the middle of the barn.

Annabella had finished looking at her phone to see if there was a reply from Theo regarding his best friend's name. There were no messages. Disappointed, she puts the phone on the side table and walks away towards Roberto. Roberto was admiring how beautiful everything looked.

"I'll be going to the waterfall to have a picnic and a swim. Would you two ladies like to join me?" asked Roberto "Oh my god I have seen the pictures you have sent me Annabella, I'd love to go there just to be in the moment, it's a yes from me!" said Stephanie enthusiastically "Thank you Roberto it is a yes for me also!" replied Annabella

"I will ready the horses." Roberto heads to the stable, Annabella calls out

"What about Maria?" "Maria is making preparations for the BBQ tonight; she's baking a cake for us!"

Two hours later they were all on horseback and were at the top of the mountain that looked down slightly to the waterfall. Roberto stops all the horses so they can get a good view and take a few pictures if they wished and they did just that.

Nudging his horse Beauteous they make their way towards the waterfall.

The horses are stopped, drinking the cold water from the cold lake that came down from the gushing waterfall.

Roberto's ritual was to pick up a stone and put it on the pile, which he did, followed by Annabella and then Stephanie. Roberto takes the shotgun from the horse and puts it near Annabella and Stephanie and begins stripping by the side of the lake.

"What is he doing?" asked Stephanie

"He's going for a swim." replied Annabella

"Is the water warm?" "No, it's freezing!" responded Annabella "Don't worry he has been doing this for years!" Stephanie looks at the shotgun stacked against a rock close by

"What's with the shotgun?" asked Stephanie

"Have a good look around you. We are in the wilderness and there are wild brown bears, wolves, wild boars, and royal eagles."

"There is a waterfall in the book I read, you know the one, "Emotional Rhapsody" and it's under the tropical waterfall the character first encounters the woman of his dreams. She was washing her long hair, and the waterfall acted as a shower. He was so mesmerized by the beauty of this woman that he could not even approach her to say hello.

Instead, he enjoyed her beauty. He drank up all her movements, all her expressions, the way she breathed, the way she washed her hair, the way she turned under the waterfall, the way she closed her eyes as the water ran down her head and body. He watched in silence as she washed her thighs. He lived a thousand years of love in that moment and he never even knew her name.

Distracted by a friend who called out to her from nearby, that the picnic was ready; he watched her walk. Her wet long hair and the beauty of her balance, as she stepped from stone to stone, to get to the edge of the dry land sent him over the moon."

At that moment, everything he had seen of her was engraved in his heart, soul, and mind, and it was then that he knew, he'd fallen in love with her."

"Did the story have a good ending?"

"They ended up marrying." said Stephanie

"So why were you crying that night when I called? You were crying like a baby, why?"

"I got emotional and cried when he opened up and told her his feelings. The words were so poetic and so beautiful, it made me cry." "Well, what did he say to her?"

"One of the lines he used was something really close to this; "I have died a million times over the years, waiting to stand before you to look into your soul and to see if I can see myself there." "I don't think there is a single woman in the world who does not long to hear such words from the person they are in love with."

"I have to admit, even though I have given up all hope of ever finding that kind of love; I still love hearing the words. What else did he say?"

"Oh no! You'll have to read the book to find out! I am certainly not going to deprive you of your emotional tears when you cry! Believe me, you will cry!" Just then, Roberto climbed out of the lake, exhaled a large breath, picked up the towel and started to dry himself. Annabella's eyes were glued to the beautiful waterfall.

Wondering what had this man said to the woman that made Stephanie cry uncontrollably that night on the phone.

The majestic waterfall stood in the background as Roberto stopped the horses on the side of the mountain so they could take one last look before heading back to the house.

After a few minutes, Roberto nudged his horse and they began the trip back. Tonight, there was to be the BBQ and of course, Roberto was in charge!

This place was like another world, no wonder Maria and Roberto referred to it as "The Garden of Eden." Full of mysterious mountains, wildlife, and almost hand crafted by God himself, a landscape that went far beyond the human eye and straight from the heavens.

Millions from around the globe travelled each year to visit and experience this little piece of heaven on earth. It was truly a sanctuary of lakes, rivers and plush green rolling hills, it was said to be sacred, but, to Roberto and Maria it was "home."

When they arrived at the house, Roberto took the horses to the stable to feed and unsaddle them. He tended to the other animals and feed them as well. He enjoyed this connection with the animals and he respected them for the gifts they were.

Maria as usual, had cleaned two of the rooms on the first floor in the big house, and made sure the downstairs was immaculate. There was a note left for Annabella to let her and Stephanie know that there were some freshly made sandwiches in the fridge. Annabella had never known such consideration and understood now why she felt her loving connection to both Maria and Roberto.

Back in the cottage kitchen, Maria was sorting out the venison steaks, lamb chops, and wild pheasant. She was making fresh salads with wild herbs. The food was her department, and the BBQ and the cooking was Roberto's.

Annabella checked her phone for messages several times during the morning and it was now two in the afternoon with still no reply from Theo. Not knowing the man's name was unsettling for Annabella as thus far Theo had been very accommodating and always replied to her messages. Not today. Annabella felt uneasy she has always felt uneasy ever since she was a child.

It was "the not knowing" that always triggered the childhood memories and thought patterns. Even though she comes across as confident and self-assured at times, this was all just a front, for her. Always in survival mode.

After playing with Paris and Venus, and giving those hugs and cuddles, Annabella wanted to take the car and go into Andorra to pick up some black and white prints in frames to put on some of the walls in the barn. Annabella persuaded Stephanie to go with her and the two took off with the top down, sun shining on their beautiful faces.

They only had about four hours to spend away from the house. The winding roads and the lush green mountain sides all dotted with small farms and white sheep grazing left Stephanie in awe. Looking at Annabella, Stephanie asks

"So, there's no news then?"

"No news about what?" Annabella replied

"News about Theo and his best friend's name." Just as Stephanie asked the question, the flat road was now at the bottom of a steep road. Annabella put her foot down on the accelerator and the Mercedes responded with a roar; scaring sheep and birds to run. Stephanie's head is pushed back onto her headrest by the G force.

"No news as yet." replied Annabella calmly. The car reached the top of the hill and Annabella took her foot off the gas.

Stephanie was doing something with her breast looking for something inside. Annabella does a double take and looks at her

"What are you doing Stephanie?"

"I am looking for the one breast that I have, to see if it's still there! For a second I thought it ended up in my stomach with the way you put your foot down on the accelerator!"

Annabella smiles, then the smile turns to smirk, then into uncontrollable laughter! Stephanie joins. Their laughter together was more beautiful than the Mercedes. Andorra was ahead in the distant hills.

In Andorra, they park the car outside an art décor shop that deals with prints. Annabella and Stephanie are looking around the shop; they both pick out several prints they think will be perfect on the walls of the barn. They stop at a large picture in a frame.

"You've been miserable all day!" said Stephanie without taking her eye of the large black and white print on the wall. The print depicts a man in an evening suit, and a woman with wearing a long dress, that has a split on the side that goes right to her hip flashing her beautiful leg and thigh.

"If I was to name this picture, I would name it "Eyeful." "Look at those thighs! I wish mine were like that again!" replied Annabella trying to deflect the conversation from answering the question. Stephanie turns and looks at Annabella "Are you going to answer me?"

"I haven't been miserable, I have been concerned that's all."

"You don't know this person, you have never met this person, and yet you are concerned!" The only thing you are concerned about is, Theo has not replied to you in the same way as he has done before.

Maybe, it is a surprise for you not to know. I mean, maybe he's trying to keep you in suspense?" Annabella looks at her lovingly coming back to herself again.

"No woman at my age wants surprises! We want calm and stability, trust and honesty. Look what life has done to us, and you still want surprises and suspense!?" " Well, you can have my share; I am done with all that suspense, and surprises stuff!"

Annabella heads to the cash register to pay for the prints.

Coming out of the shop Annabella gets into the car, turns on the ignition key, and closes the roof, so they can put the pictures into back. She comes out opens the back and they lay the prints flat, then they both get in the car. Annabella opens the roof again, turns on the car, and notices that the whole street of people walking past them is looking at the car.

"You might be done with surprises and suspense, but, believe me, life is not done with you! I am sure you will have a few more great years before your day is over!"

"Put your seat belt on!" demanded Annabella, ignoring what she'd heard. Annabella begins to drive and Stephanie bursts into life again.

"That's exactly what I mean!" said Stephanie furious at something.

"What? What are you talking about now?"

"Here we are in Andorra, in a new Mercedes convertible, and everyone is looking at us. That's what I am trying to say!"

"I don't know what your point is or what you are trying to say here little sister!"

"The point is everyone who looks at us thinks that this is our car, and they are judging us!

They think we're rich, famous and glamorous show offs!"

"Is that your point?" asked Annabella

"No, the point I was trying to make was; people's perception can be so wrong! We are sitting in a convertible Mercedes that does not belong to us, but these people believe it does! They are stigmatizing us!" Annabella sees the reasoning

"You're right, but they have one perception that is right!"

"What's that?"

"We are glamorous!" Stephanie holds her head up high and straightens her shoulders.

"We are not just glamorous, we are two mature women in the prime of our life, and we're sizzling hot!"

"I haven't been sizzling hot for ten years!"

"Please Annabella; on the home stretch please don't put your foot down too hard, ok? You might discover that what you think is my hair is in actual fact a wig" said Stephanie giggling.

"Now that would be a surprise!" Annabella replied as she turns the corner towards the open road that leads to the house. Putting her foot down hard on the accelerator, the car flies down the road. Stephanie is screaming, "Whooohoooo!"

It was late afternoon, night was drawing closer.

The sun was low on the mountain tops and the sunset was breath-taking. Arriving home, Roberto, had already organized and lit the BBQ. Music is playing; it's the Italian version of "*My Way*" This song always makes Roberto happy and sad at the same time.

It was his late father's favourite song. Sometimes he would burst out into song, trying to sing along with the lyrics, as if he was singing to the whole world.

Maria, Annabella, and Stephanie, come out with the trays of food and put them on the table. Maria places the cake she baked on the side of the table. Roberto grabs Maria and starts to slow dance, for the last part of the song, holding her close in his arms, they did this many times before, and it was nothing unusual for them.

Annabella and Stephanie looking on lovingly at the beauty of the two of them dancing and obviously very much in love. The song finishes, Annabella and Stephanie are clapping and smiling with such love in their hearts. It's moments like this that one "freeze frames" in their minds forever.

"The first time I held her in my arms and danced with her, I thought I was in heaven! Her hair smelled like a fragrant garden, her eyes shone like the stars at night. When I got home that night from the dance, I told my mother and father that I had just met my future wife."

"You are both very lucky, and a blessing to each other!"

"That we are!" "Your husband is a good man!"

"And how would you know that Roberto?"

"I heard him speak with you on the phone. The day he was here, taking pictures and flying that contraption around that frightened the life out of me!"

"Do you have a habit of listening to other people's conversations? How would you know he was not speaking with his mistress instead of me?"

"What? Him, a mistress, Ha! If he was having lunch and a naked woman was dancing on his table, he wouldn't lift up his head to look at her, not unless the woman in question that was dancing on the table where you!"

Stephanie blushes, Annabella smiles.

"How can you tell what a man is like, or what a man is likely to do if he is aroused Roberto?"

"Forget about the aroused stuff! Another woman wouldn't even get as far as the arousal department; he would put out the fire before it spread!"

"Yes, but how can you tell from overhearing one conversation between us?"

"His tone of voice, the words he used, the vibration of those words and the feeling mixed with those words.

 The glow in his eyes and being totally oblivious to everything around him. That is not a man you want to worry about straying; that man will never stray."

"Have you ever thought about fortune telling Roberto?"

"Stephanie, just tell me I was wrong, and we have a decision based upon your personal experience with this man."

"I can't because what you have said about him is true. The last thing that comes to my mind would be him straying."

"I know."

"Yes, but how do you know?"

"That part is a little hard to explain. The truth is, I don't know how I know, but I do know that I know."

"Roberto will you stop embarrassing our guests, are you going to tell them about the cake?"

"You baked it, you tell them."

Stephanie and Annabella look at each other and then back at Roberto and Maria.

"What do we need to know about the cake?"

The cake looks like a six-inch pizza on the plate; Maria has cut the cake into four equal pieces.

"I can't ask you to eat something that I've baked without you knowing the ingredients."

Annabella and Stephanie exchange a curious glance between them, Maria continues

"It has been given many names over the years, such as cannabis, dope, hashish, Ganja, joint, reefer, and weed."

Annabella moves her head back in shock and looks at Stephanie and then to Roberto who shrugs his shoulders and then to Maria, who is standing next to the cake waiting to serve it up.

"I think they get the picture Maria."

Annabella looks on with her mouth open. Stephanie smiles and nudges her with a twinkle in her eyes.

"I grow it for my arthritis. It helps me, especially in the cold winter months here. You don't have to have any; we have plenty of other food for the night."

Stephanie moves forward and grabs a piece and starts eating it.

"What is it they say? "When in Rome, do as the Romans do!" "I'm not an angel; I'm here to party and have a good time!"

Maria and Roberto grab a piece of cake and begin to eat it.

"What would Gabriel say if he knew?"

"He would probably complain that I never brought some back for him! Will you stop being such a goody two shoes and join in! Anyone would think you were a fifteen-year-old virgin, the way you are acting!"

"I've never eaten hash cake before! I'm just asking will it make me hallucinate."

Roberto nearly spits his mouthful out, trying not to laugh at what he has just heard. Maria looks at Annabella, rolls her eyes. Stephanie has already finished her piece of cake.

"I have a question for you?"

"Ask"

"Has any harm come to you, from me or my husband during the time you have been here?"

"No! You have both been very kind and generous to me."

"Hey, you are my older sister. If you were my aunt, I would have a lot more to explain."

"You can be sure Annabella that no harm will ever come to you, from me, or your brother Roberto. Only good will always come, to you, from both of us!"

Annabella knows Maria is speaking from her heart. That's just one of the qualities she loved about Maria. Annabella takes the piece of cake and starts eating it. Looking over at Stephanie, she is already looking for more. She tries to speak, but her mouth is full.

"The party is just beginning."

Annabella takes a bigger mouthful of the cake, "It tastes good!" she mumbles to Maria and

Roberto who have nearly finished their pieces.

After forty minutes or so, Roberto is dishing up the venison steaks that he's cooked, with the help of Maria, who acts as an assistant chef putting on accompanying food on the plates. Roberto hands the first plate to Annabella who looks at the plate and is shocked, the plate is totally full.

"I won't be able to eat all this!"

"Take it! What you don't eat, leave on the plate."

Roberto takes another plate from Maria and puts another big chunk of steak on it and passes it on to Stephanie. Without complaint, she starts to eat with her hands. Annabella is watching her, drops her knife and fork, and begins to eat with her hands as well.

Roberto has eaten as he was cooking; it's a privilege that is bestowed on whoever cooks the BBQ. Pouring out four large glasses of red wine, he passes them around. Stephanie is nodding her head in delight that the food is great! Annabella nods her head also acknowledging her that it's all good. Roberto interrupts the party holding a glass of red wine in his hand "A toast!" everyone grabs their glass and waits for Roberto to speak.

"My beautiful wife and I would like to thank you both for coming into our lives. You've enriched our lives and brought us joy. We wish upon you only good health, good life, and a multitude of endless blessings. He makes the sign of the cross. We stand before you blessed, for the good company you have blessed us with by being here! To you two beautiful souls; Salute!"

Raising his glass up, everyone clinks their glass against his they all say; "Salute!" "Now it's time to really get the party started!" Roberto turns to the big stereo and puts on an Italian song *La Ziletta*, a version that is played at raves for the younger people. Grabbing Maria by the hand, she just about manages to put her glass down on the table without spilling it, they are on the grass by the side of the pool, facing each other than they start to dance like two rams locking horns.

 Maria moves her body around then she moves and takes Roberto hand and they embrace swing around and they part; still holding hands.

Roberto pulls her in again and so they continue. The dance looks like samba, cumbia, lambada and rock and roll all in one.

Annabella and Stephanie start to dance to the song improvising as they go along. They look like they are doing some sort of belly dancing and flamenco combined; bouncing their hips off each other while they are curling and stretching their hands into the air. The sound of giggling and laughter fills the night air as they continue with the dance.

The sun is down behind the mountains in the distance, another dance song is blasting out of the speakers this time a Latin, Spanish favourite disco song called *LaColegiala* by (Rodolfo Aicardi con Los Hispanos) they are dancing, mostly they are improvising. Different movements to the fantastic upbeat song that would get anyone dancing once hearing its rhythm. More giggling and smiling. They are all stoned and half-drunk now but are all having a fantastic time!

Ten o'clock at night the sky is dark, the lights around the pool are on, all the plates are empty, and the BBQ has gone out now.

There are several empty wine bottles on the table now as Stephanie put her arm around Annabella's shoulder and leans in close to Annabella's ear.

"Are you having a good time?" Annabella just burst out laughing, she had the giggles. Stephanie joins her, now they both have the giggles. Roberto looks at Maria"

"Maria our guests have a case of the giggles." Maria chuckles. The last song for the night is, *"I Will Survive"* by Gloria Gaynor. A seventies classic disco song a woman's anthem from the seventies.

Stephanie pulls Annabella to dance. They dance and sing along to the song, joined by Maria. Roberto approaches Maria and indicates with his eyes towards the pool.

Maria and Roberto are holding hand's as they take a running start and jump into the pool with their clothes on. Both are laughing in the pool playing water splash and then they kiss gently on the lips and hug gently. Upon seeing this Stephanie lets out a scream, "Yeahhhhhhhhhhhhh!" She runs and jumps into the pool. Annabella shouts, "Whoohooooooooooo!" She runs and jumps into the pool. They are laughing and playing water splash, singing along to the song that is blasting from the speakers.

Half an hour later, they all stumble into the kitchen soaking wet. Roberto is carrying with him his glass of wine. Annabella and Stephanie are holding an open bottle of wine each, their hair all over the place, they look like they have been dragged through the bushes, They are looking at Roberto as they knew he was about to speak.

"Ladies all good things must come to an end, and so, I wish you good night and sweet dreams."

Roberto unsteady on his feet, downs the glass of wine in one gulp, grabs Maria by the arm, and swings her over his shoulder, slapping her on her bottom.

"Good night, sweet dreams!" Annabella managed to get out of her mouth followed by a hiccup.

Maria lifts up her head, smiles, and waves bye and good night as she is carried away.

Stephanie manages to move her fingers to say good night, swaying as if she was on a boat in a middle of an Atlantic storm. Roberto carries Maria out the front door of the house; she manages to pull the door shut behind her. Annabella is trying to walk upstairs swaying all over the place.

"Damn stairs who invented them, they are not much use when one is drunk and high on hash cake!"

She breaks out into an uncontrollable giggle; Stephanie sits on the second step of the stairs. Annabella is four steps above her looking down at her, she brings the bottle to her mouth to have a drink, but it's empty.

Lowering the bottle down and looks at the bottle in her hand, then turns it upside down. Not a drop spills out.

"I've been carrying a bottle of wine all the way from the pool to here, and there is not a drop of wine in it!" Annabella looks down at her has a sudden hiccup that jerks her upwards, then she starts to giggle again.

"There is not a drop in the bottle because it's all in your stomach! Come on, let's go, we had our pit stop." Annabella reaches her hand down to Stephanie and grabs her by the hand pulling her up.

They start making their way up the stairs she is still clinging to the bottle.

"A few more parties like this and we will be like twenty-five-year-olds again!"

"A few more parties like this and it's more like Gabriel will divorce you, for being a party animal! A few more parties like this and we will be dead, and don't forget we have a guest coming tomorrow! A mystery best friend, of a mystery man, that no one knows!"

"Not me! The "mystery guest"   is your guest, not mine!"

At the top of the stairs, they steady themselves and straighten themselves up a little.

The phone is ringing in Stephanie's room. It's Gabriel, calling on video chat to say Good Night.

"Good Lord, I am in Stuttgart now." as she takes a step towards her room Annabella lifts up her hand to say bye, but before she lowers her hand Stephanie, spontaneously grabs her hand and drags her towards her. She opens the door and drags Annabella into the room, picks up the ringing phone on the side table of the double bed, and answers it.

"Hello darling did you miss me?

"What the hell happened to you?"

"Wait!" she swings the phone around so Gabriel can see Annabella in the same state holding a bottle of wine in her hand

"What the hell happened to both of you? Are you two drunk?" Annabella takes a swig from the bottle. "We're not drunk, we are extremely drunk, get your facts right my darling lawyer."

"We are not drunk, we are intoxicated!" Annabella lowers the bottle from her mouth and she hiccups up and burst into giggles.

"Whose idea was all this?"

"Not mine, your wife is a bad influence on me, and in my defence, all I'm going to say and plead is that she led me astray."

"That's it blame it all onto me, you traitor!" They start giggling again

"I can see I am not going to get any sense out of you two tonight."

"The only sensible person is the culprit! He became a fugitive a little while ago, carrying a woman off into the night. He's probably making love to her by now. And where is the love of my life? Six hundred kilometres away in Paris!"

"I will be there first thing Friday morning to conclude the last piece of business."

"Yes! As you can see we had a fantastic time, and the night is not over yet, we're just getting warmed up. By the way, you tell that rat Theo, whoever he is, that I am very cross with him."

"Stephanie, don't bring Theo into this. The poor man he hasn't done anything wrong."

"Leave my client out of this conversation."

"You see that's my point, you are both defending him, she's never met him and you won't divulge any information about him."

Gabriel in a soft voice, "I miss you."

"That's not fair Gabriel!"

"I love you, I miss you terribly."

She hands the phone to Annabella, who has various expressions coming and going on her face trying to compose herself.

Stephanie throws a pillow on the floor and kicks it against the wall

"Did you have a good day at the office?"

"Annabella, please look after her ok? I will see you girls Friday morning. I will call Stephanie tomorrow. Remind her that I love her! Good night."

"I will, I Promise!" they end the call. Stephanie is crying

"He knows all my buttons, even a few I didn't know I had, and he knows which ones to press and when to get the desired effect."

"I know you miss him."

"That's just it, he knows I miss him, and he knows how to play me."

"Well, he will be here in less the thirty-six hours and you will be together, it's not that long."

"When is your prince charming going to turn up?"

"You mean Theo's friend?"

"No, I mean the man who you will fall madly in love with, someone you can share your life with, what's left of it. Someone to make you happy, someone to make you feel alive again, someone to have lots of sex with and lots of dirty flirting innuendoes with, that man!"

"It's been so long since I had sex, I forgot it was called sex! I don't think I am strong enough anymore to handle rejection or disappointment, it will break me for good."

"It might just make you!"

"Good night little sister, sweet dreams," Annabella embraces her and kisses her on the cheek and looks at her.

"Can I adopt you as my younger sister?"

"Sometimes you are too slow; I have already adopted you as my older sister. Good night, sweet dreams."

Annabella walks out onto the balcony of her room, still uneasy on her feet; she looks up at the glittering stars, shining in the sky, after a few seconds she sees a shooting start going across the sky. She can see the white streak, it's leaving behind it; she clasps both hands together, and starts to say a prayer.

"Dear God, I know you get millions of requests. I know you know, that I am drunk, and high and I know you will forgive me, I had a very good time tonight.

You know, because you know everything. I don't know how many requests you get daily, to write a happy ending for people but, I've never had a happy beginning or a middle, and now as you know I am on the last chapter of my life; I need to get on the "Happy Ending List!" I pray that you hear my prayer, and write a happy ending for me. Amen."

When she opened her eyes and looked, the shooting star was gone. Back into her room, she takes out a pair of white pyjamas that have little teddy bears and hearts printed all over them. Staggering into the bathroom, she brushes her teeth and changes. Now she was ready for bed, but she could not resist the temptation, and she looks one more time at her phone to see if there are any messages from Theo.

 No messages. Placing the phone down, she rests her head on the pillow, curls up like a little girl, she begins to cry softly.

Chapter Twenty

Unexpected Visitor

The next morning Annabella opens her eyes and looks at the phone. Eyes wide open she jumps out of bed. Quickly taking a shower, she finds her loose summer dress and some sandals. Knocking on Stephanie's door, she hears a grunt; "Yeah" Annabella walks in, Stephanie is still in bed, starts to stir awake.

"What is it?"

"Do you have the right time?"

She reaches to the small table and picks up her phone and looks at the time,

"The time is not working on my phone it says it's ten o'clock. Can that be right?"

"It is right! It's ten o'clock in the morning!"

"Is the rooster sick or has he died, he usually crows for hours?"

"He is neither sick nor dead; we slept though the morning crow. Come on, time to get up we have the visitor arriving today, and we don't know what time he is going to show up."

"That means I slept for ten hours."

"We both slept for ten hours."

"I am going to ask Maria, if she can bake a cake for me, to take back to Paris."

"I am going downstairs to have a coffee, and then I am going to the barn to put up the pictures on the wall."

Stephanie gets out of bed half dead, and starts walking towards the bathroom.

"I am going to take a shower and I'll see you at the barn shortly." Annabella walks out of the room.

Annabella walks into the kitchen and finds Maria fully awake with a smile on her face.

"Good morning, what would you like for breakfast?"

"Not anymore cake that's for sure!" They both start giggling. "I'm still full from the BBQ we ate last night. Has anyone turned up to pick up the car?"

"No."

"Where is Roberto?"

"He took his horse and went out hunting about three hours ago, he will be back soon." "Oh! What time did you two wake up this morning?"

"The usual time five, or five-thirty. Why do you ask? Is there something wrong?"

 "No, nothing is wrong. I just wondered that's all. I am going to make a coffee and then off to the barn to hang some prints we picked up in town yesterday."

"Don't bother."

"Why not?"

"I took an electric kettle down there for you, along with coffee, tea, sugar, and milk."

"Thank you, that is so very thoughtful of you Maria!"

"Also, you will find Paris and Venus running around the barn, I was about to take the wooden box there for them."

Annabella looks at the empty wooden closure

"I will take this to them."

"I have put some food and water for them in the box, just in case they get hungry."

"Thank you, Maria. When Madam comes downstairs, she will probably ask for some cake for breakfast!"

"Did you have a good time last night?"

"The best time! Thank You! I've not had so much fun and laughter for years!"

"I am glad you had a good time!"

"Me too! I'll see you later." Annabella gives Maria an unexpected hug; Maria returned the hug with a great deal of love.

Annabella picks up the wooden enclosure for Paris and Venus and leaves the kitchen.

Opening the door of the barn, she stands in the door, and looks at Paris and Venus running around playing, she smiles. The two are sliding on the polished wooden floors. She brings in the wooden enclosure for them, closing the door behind her.

Stepping down into the open plan room she places the wooden enclosure on the floor. Paris and Venus run to her with their tails wagging as she picks them up in each hand and puts them to her face, smooching and hugging   them.

231

"You want some loving, eh? You want some loving, yes you do! Shall I kidnap you both and take you both to Morocco with me? Mmm, Yes!"

She puts them both down onto the floor and they playfully chase each other around the large room, the door of the barn opens Annabella turns and looks quickly to find Roberto standing on the step just inside the door.

"Good morning!"

 "Good morning little brother!"

"I'm glad to see that you've survived last night's wild party!"

"You and Maria sure know how to throw a pool party!"

"No green monsters, then?"

"No green monsters."

"Glad to hear it! I'll see you later."

"Roberto?"

"Yes."

"You and Maria, your hospitality has been magnificent and so loving! Thank you!"

"Well, our middle name is Magnificent, as for our hospitality, we don't go by normal rules, but your presence here, has made us extremely happy!"

"Thank you, Roberto!"

"My pleasure! I'll see you later." He walks out closing the door behind him.

Twenty minutes later Stephanie steps into the barn closing the door behind her.

Annabella has the pictures all on the large dining table looking at them and trying to decide in what order they should go on the wall leading to the top of the stairs.

"I think the ones in the front here can go on the wall leading to the top, six feet in height so that way they will be consistent to the eye line going up or downstairs, what do you think?"

"I think I need a coffee and twenty minutes rest in the garden before I can make any kind of sound judgement this morning."

"That's a good idea; I think I'll join you."

A taxi stops outside the big house. Roberto walks to the taxi opening the rear passenger door. A gentleman in his late fifties exits wearing a cream coloured summer suit, holding a cream coloured Panama hat in one hand and a black walking cane in the other. The taxi drives off.

"Are you the man who has come to pick up the car?"

"Yes."

"You spoke with my wife Maria, she said you also wanted to speak with Annabella is that right?"

"Yes, that's right."

"Please follow me, sir. The ladies are in the barn, putting on the finishing touches with some black and white prints they purchased yesterday from Andorra. My name is Roberto De La Mancha Surgio."

Roberto opens the front door to the barn and walks in. The gentleman stands still in the doorway. Roberto walks towards the end of the large room, he can hear Stephanie and Annabella in the garden talking, and he walks out and looks at Annabella.

"There's a gentleman here to see you Annabella."

Annabella and Stephanie look at each other as they ease out of their chairs. Roberto walks back into the large living area, followed by Annabella and Stephanie.

Still standing by the door, the gentleman could not be seen properly as the sun made him look much like a silhouette holding a walking cane and a Panama hat. Annabella stops, looks at the man, but cannot make out who he is.

"Hello, you must be Theo's friend that has come to pick up the car."

"Hello Annabella"

"I'd know that voice anywhere!" exclaimed Annabella

Annabella moves forward to see the person clearly. It was indeed Santiago the man she was in love with, the man she was supposed to meet in Paris. Annabella smiles for a second.

"Santiago?"

"Yes."

"You know each other?" Asked Stephanie with surprise.

Annabella smiles. "Yes." Santiago, I'd like you to meet my younger sister Stephanie and my younger brother Roberto."

"Nice to meet you both."

Knowing that Annabella has no siblings, Santiago is giving them a strained and uncomfortable look without giving it away that he knows they aren't related at all.

"Right! I will be at the house if you need me."

Roberto leaves, closing the front door behind him. Santiago is looking around the barn.

"You have done a great job here! Everything looks beautiful!"

"Thank you!"

Stephanie steps forward. "Are you the same Santiago, who never showed up to meet Annabella in Paris?"

"Yes."

"I think you two need some privacy, I'll be at the house if you need me."

As Stephanie was about to take a step forward, she is stopped in her tracks

"Stay where you are!" demanded Annabella

"I could do with a witness. Please stay." pleaded Santiago

"Oh boy!"

"Well, what are you doing here?"

I came to pick up the car and hopefully spend the day with you or what's left of it."

"I did not expect it to be you that is Theo's friend."

"Are you disappointed?"

"No, just surprised!"

"Well, as you know I'm full of surprises!"

"Did you know I was here?"

"Yes."

"And how do you know Theo?"

"Theo is my best friend."

"You never mentioned him in all our conversations that we'd before."

"I was too captivated by you. I could only think of you."

"Well, Mr. Captivated, if you've come to tell me that you love me, and all that nonsense, then it's best you forget it."

"For God's sake Annabella! For once be nice! You make me so nervous."

"I make you nervous? It's you who make me nervous and frustrated. Why don't you just give up and leave me alone?"

Stephanie jumps into the conversation trying to make light of things

"I know someone like that. Look you are both making me nervous. Shall we all take a deep breath and relax please? Ok, Annabella? Please it's Santiago, right?"

"Yes."

"Please come and have a seat."

Stephanie sits down Annabella lowers herself into a seat next to her

Santiago starts to walk towards the large table, using his walking cane.

"Why are you using a walking cane?"

"I have arthritis in my hip, it helps me."

"You never told me that before."

"You've never given me a chance. You haven't spoken to me properly for the past four years."

"You're lucky; I've spoken to you at all, after what you did to me."

"What do you mean? "What I did to you?" " I've never done anything to you. Now will you please calm down?"

"Don't you dare Santiago De la Cruz, tell me what to do! You're not my husband!"

"I am not telling you what to do. I'm merely suggesting you calm yourself Annabella."

"Good."

Santiago slowly sits down across from Annabella and Stephanie

"I think that you two should be left alone to have this conversation."

"Stephanie don't you dare move from that seat."

"Ok! Let's hear what Santiago has to say, without shouting or getting excited please!"

Annabella calms down a little and looks at Santiago

"Thank you! On the way here from the airport, I stopped the driver in the middle of nowhere on three different occasions. I got out of the car and pretended I was looking at the mountains but, in reality, I was so nervous to come and meet you today that I was vacillating back and forth with myself about actually showing up. Finally, there was no doubt I had to come and see you."

"Why? What do you want to see me about?"

"I wanted to spend a day with you and talk with you."

"Annabella give the man a chance, will you?"

"It's taken me one thousand four hundred and sixty days to get here. It's taken me two hundred and eight weeks to get here. It's taken me forty-eight months to get here. It's taken me thirty-five thousand hours to get here to be here with you today.

All of this time just to spend a few hours with you, to talk and have a chance to explain what happened."

Annabella looks at Stephanie. She knows she has nowhere to hide.

"I think it's a great idea to spend a few hours together, Annabella has told me wonderful things about you."

"Stephanie!"

"Wait, sorry."

"I will spend a few hours with you, on one condition."

"Name it."

"That if you upset me, you will bring me right back here."

"I promise."

Santiago looks at Stephanie, and then in a soft, grateful voice says

"Thank you."

Annabella leaves the barn, Santiago holds the door. Walking to the car, Santiago rushes and opens the car door for Annabella to get in; something that no one she's been involved with has done for her before. Santiago gets in the car and puts his seat belt on and starts the car.

Annabella is putting her seat belt on, Santiago releases the roof, and the car turns into a convertible, all along Stephanie is watching all of Santiago's actions towards Annabella.

"Do you know how to drive this car?"

"I think I can handle it."

"It's a beautiful car; it draws a lot of attention from people."

"It's a beautiful car, in a world full of beautiful cars."

"Santiago slowly drives the car down the road, as Stephanie watches from the barn door.

Hoping Annabella can hear her telepathically, she speaks quietly; "Don't mess this up sister." Stephanie watches as the car disappears and returns into the barn.

Chapter Twenty One

Not So Fabulous Day

DRIVING THROUGH THE VALLEYS

"Let's try not to make each other any more nervous than we already are, shall we?"

"I am already nervous."

"Me too, but I am trying not to show it. I'm trying to show the macho side of me, but it has deserted me. You are, as I imagined you would be like in real life, beautiful in every way."

"Thank you. You have seen me so many times on web cam chats, I'd think there were no surprises for you regarding me."

"Not for the past four years."

"That was your fault."

"My fault?"

"Yes, it's your fault, you let me down. You never came to Paris."

"I'm going to explain all of that you once we settle down and have a coffee."

"How do you know Theo? Is he really your best friend and are you really here to pick up his car or is this something altogether different?"

"Yes, Theo is my best friend!"

"If he's your best friend, how comes he has never helped you with money? You live in poverty in a room; what kind of a friend is that?"

"Well, he gave me good advice, and through that good advice, my life has totally changed."

"I'm happy that your life has changed. My life is still the same, nothing seems to ever change, except for this opportunity to spend time on the estate and live the past three weeks. It is like I am living in a Fairy Tale. I've been blessed to now have a family that truly cares about me and they have enriched my life so beautifully."

"This might be the beginning of new things for you. I am very sorry about Fluffy."

"Let's not talk about Fluffy. I'd prefer not to get emotional and cry I still haven't recovered from losing her."

"Understood. I didn't mean to appear insensitive. How is the situation with you and Ibrahim?"

"The same. Another subject I'd rather not discuss for fear of depression setting in."

"How is your health?"

"Everything is falling apart, my body aches. When I think about you, my head aches."

"So, are you happy to see me?"

"You are one of my greatest nightmares!"

"I wanted to see you. I wanted just to spend a day with you, a day that even if you said "Goodbye" I could keep the day with me forever. May we please have a beautiful day together Annabella?"

Annabella turns and give Santiago a long hard look. Santiago turns to look at her and then turns back to the road.

"You are such a Stupido! You know, you are a little kid trapped in a man's body and you will never grow up!"

"Given the circumstances, I think I deserve a higher praise! How about; "Mr. Super Stupido", if I'm going to be special I want the highest praises."

Annabella gives him another long hard look and then she turns and stares out of the window to the fields and the mountains dotted with sheep on the hillsides.

SAINT-CYPRIEN BEACH FRONT

Santiago stops the car by the beach close to the restaurants and coffee shops. Getting out he takes his walking cane and makes his way around the car to open the door for Annabella.

Annabella comes out of her seat gracefully and says

"Thank you."

"Would you like some breakfast? Perhaps, after we could go for a walk on the beach?"

"I have already had breakfast. I'd like a coffee, please."

SAINT-CYPRIEN BEACH FRONT CAFE

Sitting outside looking out to the sea the sea air is beautiful. People walking the streets, shopping and relaxing in the sand on this beautiful sunny day yet the two a full of nervous energy. Everyone seemed in an enchanted trance, and this part of France was the perfect spot for enchantment. The waitress approaches, bringing two coffees, places them on the table and turns away to other customers. There is a moment of stillness and calm, as they make eye contact for the first time.

"I want to talk a little about Paris."

"There's nothing to say about Paris, except to say; that you failed to show up."

"Well, I'd like to explain that."

"I'd like to see you try."

"Annabella please be nice to me. It took all my nerve and courage to come here. Courage I did not know I had but, I had to come and see you."

"Why did Theo offer me the job? I believe he could have chosen anyone to do this for him."

 "Well, when he told me he bought the place and that he wanted the barn furnished, interior designed to make it look comfortable, and I recommended you."

"Why?"

"Well, I thought you could earn some money, and it would give us a chance to meet. I thought you might appreciate getting out of the house in Morocco for a few weeks. It's not every day that one gets the opportunity to spend time in a place like this."

"Ok, now that we're here, what would you like to talk about?"

"As you know, I did not have money. I was living in a rented room when you decided to go to Paris, and for us to meet.

I could not raise the money fast enough to make the trip; it was impossible to arrange it in time to meet you."

"It doesn't matter anymore Santiago, that's all in the past now."

"Not for me! It matters to me! That's why I'm here today. You couldn't possibly imagine what it's like for a fifty-five-year-old man, madly in love with "the love of his life" to not have enough saved, to cross the sea, to meet her in Paris. I didn't know such shame could exist in me."

"That's because you're a dreamer, Santiago, and that's why you couldn't do it."

"Don't I have the right to dream?"

"Everyone has the right to dream. Most people make their dreams come true by the time they reach our age and most people are planning to retire."

"Well, at least I made one of my dreams come true."

"Oh? What dream is that?"

"Being here, with you, today."

Annabella is taken aback and the silenced emotions have been stirred in her after looking at Santiago. Annabella turns and looks away towards the sea.

Santiago continues.

"I know were and are deeply disappointed in me."

"I was not disappointed in you. I was mad at you, and I am still mad at you!"

"Well, I hope after today, you won't be so mad at me."

"Don't be too sure about that."

"Why did you decide to end what we had?"

"Because you're a dreamer Santiago that's why I ended us."

"You said; "there is no future for us and it's best we stay friends." I accepted that on the grounds that I would not lose you completely. Losing all that we had, made me realize that I was not only poor, but I felt I was totally degraded and not because my circumstances have changed but, because I lost you."

"I am sorry. Did you come all the way here to tell me this?"

"No, I have a few other things to say. Making a long story short, I felt, like I had died inside, after you'd finished with me. For about a month, I did not go out, I sat in my room in the dark.

I lay in my bed thinking, and realized I had to do something if I was ever going to meet you, I'd have to put my hurt and pain aside so that I could spend one single day with you."

"Santiago are you telling me you got a job? Have been saving for four years, to be here today with me?"

"No"

"Did your best friend Theo know about your feelings and about us?"

"Technically speaking, yes I'd like to move along with my present situation, if that's alright. I got to work on an idea that had been in my mind and began to work hard on it. Suddenly, my fortune changed, but I have not changed. I am still the same Santiago inside.

I wanted to tell you about the changes that were taking place in my life but, you deleted me from all social media connections we had together.

My last refuge of staying in contact with you was through emails, and even then, you would only say a few words, encouraging me to stop, telling me that there was nothing left between us."

"Well, every time you wrote to me, you would write a whole page, and it made me so upset when you spoke of us and love. Honestly, I felt it was better to finish it all, but you wouldn't give up. Are you finished with what you wanted to say?"

"No"

"Ok, what else do you have to say?"

"My situation has changed drastically as far as money is concerned, but my thoughts about you have never changed. I flew out to Morocco last year."

"You did what? You flew to Morocco! What for?"

"Yes, I flew to Morocco; I came to see you, where you lived."

"Oh my god! You're crazy, such a "Stupido!" Please tell me you did not knock at the door and ask for me."

"I haven't got to the crazy and "stupido" part yet. For one hour, I struggled with myself there outside your house. It was three o'clock in the morning.

I was looking at the house, it was totally dark. I knew you and Ibrahim had gone to sleep. I lost my nerve, or in other words, I came to my senses. I wanted to knock at the door, see Ibrahim, and tell him that I was in love with you. I was going to ask him to give you a divorce.

I thought about the possibility that you were really finished with me, and you didn't want me in your life.

How could I do this to someone I love?

If I had done that, I know he would have thrown you out with nothing, and that you'd have killed me altogether.

So, I left, and went home."

"Santiago you need to see a doctor! No, you need a specialist! On second thought, I think I need a specialist for ever having had you in my life in the first place."

"Hey, easy, with the specialist stuff! I am not that bad you know."

"You're not that good either."

"Annabella why can't you be a good girl for me? Please be nice to me. Will you?"

Annabella giggles briefly and then stops

"I remember you used to say that to me when I made you mad sometimes."

"Well, I'm glad you remember something about me."

"Yes."

SAINT-CYPRIEN BEACH

Annabella and Santiago are walking on the sand,

"I did not tell you the rest of what happened while I was in Morocco."

"How long were you there for?"

"I was there for a week."

"Did you know anyone there apart from me?"

"No."

"What else happened while you were there? You haven't told me the worst part yet?"

"I hired a car as soon as I got there. The first night I wanted to knock at your door, and then I spent the next three days sitting in the car parked down the road looking at your house just to get a glimpse of you."

"Santiago! That is called "Stalking!"

"I don't care what they call it. I wanted to see you."

"Did you see me?"

"Yes, I saw you on the third day. You came out, got in your car, and I followed you to the beauty salon. After you went, in I drove away."

"Did you feel good after all that?"

"No, I felt worse, because I couldn't talk to you, I couldn't express myself, and the worst part was knowing that you were going back to an unhappy marriage in an unhappy home."

"We can't change some things Santiago."

"Do you wish to know what I remember the most, apart from seeing you briefly?"

"Yes. What?"

"I ended up by the seaside in a café. I was drinking my coffee; the sun was going down and I thought to myself; why can't Annabella be here with me to share this beautiful moment in time with me?"

"Sometimes dreams are better left as dreams."

"You know the great theme of all romance novels and films is the poor jilted man or woman, goes off, and does something with their life that brings them money. They come back to ask the immortal questions, "Why? Why did you leave me? Why didn't you believe in me? They come back for revenge, only to realize they are still in love with that person and that love they felt, never, died."

"I am not going to stand here and tell you that what we had five years ago was a lie, because it was not. It was real, and we had something very special."

"It's still special to me."

"Santiago it was a long time ago! Perhaps, it was a time we both needed someone in our lives to make us feel special. I'm not going to say what I felt for you wasn't special, it was more than special."

"I don't understand a lot of things the way things happen in life that shapes and changes people's lives, but I understand this much; being here with you today is the best thing I have ever done. Maybe it wasn't the right thing to do, but it IS the best thing I have ever done!"

"Have you been to this place before?"

"No, Roberto told me about it. He said it's a good place to have lunch and talk."

"Yes, I can always count on, "Roberto the Great," my younger brother, to come up with a beautiful setting like this for us to talk. He's shown me so much beauty here, his suggestion doesn't surprise me.

"Your brother?"

"We adopted each other as brother and sister."

"Was it easy to adopt each other?"

"Yes, all it took was a few words, and some wet earth and we were brother and sister. Everything in life should be that perfectly simple and beautiful at the same time."

"May I adopt you as my lover?"

"Don't push it Santiago. I'm still mad at you!"

"Will you be nice?"

"No, I will not be nice! You've broken my heart. I think I've told you that repeatedly."

"Well, what about my heart? My heart is broken. You know you're not the only one with a heart."

"You broke your own heart, by being a "Stupido", by not coming to Paris."

"There are so many things I wanted to say to you. I came here today in the hopes that we could just spend one beautiful day together and a chance for me to explain why I wasn't in Paris. I thought we could just enjoy the time today, being together. I've made a mess of it. Not only have I made a mess of it, I don't have a plan B."

"Santiago it's all in the past. Please, let's just leave it there Ok? Would you please take me back now?"

"Sure."

They arrive at the car and Santiago like a true gentleman opens the door for Annabella, she sits in the passenger seat and puts her seat belt on, and Santiago gets into the driving seat and thinks for a few seconds.

"After today, I will not bother you anymore, I promise! The reason why I'm here today was to say I am sorry if I have hurt you by not turning up in Paris. I've said it before and I mean that from my soul.

I'm so sorry if I have disappointed you, and I'm sorry if I have ruined a part of your life that was spent with me. Even though it was only on the internet, I want you to know it was the happiest time of my life. I want to tell you, I have never loved anyone as I have loved you."

"Thank you. You're a big hit with the ladies. They all love and adore you." Annabella replied slyly

"Is that why I'm still single?"

"I'm sure you will find someone who will make you happy. You'll forget me in time."

"Never! Never in a million years! I tell you, my last vision in life will be your face, my last breath will be your name."

"Santiago, it will never work between us! Please forget me!"

"Be nice will you."

From the hillside, the car approaches the Estate.

Santiago pulls up to the barn. As he'd done earlier, he opens the door for Annabella. She gets out and walks into the barn. Stephanie is anxiously awaiting her arrival. Santiago enters the barn carrying his walking cane.

"Come and sit down. I will get some refreshments for you."

"No thank you I am fine. I will sit for a few minutes and then I will have to go. I have a long drive   ahead of me."

Santiago lowers himself and sits at the big table joined by Annabella and Stephanie, who sit across from him. There is an awkward silence for a second, creating a feeling of being uncomfortable. Suddenly Paris walk's up to Santiago and brushes against his leg; he looks down and picks up Paris.

"Hello Beautiful! Which one are you? Paris or Venus?"

Annabella looks deep and long into his eyes.

"Paris and Venus? How did you know their names? Was this your idea?"

"Yes, I thought they would be good company for you while you are here."

Suddenly Annabella realizes that everything that had happened to her has been arranged by Santiago.

"There's never been a Theo has there? Theo is you! You are Theo! You arranged everything! The job offer from Gabriel? The private jet, the car, the dogs, it was all you!?"

Santiago lowers his eyes. He can't look Annabella in the eyes after she said all that. Stephanie is looking at Annabella and Santiago searching for answers.

"That's impossible! You'd have to be a drug dealer to be able to pull something like this off! Did my husband know about all this? Are you one of the drug cartels?"

"Gabriel knew everything, but I am not involved in a drug cartel, you have my solemn word."

"Just what is it that you now do Santiago to afford you so much wealth?"

"I am an inventor, I invented something, and it's done very well."

"An inventor? And you are my husband's client 'The Mystery Man who owns all this?"

"Yes, I am a client of your husband."

Annabella's eyes fill up, but they don't overflow.

"Stephanie stop wasting our breath! The man is a serial liar!"

"No, I have never lied to you."

"Theo, or Santiago, whatever your name is, Get Out!"

"Annabella Please!"

"Don't you ever come back here, I never want to see you again!"

"Annabella please give me a chance to explain."

"Get out!"

Santiago stands up slowly, his face filled with sadness, never taking his eyes of Annabella.

"I'm going now, but not before I tell you this; of all the things I have envisioned in my life I never envisioned that we would ever stop loving each other.

Such was my commitment, my loyalty, my love for you."

Annabella looks at Santiago for a long few seconds and then starts walking towards the back door, but turns into the kitchen.

Santiago looks at Stephanie for a few seconds turns around and starts walking off towards the door. Stephanie looks at him as he opens the front door, steps out and closes the door behind him. Stephanie runs into the kitchen, Annabella is crying.

"I knew there wouldn't be a good ending to this story. I am the one who is a "Stupido."

"Well, if it wasn't finished before, you sure killed it now!"

Stephanie hears the door open, she indicates with her index finger to Annabella to be quiet Stephanie rushes out to find Santiago; he is standing in the doorway with tears in his eyes.

"I just came back to say I am so sorry. Please tell her, I said I'm sorry.

I know it was stupid what I've done and yet, I would do it all over again. For me it has been worth it, to see her for an hour or if only for a moment."

Stephanie approaches Santiago, who is standing there his eyes filled up about to burst, he looks at Stephanie and then continues

"The hardest thing in the world is, having all the good intentions, to make someone you love happy, and then it all goes wrong."

"Please go to the house and wait. I will speak with her ok?"

Santiago looks at her with compassion in her eyes, turns and walks out the door, closing the door behind him gently. Stephanie rushes back into the kitchen to find Annabella angry and crying.

"He's gone."

"He can go to hell as far as I'm concerned."

Santiago gets in the car and drives up to the house just as Roberto is coming out of the house. Santiago turns the car around and stops, he gets out the car, and starts looking over the mountains his eyes filled with tears. Roberto approaches him; he can see he is deeply emotionally wounded.

Santiago looks at him and then looks away into the distance across the beautiful mountains. Roberto turns and looks at the same mountains, Roberto trying to make light of things

"There is nothing more beautiful than looking into the eyes of nature, not unless one is looking into the eyes of the woman they love."

"Yes."

"People living in the city when they have a wounded animal they take it to the vet to have it put down based on the moral grounds of compassion. Here in the wilderness we have vets to but we have something even better called the gun that we use on compassionate grounds.

Santiago turns and looks at him with a serious look, Roberto is still looking out into the eyes of nature.

"The only problem with love is that no vet, no shotgun, can solve that problem."

"How do you know its love?"

"When I asked you if you also wanted to speak with Annabella, your eyes betrayed you.

When I introduced myself to you, you did not tell me your name because you wanted to surprise her and when you asked me to tell you a beautiful place where you can spend a few hours."

Santiago lowers his eyes and then looks up panning the beauty of nature

"Shall I get the shotgun?"

Santiago turns and looks at Roberto with a shocked look on his face.

In the barn Annabella continues to cry, Stephanie is trying to defuse the situation.

"So why are you crying? After all, you have so many admirers, who are all lining up to make plans for the next four years so they can spend a single day with you."

"I am crying because he lied to me."

"Is that the only reason you are crying."

"I hate him!"

"Do you? Why?"

"He always makes me emotional, and he lied to me!"

"Well, you don't have to cry anymore, he's gone for good now. He promised me. He will never bother you again."

"He said that?"

"Yes."

"What else did he say?"

"He said he was sorry, and that he would do it again, just to spend an hour or a moment with you."

"Is that it?"

"No, he said, the hardest thing in the world is, having all the good intentions, to make someone you love happy, and it all goes wrong."

Annabella put both her hands on the huge table. Breaking down, she lowers her head and cries inconsolably. Her back, her body shaking as though she'd been jolted by electric current

"Soon as you said his name, I knew you were still in love with him."

"Santiago De la Cruz, spent four years of his life plotting, so he can spend a few hours with me?"

Annabella picks up a tea cup from the table, she screams "NOOO!" Smashing the cup so hard against the wall it shatters into a thousand pieces.

"And I thought he never loved me."

She grabs another cup, screams again, "NOOOO!" Smashes another cup against the wall, that also shatters into a thousand pieces, she turns, and looks at Stephanie, still crying hysterically.

"Santiago De la Cruz the man I have been so cruel to, the man I have been so cold to for the past four years, so he could forget me. I tried to end it with him many times. I thought he stopped loving me. I thought he would forget me! I thought he would find someone else to love... and Santiago De la Cruz loved me, when I did not even love myself. Santiago De la Cruz never stopped loving me."

"Annabella listens to me it's not too late, go and speak with him, he's in the house."

"What like this?"

"When he came back just now to say sorry, he was openly crying, well almost."

"What?"

"He was nearly crying; his eyes were full."

Annabella quickly turns on the faucet, splashes some water on her face, and quickly dries her face with the tea towel and dashes out of the kitchen. As she comes out of the kitchen the Mercedes, dashes past the front door, leaving a trail of white dust behind it comes from the dirt track.

She reaches the door, opens it and runs out, the car is going away from the house, Annabella runs calling out; SANTIAGO, WAIT,

SANTIAGO! Falling down on the dirt track, in front of her she collapses. Stephanie comes out and rushes to her, picking her up.

"What have I done?"

"It's going to be alright. Come on, it's going to be alright, let's go to the house so you can rest."

Roberto runs down from the house, grabs Annabella and puts his arm around her waist, and puts her hand over his shoulder, Stephanie had done the same thing on the other side of her, and they are walking her towards the house.

Ten minutes later they're settled. Annabella is outside on the porch of the house that leads into the kitchen. Roberto gives her some of his special brew in a glass to drink, and has the bottle in his other hand. Maria brought a blanket, and covering her from the waist down to keep her warm. Annabella looks up at Maria

"Thank you."

"Drink this, it will steady you."

"This stuff will kill me."

"It will kill all this madness and all this emotion you have inside you, unfortunately it does not kill love. Don't worry, if he comes back, I will shoot him!"

Roberto takes a good swig from the bottle and lowers it; Annabella takes a Roberto's hand

"You are the best. Thank you, Roberto, for being you."

Roberto leans down and kisses her on her head and stands up straight takes another swig from the bottle.

"Rest, I have work to do. If you say any more nice things about me, I am liable to get emotional and   cry myself."

"Even hero's cry sometimes."

Roberto leaves Stephanie comes through with a glass and a bottle of brandy, she sits in a chair close to Annabella, her phone rings it Gabriel on video chat.

"Where have you been? I've called you three times in the last fifteen minutes."

"I was in a meeting what's wrong?"

"Santiago was here and he had some words with Annabella and he has gone off. I need you to call him and tell him to come back here to the house. Please do it now!"

"Ok, let me call him and I will call you right back."

After several minutes the phone rings again, it's Gabriel

"His phone is off. I will try him later ok?"

"Thank you darling, I love you."

"I love you too."

Stephanie closes the phone and pours out a shot of brandy for herself and she clinks the glass against Annabella's glass, "SALUTE!" she takes a big swig

"What we need is some of Maria's cake right now!"

"What do you think I have a Hash bakery here? Have a few more drinks that will do the trick."

"The day is not over yet, and we've had a month's worth of drama in one hour. Nothing this exciting happens in Paris!"

"I hope he is alright."

"He'll be alright. I hope when you both calm down, you can meet again and talk things through. Let's hope he turns his phone on and Gabriel talks with him."

"He won't answer his phone, and I don't think we'll ever meet again. Life sure packs a punch. It's the bitter with the sweet or however that saying goes, this is so painful!"

"Doesn't it just! What do you plan to do when you go back?"

"I don't know. I think I want to be on my own for a while. Maybe rent a room in Paris."

"What about Morocco and your husband?"

"I have heard more tender words from Santiago, in half an hour this morning, and then I have heard from my husband in the past ten years."

"I have to hand it to him, he is very charming, and he has that certain, Je ne se qui."

"When he said, Hello Annabella to me, I nearly died. My emotions went wild, I felt so happy, and yet so afraid."

"Afraid of what?"

"Afraid, that he might be disappointed in me."

"Why would he be disappointed in you? Imagine the guts it took for him to come here to face you. That takes courage!"

"We spoke every day for hours, I never had that before with anyone, he knew everything about me, and I fell in love with him."

"Try and be good next time you two meet."

"When I was a little girl, I used to dream, that someone mysterious, would do all these things for me to win my heart. When I got to the airport with Pierre, and I saw that I was going to fly on the private jet; it reminded me of my childhood.

When Paris and Venus were delivered here, again, it reminded me of my dreams. Then the car, each thing that happened along the way, in my heart and soul I wished it was Santiago.

When I realized it was all his doing, I felt ashamed and I didn't think I was worthy of him; especially after the way I've treated him over the past four years. And when you were telling me about Gabriel, and how he was with you for months on end, it reminded me of me and Santiago, he is a good person."

"Why are you telling me all of this? It appears that you should be telling all this to him?"

"Today, I think I have killed everything. Every chance of ever having the opportunity is gone. Dead the way I could only kill it. I am going to go and have a nap upstairs.

"You do that. If I hear anything from Gabriel I will let you know."

Annabella walks into her room, lays on her bed, and looks at her phone no messages from Theo. She thinks for a few seconds and then closes her eyes and falls asleep.

Chapter Twenty Two

Astonished

Two hours later, Annabella is sitting out on the balcony, there's a knock at the bedroom door, and Stephanie walks in with a tray of food and some fresh squeezed orange juice.

"Are you receiving visitors?"

"Yes, come on in."

Stephanie lays the tray on the small table on the balcony.

"Compliments of Maria! How are you feeling? Did you sleep?"

"I rested my eyes for about half an hour, and ever since then, I have been out here relaxing and thinking.

"It's so peaceful here."

"Yes, the sounds of birds, when there is no other sound around, always remind me of a cemetery."

"Maybe because we go there knowing it's quiet, no one argues, or fights and everyone is at peace and harmony."

"I wish it was like that above ground."

"I talked to Gabriel. There is still no news from Santiago. His phone is off."

"I don't think I will hear from him again, not that I blame him. I have been too hard on him."

"Well, maybe it's time you chased him, instead of him stalking you. Maybe it's time you started doing a little stalking yourself."

"How does a person go from living in a room to buying a multi-million euro's house, a Mercedes sports car, and hiring a private jet? I feel like such a "Stupido!" Did I tell you that he never told me where he got all this money from?"

"No! I know one thing; Gabriel would not represent anyone who did not make their money legally. Where did you learn that word "Stupido?"

"He called me once when Ibrahim was out in the garden. Luckily, I was in my bedroom, and I said to him, "My husband is here, what are you a Stupido?" It stuck... I think it's Italian. I called him that often when he used to make me mad he never minded."

"Well, judging by the evidence earlier, I would say the poor man can't do anything right in your eyes."

"He is such an amazing man. He is everything I ever wanted in a man, but as you can see we are not compatible."

"I can only see one thing here, and that is that you are in love with him, but you are afraid it might not last. As for his wealth, we can rule him out of being connected to any cartel!"

"He could never lower himself to do something like that. He's too straight. I know him better than I know my husband."

"You know the saddest thing in the world is looking at someone crying, and knowing how broken they are. You see all his pain pouring out of their eyes."

"Please don't make me feel any worse than I already do."

"When he came back to say he was sorry, what I saw in his eyes, it broke my heart."

"He knew my Fluffy died, and he knew I would be happy with Paris and Venus, I guess that's why he got them."

"Well, it wasn't such a bad gesture after all, was it?"

"I also know why he gave me the job."

"Why?"

"He knew I had no money to leave Ibrahim so, by giving me twenty-five thousand Euros it would get me to France. I'm sure he thought I might be able to get a little flat as well. He knew how unhappy I was. I can't think of another reason."

"You know, even with all doubt hanging over him regarding you and him, he still took action to do something good for you. That quality in a man is very rare to find now days."

"I still wonder how he made his money."

"Personally speaking, after meeting him today, I have no doubt that he made his money legally."

"He told me he invented something and it's done well but, he never said what that something was. Only a STUPIDO like him would leave me guessing."

"I'll leave you to figure that out. I am going to take my book and go sit by the pool. Reading always relaxes me. Why don't you have something to eat and then come and join me?"

"How many times are you going to read that book?"

"I'm not sure. It's riveting! I hope Mr. Ivan Baranowski, writes another book soon!

He really knows how to live in another dimension. It's really very intriguing."

"Ok."

Annabella had a few mouths full from the food, drank a little orange juice, but she was still feeling drained. Her mind was racing with questions that she could not answer. She thought about Santiago, she hoped and prayed that he was safe.

Annabella went and joined Stephanie by the pool. They talked about going back to Paris, and how Gabriel will be arriving tomorrow morning to finish the paperwork he had on the property. Stephanie reminded Annabella that they would all be heading back to Paris together once the final business was concluded. Annabella's mind was filled with thoughts of all things Santiago. Remembering all the wonderful times they shared getting to know each other on webcam. The funny and tender moments they shared, and how Santiago made her laugh out loud. He had declared his love for her; she'd fallen madly in love with him. Of course, they shared a very special song that he'd dedicated to her; *"Do You Love Me,"* by Sharif Dean.

Annabella's thoughts were filled with the lyrics to that special song, her heart was aching.

That evening they all had a meal together. Roberto was talking about them leaving tomorrow, and how quite it would be without them. He and Maria had made two friends that they might never see again. Maria suggested they come back anytime they wished; she had grown so very fond of the both of them. Annabella decided to have an early night, it had been a long and stressful day; she was still feeling weak and her emotions were running high even though she kept them in check. Entering her room, her mind was filled with the lyrics to the song Santiago dedicated to her again.

Stephanie visited Annabella in her room to say good night. They hugged as Stephanie reassured her that everything was going to be alright and she went next door to her room.

Annabella took her phone and earphones with her and walked out onto the balcony. Turning on the song *"Do You Love Me"* by Sharif Dean listening privately so as not to disturb Stephanie, she sang the lyrics in her head.

With every word of the song Annabella recalls different memories together with Santiago, like the time they talked about getting a tattoo together, and their dreams of living together in a log cabin.

So many times they took pictures of themselves and sent them to each other.

The song continues as do the memories of all the long and meaningful messages Santiago sent to her.

Everything in the world seemed perfect when they were on webcam together. Every smile, every laugh, every silly romantic thought were etched in her memory permanently.

They had talked for hours about life about themselves, details, and desires that she had never shared with anyone else.

Annabella recalled the day she made a video while in her telling Santiago that she was madly in love with him.

All these images and memories come flooding back to Annabella and she realized that she was still as madly in love with him, as he is with her. There's no getting away from this truth or denying it. The immortal question now was; "What is going to happen next?"

Knowing this was her last night in this magical "Garden of Eden" she wanted to look at the stars. She did not say a prayer but, rather enjoyed the beauty of the dark sky and the glittering stars darting around in the heavens. This place had become not only a safe and tranquil haven during a raging storm in her life but, it was also how Annabella imagined a "True Heaven" to be when life here on earth was over.

Thinking about Santiago, she checked her phone, no message from Theo/ Santiago. Her heart and mind were filled with love and concern. Around ten thirty, she climbed into bed and closed her eyes and fell asleep exhausted.

The following morning, Annabella's mood was still sombre. She ate a little breakfast so as not to offend Maria. There was small talk at the table.

After breakfast, Annabella and Stephanie went to the barn carrying Paris and Venus with them.

Once in the barn they let them run around but closed the kitchen door barring them from the kitchen so they would not get under their feet. They got to work trying to find the pieces of cups that were shattered on the wall the day before.

The glass was everywhere! After about five minutes, they heard Gabriel's voice calling out to Stephanie.

They stop what they are doing and slowly walk out the kitchen Annabella closing the kitchen door so the puppies didn't go in there. Gabriel was smartly dressed as usual, with a bulging briefcase in his hand, looking troubled about something. Stephanie walks over to him and kisses him on the lips.

"Hello darling! Did you have a good flight?"

"Yes."

He looks at Stephanie and Annabella with a note of concern in his eyes.

Annabella walks over to Gabriel smiling and kisses him on both cheeks.

"Welcome Gabriel!"

"Thank you."

"Can I get you a tea or coffee?"

"No, thank you. It's best I close my business and then I can think about a drink."

"Ok then, you go over to the house to close your business. Stephanie and I will see you there in about a half an hour."

"The business, I came to close concerns you Annabella."

"Me?"

"Please sit down."

Annabella takes Stephanie by the arm and shows her to a chair. Sitting herself down, she's looking at Gabriel. Gabriel is nervous and he is trying to collect his thoughts. Stephanie leans forward on the chair, and says; "Gabriel?"

"Ok. I have three things to complete here, first things first."

Gabriel opens the briefcase and takes out a drafted document.

"This is for you Annabella. Please sign on the dotted line here at the bottom of the page."

Annabella signs the document thinking it the contract for the twenty-five thousand Euros.

Gabriel thanks Annabella and then produces a letter in a sealed envelope. "This letter will explain everything." He hands over the envelope to Annabella who looks at Gabriel examining his face for some expression but, he is expressionless.

Stephanie looks at Gabriel trying to get some reaction from his face, nothing. Gabriel is waiting for a reaction from Annabella who has opened the envelope and she is reading its contents. The letter is from Santiago. Annabella reacts with absolute astonishment.

"No!"

She reads some more

"No!"

She looks away and then she reads a little more

"No! Nooooooo!" Annabella breaks down crying and shaking all over.

"Annabella, What is it?"

Annabella passes the letter back to Stephanie, who reads it aloud.

"A long time ago, you told me about what you had gone through during your divorce with your first husband. You had explained that you had lived in a chateau outside Paris at that time. Further, you stated that you wanted your husband to give you the barn in the divorce settlement and how he had refused you.

The barn here is my gift to you. A gift for enriching my life during the short time we were together."

"Gabriel, did he do this because of what happened here yesterday?"

"No, this was done six months ago, the day he bought the house.

When I showed him the pictures of the house and the property, he immediately gifted the barn to Annabella. It was then, that he had the idea to bring you here on the pretext that you would be decorating the barn. In reality, he just wanted to spend one day with you. We talked about this, and I agreed to arrange everything. I agreed to do so because we were not breaking any laws."

"I pleaded with my ex-husband to let me have the barn on his estate as my home because I had nowhere to go but, he refused. In passing conversation I told this to Santiago, and Santiago De Le Cruz, that Stupido, kept it in his heart. Santiago De Le Cruz never forgot it. Tears streaming down Annabella's face were evidence of her now being able to see that Santiago was true to his words when he said he loved her above all else.

Annabella turns and faces Stephanie and Gabriel she wiping her eyes with the back and the palm of her hand. Annabella tries to compose herself. "Any more surprises?"

"This is also for you." Gabriel stretches out his hand with another note. Annabella takes it and reads it.

Looking at Stephanie, she passes the document so that Stephanie can read it as well.

"You will have an income fifteen thousand Euros a year for life." "Gabriel where did this man get this kind of money from, is all this real?"

"It's real. We will get to that in a second."

He looks at Annabella and Stephanie then takes out a brown wrapped envelope that looks like a book and passes it to Annabella.

"You wanted to know where he got his money from, well the answer is there."

Annabella unwraps it. It's the book that Stephanie has been raving about. "Emotional Rhapsody" by Ivan Baranowski. Annabella opens the first page; it is signed with a message.

"To Annabella, Thank you from my heart for inspiring me to write this book.

Signed, Ivan Baranowski, Santiago De La Cruz"

"Oh my God! Ivan Baranowski is Santiago! Gabriel how long have you known this?"

"From the beginning."

"The man I call Stupido wrote this?"

"That "Stupido," as you like to refer to him as, is a great man. Most men would have been basking in the limelight of their success but, not him. He can go anywhere and no one would bother him because no one knows him. You both are not to mention this conversation to anyone is that understood?"

"Gabriel, you have never lied to me, apart from small white lies to save my emotions. I will not get upset. Tell me the truth; did you speak with Santiago last night or this morning?"

There is a brief silence. Gabriel looks at Stephanie. She knows something is wrong. Looking at Annabella, she is focusing her eyes into Gabriel's soul and she can see something is wrong, he lowers his eyes.

"I was hoping this part of the conversation, wouldn't come up."

Annabella stands and moves forward looking directly into Gabriel's eyes.

"Is he alright?"

"I don't know."

"You spoke with him? Gabriel, I'm begging you, please, tell me, what do you mean by you don't know?

"He asked me to deliver a message for you here today.

I refused on the grounds that it was too much of a burden on my conscience. Everything has gone too far, and everything had to stop."

"What was the message?"

There is another moment of silence. Stephanie gives Gabriel one of those looks that says; "You better tell!"

"He wanted me to tell you that he died in a car crash last night."

"Why? Why would he ask you to do that? You don't think?"

"What? That he would take his own life? He might be a "Stupido" as you call him but, I doubt he is that stupid. As you may know, in law, we always go by facts. I tried to call him several times last night and this morning, his phone is turned off."

Annabella starts crying uncontrollably.

"Just when I thought I was starting to get over him and forget him, now this? One month ago, I was living a boring life. He comes into my life as a total stranger for three weeks and turns everything upside down. All the strides I made in trying to forget him went out the window with two words; "Hello Annabella" I'm now a emotional wreck!"

"Annabella my personal view is that he said what he said last night, in order to make a clean break. He wanted to give you a clean break so that you had a chance to start your life without worrying about him, worrying about a home, and without worrying about money."

"Gabriel's right. I agree. I think he said what he said so, you could be alright."

"How can I be alright Stephanie? I'll probably cry for the rest of my life! Santiago De La Cruz Oh God, of all the men in the world, God had to give me Stupido!"

"Truly Annabella he is a great writer, a good man and a good client."

Annabella turns to Stephanie; Stephanie could see she needed a hug. Stephanie hugs her. Annabella falls into Stephanie's arms crying like a baby.

"The man that I call "Stupido" turned out to be my best friend. I broke his heart and sent him away. The man I call "Stupido" that lived a little room has turned out to be more of a gentleman, than most gentleman clubs have members, and I turned him away.

The man I call "Stupido" turned out to be a genius, and I insulted him. My "Knight in Shining Armour", I killed his spirit. What am I going to do? If I don't find him, I'll die from guilt!"

"We are going to find him dead or alive!"

One hour later, they all sat at the table in the garden having lunch and some wine. The mood is sombre and uninspired, the energy levels are low. Annabella, Stephanie, and Gabriel hardly touched their lunch. Maria and Roberto are at the table; Roberto slowly stands up with the glass in his hand.

"In life we will face difficult times. We will face good times. Life will present us with painful times, life will present us with truly good friends, and life will present us with false friends. True friends delight in knowing that something good has happened in your life, true friends understand that life is hard for everyone, and yet they celebrate your achievements with no thought for anything else but goodwill from their hearts to your heart.

True friends celebrate your good fortune and your blessings that you earned and paid for with your own just acts, compassion, understanding, and your high standards.

These qualities a person can take anywhere and yet this unshakable quality in a person's character, is to be found in how true they stay to their word. When you face terrible times, the false friends take flight like rats abandoning ship. It's as if they take joy in knowing that something bad is happening to you, as if they are going to personally profit from such tragedy. Cruel in their flight, they show their true colours.

Above all else, true friends will count their blessings and pray that false friends are no longer   among us.

It is not the clothes that make the person, nor the money, titles, or status in life can makes a person of quality and worth. What makes a worthy and quality person is what they think, what they stand for, and who they stand with.

Today and all the days ahead, I stand proudly by the side of Annabella! She came to us to furnish the barn and instead she furnished our hearts and souls with her goodness, kindness, friendship, and if that wasn't enough; she adopted me as a younger brother!

Dear friends, we know you will be leaving us soon, and wish you a safe journey. I make a toast to the beautiful souls who sit at this table and grace our presence with kindness, understanding friendship and love. A toast to forever friendships!"

Roberto raises his glass. All stand; raise their glasses of wine, gently clinking the glasses in mid-air, above the table to celebrate the love of friendship. Annabella has tears of love and admiration in her eyes, knowing that each word Roberto said came directly from his amazing and loving heart. Roberto and Maria are her family now and she could not have imagined in her wildest dreams how lucky and fortunate she was to call these fine people her brother and sister in-law. Her heart was filled with joy and she counted herself as totally blessed. Leaving here would be like leaving her true home.

Two hours later, the taxi has arrived waiting outside the house. Gabriel helps with Annabella's and Stephanie's luggage. The taxi driver takes over and puts the luggage in the trunk of the taxi. Roberto came across from the cottage with a box in his hand. Handing the box over to Gabriel. Gabriel opens the open box. The box contained bottles of wine. He takes one of the bottles out and looks at it.

"That one is for you to take to your office. This you give your clients after you tell them how much the bill is, and if you are having a very bad day you take a sip yourself it will kill all frustration and everything that is not supposed to be there."

"Thank you, Roberto!"

"The rest is for the girls."

Roberto walks into the house as Stephanie and Annabella are coming out. Both have freshened up with their hair combed, a touch of makeup, both dressed in beautiful summer dresses.

The two stand next to Gabriel, Maria comes from the cottage carrying a cane basket.

Walking up to Annabella and Stephanie, and she pulls back the tea towel that is covering a small cake and several bottles of lavender perfume that Maria has made herself. Annabella and Stephanie look at each other wondering if this cake had the same ingredients in as the hash cake they had the other night at the BBQ

"Don't worry; it is not the same cake! The main ingredient is missing. The cake is to give you energy, the perfumes to make you smell nice and help you to relax. Thank you for spending your time with us. I do so hope we see each other again as soon as possible!"

Maria's eyes fill with tears. Annabella leans forward and hugs her tightly.

"I promise, you will see us again, just as soon as possible!"

Roberto walks out of the big house with a brown box. He is carrying Paris and Venus, Stephanie steps forward and hugs Maria.

"Thank you for everything!"

Roberto opens the back door of the car and puts the box between the two seats. He turns and looks at Annabella for a long few seconds before saying goodbye. Annabella and Roberto lean into each other and Roberto hugs her and pats her on the back. Annabella hugs him tightly in return.

"If you don't come and visit your younger brother and sister in-law from time to time, I am going to be very cross with you!"

"Thank you, my sweet brother Roberto! I promise I will come and visit!"

Stephanie steps forward and hugs Roberto; he pats her on the back

"Thank you for everything!"

"Are you thanking me for introducing you to wild BBQ parties?"

"Yes and so much more. This was by far, the best time I have had in ages!"

"Look after him."

Pointing with his eyes to Gabriel, Stephanie leans in and whispers

"What makes you think he needs looking after?"

"He is a man! Without a woman, we are hopeless, worthless, and useless!"

They all exchange smiles. Stephanie and Annabella get in the back of the car they sit on either side of the puppies Roberto had put in the back seat. Gabriel gets in the front passenger seat and closes the door.

Maria stands next to Roberto who puts his arm around her. The taxi begins to drive away from the estate. Annabella and Stephanie look into the box and to their delight; Paris and Venus are looking up at them wigging their tails in happiness.

They both pick one each and start hugging them and making a fuss over them. Gabriel turns and looks at them, smiles and turns back, looking ahead of him. Leaning forward, he looks into the side mirror on the door; he sees Roberto and Maria standing together cuddled up looking at the car driving away from them.

Chapter Twenty Three

Return Flight

Sitting in the private jet for the return journey to Paris, there is a melancholy silence. The plane is taxiing along at great speed, and lifts into the air. As the plane climbs higher, Annabella looks out the window at the Pyrenees Mountains below, how beautiful and majestic they look from up high. Emotionally, Annabella was drained from the past two days and what had taken place.

She reflected on seeing Santiago for the first time standing there in the barn. She recalls the day she saw Venus and Paris for the first time, so beautiful and cute.

Stephanie and Gabriel sat together relaxing looking out of the other window onto the beautiful landscape and horizon. Stephanie leans over and kisses him on the cheek, Gabriel looks at her

"What are you after now?"

"Just you, you are enough for me." She rests her head on his shoulder.

"When we get back, me and you, we are going to have a conference."

"Conference, about what?"

"About hash cakes and wild poolside parties; no lingerie is going to get you off the hook on this one!"

"Darling!"

"Yes?"

"When we get home, why we don't play some role-playing games, I can be anything you want."

"Anything I want?"

"Anything you want."

Stephanie leans to Gabriel's ear and begins whispering things in his ear only he can hear. Gabriel can feel her hot breath in each word she says, he looks around him as a distraction but no avail, she has him where she wants him and he cannot resist.

Annabella rolls her eyes and shakes her head while trying to get comfortable in her seat. Closing her eyes, she begins to playback all of the spectacular memories from her time on the estate.

The visions of the beautiful waterfall cascading out of the clouds on the mountain. The trip with Maria driving the Mercedes and their hair flowing in the wind. The delivery of the puppies, the smell of the fresh mountain air and the herb garden. Eyes closed she smiles. The crazy BBQ when they all jumped in the pool and the hash cake and wine,

Her heart was so full at this moment. Of course, seeing Santiago, standing in the doorway of the barn as a silhouette, then hearing his voice, her insides were reliving the excitement of that day and again by the seaside talking with her while having coffee. Her skin is now warm as she sees him in her mind, walking along side of her; just the two of them, the rest of the world had fallen away.

Trembling now as she recalls the look upon his faces when she told him to get out of the barn.

Annabella opens her eyes. A single tear cascades down her face. Glancing at Stephanie and Gabriel with their eyes closed resting; Annabella wipes away the tear and looks out the window again.

When the jet landed, Pierre was waiting there with the car to take them home. As they came into Paris and drove along the streets towards Stephanie and Gabriel's nowhere felt like home to Annabella.

Pierre stopped the car next to the River Seine. Getting out of the car, Pierre removes Annabella's luggage. Stephanie announces, "This is us!" and steps out of the car. Annabella gets out the car confused and looked around.

"Call me when you are ready to go home Stephanie, I'll come and get you."

"I'll call you when I have settled this young woman into her new home."

She leans into the car and looks into the opens the box that held Paris and Venus. The two of them are wiggling their tails happy to see her again. She takes out Venus, and closes the back door. Heading to the front of the car, she leans in and kisses Gabriel.

"I'll see you at home darling." Annabella is waiting for Stephanie to explain what's happening. "I hope you will be happy here Annabella."

"Thank you, Gabriel." Pierre smiles and returns to the driver's seat. Pierre and Gabriel are off down the road. The River Seine is on one side, apartments, and shops on the other.

"Where are we going?"

"Come with me, I'll show you." Annabella grabs her small luggage and starts pulling it along. Stephanie stops by a break in the railings that has steps going down to a   beautiful boathouse.

"Oh my God! You've got to be kidding me!"

"You don't get seasick, do you?"

"No."

"Good! Let's go."

"Stephanie is this rented?"

"No, it belongs to Gabriel and me. It keeps our marriage alive. One day I'm a hooker here, the next day I am a maid, another day I am a powerful businesswoman."

"Are you serious?"

"Of course not! Don't be silly! It's a place for us to relax, and spend some quality time together. Come on please."

As they walk down the stairs towards the entrance of the boat house, Stephanie turns and looks at her half way down the stairs.

"You have Venus to keep you company. Paris did not have good memories for you. After we settle you in, we'll go and get her some food and some food for you as well!"

"Anything else?"

"Do you really want to find him?"

A confounded look appears on Annabella's face.

Inside the houseboat Stephanie stands in the middle of the main salon and starts telling Annabella where everything is.

"Let's start at the top; over there is the kitchen, this is the salon and dining room. You have a TV and Wi-Fi. You can busy yourself as you wish. At the other end you have two bedrooms, a shower and toilet, and what you can't find, please search for it."

"Stephanie, I am truly grateful for all you have done for me."

"I need to explain something to you sister, when Gabriel brought you to the restaurant, after we ate and drank a glass or two of champagne; I fell in love with your character. It was almost like looking in the mirror and seeing me, you are physically stunning, but spiritually as a person you are so much more."

"Thank you, Stephanie! I adore you so much! If you say any more, I am going to start crying again. God! I never knew I had this many tears in me! I now know for sure, I can cry a great deal. Happy or sad!"

"The night we went for a walk and we talked, what I told you about my life it's all true."

"I never doubted you for a second that you were telling me the truth."

"Thank you. Do you remember before you went to the estate? I told you I had a good feeling about it."

"Yes, I remember."

"I have a very good feeling that you're going to have a very good ending here in Paris!"

"The way I feel right now…"

Stephanie cuts into the conversation like a knife slicing through the air.

"Don't say it! Don't say it! I have a feeling that negativity is going to fill the air!"

Annabella starts to smile, and then she breaks out into a smile that lights up the whole room.

"Everything is going to be   alright!"

Annabella nods her head in agreement, still smiling.

A week went by and Annabella was settled in the boathouse. She would spend her time walking with Venus, who is sporting a little pink lead and collar. They would walk along beautiful Parisian walkways, looking at the shops.

One day she was sitting outside having coffee in a busy coffee shop the waitress treated Venus to a bowl of water and she happily lapped it up. Annabella noticed that at the next table there was a young woman having coffee and her friend came along and sat with her. The friend was carrying a book and as she sat down, Annabella could see the title of the book; "Emotional Rhapsody"

Annabella couldn't help but hear the conversation as she was sitting at the next table. "You better get your mother lots of tissue she is going to need it!" her friend replied, "Have you read the book?" "Three times, and three times, I cried. It's all over the news. Some big Hollywood studio has just bought the rights to make the book into a movie for ten million dollars!

Can you imagine that? This is book has taken off like wild fire! The girl continues, "The only thing the public doesn't know is, who the author is!"

Annabella had heard enough and left the table. Picking Venus up into her arms, she walks down the street. Thinking all the while that she knew who the author was but that she dare not speak it.

Two days later, Annabella is pacing up and down in the boathouse crying, her phone rings. Trying to compose herself, she picks up the phone and answers it Stephanie?

"Hello."

"Hi! Are we still on for tonight on the boat?

"Yes. What time will you be   here?"

"Annabella, are you crying?"

"Yes."

"What's wrong?"

"There are certain books, certain people should never read, and they should be banned, on the grounds that they are not good for some people's emotions."

"Aha, I told you! Anyway, take a shower, get yourself together, we will be there at seven, and for God's sake don't burn the dinner! We'll be starving when we get there.

She hangs up. Annabella straightens herself up and walks towards the bathroom.

That evening they'd just finished eating the dinner, and were sitting around the table, Gabriel is pouring out some more wine.

"Annabella, I have written as you have instructed, a letter to your husband, requesting that the marriage between you two should be dissolved. I have also written a separate letter informing him that you will not be returning back to Morocco.

"Thank you, Gabriel!"

Annabella begins to cry, a cry of relief.

Gabriel and Stephanie look at each other with panic in their eyes, as the crying picks up momentum and her whole body is shaking as she is crying.

Stephanie moves around and sits in the seat next to her and hugs her, trying to comfort her.

"If Annabella had a change of mind about the divorce, it would be alright wouldn't it Gabriel?"

"Yes. Annabella does have the right to change her mind and I can stop the proceedings without a worry."

"It's not about the marriage. I haven't had a marriage for ten years."

"Then why are you crying? Is it the book?"

"Oh, Stephanie, it's not the book, it's him!"

"Oh him! I thought you would have forgotten about him by now."

"Why does a person look like shit, when they are crying, and yet so beautiful to some people. I broke down and cried in front of him one day while we were chatting on video, and he told me, I was the most beautiful woman he has ever seen crying. Gabriel is that possible?"

"I have seen my Stephanie cry, many, many times, and in those moments, I always saw something beautiful glowing in her.

A voice in my head always said, I love this woman with all my heart. When I kissed her wet, salty tears, they tasted like fresh honey to me and those experiences has never left me or changed."

Annabella starts shaking again as she soulful cries from inside.

"Gabriel, give me my bag, and get me a glass of water please."

"Sure."

Gabriel handed over the bag to Stephanie. Tearing through the contents she retrieves a small bottle of pills. Opening the bottle, she takes out a single pill, at the same time Gabriel hands her a glass of water.

"Here, take this."

"What is it?"

"It is Valium."

Annabella takes the pill and drinks the water.

"My doctor gave them to me when I was going through a bad time with my breast. I got used to them and I have been on them ever since. When I have a stressful or worry filled day, I just pop one of them and I feel calmer. I just wish the damn problems would go away, but they don't."

"The problem is the barn and the money. I can't take it, and each time I think about it, I break down. I can't help it."

"Hear me please Annabella. For what it's worth, he gave you them with a full heart and with his blessing."

"If you won't listen to a housewife with one breast, then listen to a lawyer!"

Gabriel looks at Stephanie lovingly

"In my opinion, your problem is not the barn or the money."

"Great! The only thing I had going for me was my mind, now you're going to tell me, I am losing that too?"

"There's nothing wrong with you Annabella."

"What do you mean there's nothing wrong with her? Look at her; she is going nuts with her emotions! I don't mean nuts. I meant she's suffering emotionally."

"God Stephanie, you are going to make me laugh! Only you could come out with something like that, at a time like this."

Annabella breaks out into a little laughter. "You were saying Gabriel?"

"As I was saying, your problem is not the barn or the money. I never told you why he bought the house but, I will tell you now."

"Please don't tell me he bought the house, just to sell it after he gave me the barn! I would die if that was the case. What will happen to Roberto and Maria?"

"Nothing is going to happen to Roberto and Maria, the house and the land is "Private Property," it does not belong to Santiago."

"What are you saying? How can he give me something that does not belong to him? Am I involved in fraud here Gabriel? What's going on?"

Annabella looks at Stephanie, who has just popped a pill in her mouth and washed it down with a glass of water.

"What are you doing?"

"What does it look like? I am taking a pill! Trust me; with all this going on I need it."

"Are you two done?"

"So sorry Gabriel." Annabella replied

"Carry on darling, you have the floor!" Gabriel takes a sip of wine from the large glass, lowers it, and looks at them both, "Please do not speak until I am finished."

"As I was saying, the property does not belong to Santiago.

He bought the property, but he turned it into a "Charitable Trust" for underprivileged people who demonstrate a gift in the Arts.

The trust is in place and this year it will officially become the "The Global Arts Foundation." Writers, poets, painters, sculptures, that do not have the funding and the means to realize their dreams will be given accommodations there.

There is however, a caveat. The artists staying there will have help with the land, producing organic foods as a way of generating further funds for the foundation. Roberto De La Mancha Surgio, will be in charge of the land project, he hasn't been told yet. Given the magnitude of the project; Santiago involved my company to put together the legal requirements that are necessary for the foundation. Santiago also put 5 million Euros of his money into the project to get it started and suggested that I be one of the trustees. I accepted the offer gracefully on the grounds that my wages will be one euro a year."

Stephanie is crying. She is so proud of Gabriel as well as what Santiago has done. She looks at Gabriel with glowing admiration.

"I am so proud of you Gabriel Alexandre!"

"Well, you should be! You married me! Your father was in the resistance and he had a gun in the house that helped a little to shape me into the person you see before you today."

"I feel so stupid. I don't know what to say. Every time I try to find something wrong with that man; he does something brilliant and right! Having said all that, I admire him for what he's done."

"We got to know each other pretty well. He told me something in confidence, but, I'm not sure given the circumstances that I should repeat what he said to me."

Annabella is speechless, she is too afraid to ask. Already emotionally drained, she couldn't handle another emotional story, but, she knew intuitively that it had something to do with her.

Stephanie looks at Gabriel with such a serious look that he instinctively knows he has no choice but to finish the story now!

"You have two choices Mr. Alexandre, you can go home with me on your arm waltzing along the Parisian streets happy laughing and talking, or you can be dead and thrown into the River Seine. The clock is ticking!"

Annabella opens her eyes wide at what she has heard. "Stephanie!!"

"I want to know what he said, and so do you! " Well, what did he say?"

"We had lunch to celebrate the registration and the completion of the trust. He said that he knew someone very special who loved to paint, and was very gifted. Sadly, that person had stopped painting.

He hoped that if this person saw others around her painting, she might be inspired to engage her gift and love of painting again."

Annabella takes a big swig of wine from the glass. Placing the empty glass on the table hard.

"I don't have any more tears left to cry. So, if you'll both excuse me, I am going to throw myself into the river now!"

Even the drink and the pill had not helped curb her emotions. Annabella begins crying again. Stephanie rushes to hug Annabella and looks directly at Gabriel.

"Annabella and I are going to London for a few days."

"What for?"

"We are going to go to London to find Santiago De La Cruz and we're going to kill him!"

Gabriel opens his eyes wide, Annabella turns and looks at Stephanie.

Chapter Twenty Four

Connecting the Dots

Paris Gare du Nord Station, Pierre carries two medium suitcases, one for Annabella, and one for Stephanie. The girls are walking behind him, he stops.

"This is far as I go. I'll see you ladies in two days."

Stephanie leans over and kisses Pierre on both cheeks

"Keep an eye on him."

"I will. Oh, I almost forgot; producing a white envelope from the inside of the jacket of his suit he told me to give you this."

Stephanie looks at Pierre; he shrugs his shoulders and shakes his head as if to say. "I don't know what it is."

"Ok. Thank you! See you in two days."

Annabella takes charge of the two suitcases and starts to walk slowly followed by Stephanie, who is opening the envelope to see what's inside. After she reads it, she grabs her suitcase from Annabella and they casually walk along.

"Good news I hope?"

"It's Santiago's home address."

"I already know where he   lives."

"How do you know if you have never been there?"

"I went over the conversations we've had. I did not know the number of the house, but I know the street name."

"It's number 14."

"I would have found his house easy."

"Because everyone knows him! All the restaurant owners, all the shops there close to him, they all know him."

"Ok! That's our platform and that's, our train there waiting for us!"

"Did you bring the gun?"

"What gun?"

"The gun we're supposed to kill him with."

"Trust me. Don't worry about any guns right now. When he sees you, he will probably die of a heart attack!"

"Stephanie, for God's sake be nice. You're talking about the man I love."

"Ok, if he doesn't die from a heart attack, then we shoot him!"

"Have I ever told you, that you are a blessing in my life?"

"Don't talk about blessings. Gabriel tells me that all the time! Thirty years later, I still can't get rid of him! The good news is I don't think you have thirty years left in you, me neither for that matter!"

They start giggling as they walk to the check in, producing their tickets.

They arrive at Kings Cross St. Pancras Euro Station. They are whisked away in a black London taxi, which takes them to the Hilton Hotel in Park Lane.

Later that afternoon, they go sight-seeing. First is Buckingham Palace. Both cell phones are out and the two are taking pictures together, and separately. The next stop is, Big Ben, next, the South Bank of the River Thames to the Big Ferris Wheel also known as The Millennium Wheel. St. Pauls Cathedral on the other side, and the Globe Theatre. Finally, they conclude the tour of the Tower Bridge. The Tower Bridge was built in 1886- 1894. It crosses over the River Thames close to the Tower of London.

As the night falls, they are back at the Hilton. After supper they head to their room. Stephanie talks to Gabriel on video chat, telling him everything is alright and about their sightseeing tour. Stephanie, spoke of tomorrow and how she will go to the house and see if she can confront Santiago. Telling Gabriel that she loves him, she wishes him a good night and turns off her phone. Annabella is looking at her messages still nothing from Santiago. Closing her phone, she places it down on the table near the bed. Looking at Stephanie, who is washing her face in front of the mirror, Annabella speaks.

"I wonder what the chances are of bumping into him in the street."

"The chances are, about ten million to one."

"I am very nervous about tomorrow."

"You have to confront him, and in by doing so, you will confront your own feelings and emotions, as well as your fears."

"If he's home, and he opens the door, maybe, I should tell him what you told Gabriel."

"I told you, I tell Gabriel many things. What part are you talking about?"

"The part in the office when you told him you wanted to leave work, that you were in love with someone, and they had asked you to marry them, you said you would let them know."

"Don't remind me about that. Every time I think of that moment, I still see his face so clearly. The broken spirit face, it makes me sad. I have a good feeling about tomorrow; something beautiful is going to happen!"

"Every time you say that, the exact opposite happens! I wish this good feeling of yours for me, would just turn up, I'm wasting away here."

"Listen to me please! I don't claim to know much about the man, but I do know you don't have to be a rocket scientist to figure him out.

When a man goes to the lengths that he has gone to, just to spend a day with you; there is no doubt in my mind that as sure as there are stars in the sky, he is, still in love with you!"

"Well, why the hell doesn't he just turn up? I'm more than ready to talk things out now and sort out what to do next. My heart says that I will always love him. He needs to know this for once and for all!"

"Have you just developed Dementia, in the middle of this conversation?"

"No, why do you ask such a thing?"

"You told him to get out, from the very barn, which he gave you as a gift."

"A decision I regret tremendously! Please don't remind me of that or I'll end up crying my eyes out again!"

"Don't you dare start crying? When I see you cry I start crying too! He may not be perfect, no man is perfect, but he has his pride as a man and his pride is hurt.

This thing between you two makes your favourite movie, "Wuthering Heights" look like a child's fairy tale. You two better have a good ending!"

"It's not me, it's him!"

"That's it blame it on him!

When you see him tomorrow, grab the chance with your whole heart and soul, and don't surrender until he hears you out! Life is full of chances, you are lucky life has given you a second chance.

Don't make the mistake of taking this chance for granted! Make it happen! There is a consensus among the greatest thinkers in history, past and present. Most spiritual leaders and theologians agree, that the most powerful three words in the world are; "I LOVE YOU."

Tell him, show him, you have an ocean of love in you, don't deprive him, don't deprive yourself, and don't deprive me and Gabriel of seeing you both happy. I am going to get some sleep now to be rested for tomorrow."

Stephanie slips into her bed and turns away from Annabella

"You are right!"

"For a second, I thought Gabriel was talking to me. You plot, whatever version of reality you want, for tomorrow, and when you see him, tell him, and show him.

When I see him, I'm going to present him with a bill for all the Counselling you've received on behalf of him.

Annabella turns off the light and she slips into her bed, lying on her back staring at the ceiling

"Thank you, Stephanie."

"For what?"

"For being you! Good night baby sister!"

"Sweet Dreams."

In the morning, they ate breakfast in the hotel restaurant. After breakfast, they flag a black taxi from outside and head for North London. The taxi stops on the high street. Annabella and Stephanie step out and look around for a moment. Annabella recognizes the restaurants. Santiago had sent her many photos and videos of the area where he lived. Standing on the corner, Annabella feels as though she'd been here before.

Stephanie speaks: "You are on your own now. I'm going to go in here, have a coffee, and you sweet sister, Go and get a life!"

Stephanie opens the door to the restaurant and walks inside. A young waiter approaches her and welcomes her, placing her at a table by the window.

She looks out onto the side street through the big window, she sees Annabella walking in the direction of Santiago's house. Stephanie smiles and takes her chair, ordering an Espresso.

Annabella stands outside number fourteen. The house looks freshly painted from the outside. There is a beautiful wooden front door and brass numbers 14 on the door. Approaching the door, she's hesitant, but rings the bell once. Thinking for a second, she turns to walk away, but hears the door opens behind.

Stopping, she feels a panic; she turns around and sees a beautiful woman in her fifties. Annabella is strong, with a million thoughts running through her mind in a split second.

Could this be Santiago's girlfriend? Maybe a lover? The woman looks at Annabella as if she recognizes her, and she speaks:

"It's you?"

"Do you know me?"

"Yes."

"From where?"

"Please come in."

Annabella walks slowly, entering the house. It has an open floor plan, it's newly decorated, and the polished wooden floors are absolutely beautiful.

Her eyes scan the room quickly, noticing stunning settees and comfortable cushions. Everything looks spotless.

"I'm looking for my friend, Santiago."

"He's not home right now."

"When do you expect him?"

"I don't know."

"Are you his girlfriend?"

"No."

"You said you knew me."

"I do know you."

"Ok, but from where if I may ask?"

"Come follow me."

The woman walks up the wooden stairs. At the top, there are three bedroom doors and a bathroom, all modern and pristine clean. The woman walks towards a door that is directly at the end of the little hallway. All the doors are immaculately painted, the house is immaculately kept clean except the door on the end it's not been touched nor painted. The woman opens the door and turns on the lights. Annabella walks in behind her.

Standing there in amazement, the wall across from her is covered in Annabella's pictures.

All in glass frames sparkling clean. The only other thing in the room is an old desk with random items on it to include a computer and a twin bed and an old chest of drawers.

"I'm the housekeeper. In this room; I can only clean your pictures everything else is not to be touched. The window is always open, sometimes I close it. I never touch anything else in here."

"When was the last time Santiago was here?"

"I think, about three months ago. I come and clean the house twice a week, my pay is directly deposited into my bank account.

It seems the last I saw him was three months ago."

"Is it alright if I stay here for a few minutes?"

"Sure! Would you like me to make you a cup of tea?"

"No thank you."

"My sister is at the coffee shop would it be ok to phone her, and have her join me? My sister is also a friend to Santiago."

"I don't want to lose my job; I don't like the sound of this."

"Please, I promise you, you will not lose your job. We will only stay for a few minutes and then we will be on our way."

"Ok, I'll give you five minutes, that's it!"

"Thank you, give me a second please."

Annabella takes out her cell and calls Stephanie

"You need to come here right away!"

"Please don't disturb anything in the room."

"I won't! Does he use any of the other rooms?"

"No, he only uses this room. I'll go and let your friend in."

"Thank you."

The housekeeper leaves the room. Annabella is alone looking at all the pictures of herself in frames. Her eyes shift to the old unmade bed, and an old chest of drawers. Opening the old wardrobe to find his clothes she takes the sleeve of a jacket and smells it. Looking at the shoes on the floor together.

 Standing over the writing desk under the pictures where the computer monitors set in the middle.

There's an ash-tray, with several cigarette butts, a few vitamin bottles, several painkillers in packets. The only thing clean in the room is Annabella's photos in frames.

Everything else is neglected and untouched. Annabella sits on the bed facing the wall looking at the pictures. Her head is spinning with what she's seeing. How could she have known that Santiago was totally and completely in love with only her?

Downstairs the housekeeper opens the door for Stephanie. Stephanie follows her upstairs and enters into the room where Annabella is.

Looking at all the pictures on the wall, then, she moves and sits on the other side of Annabella close to the window. The birds are singing.

"Now that's what I call a gallery."

"When he used to speak to me on the webcam, I could always hear these birds outside."

Stephanie finds a picture of Annabella lying on her stomach on the bed wearing a G string with her ass in the air, and a smile on her face.

"Is that your ass?"

"Stephanie!"

"Nice ass!"

"Out of all the pictures on the wall, you had to go and find my ass!"

"Sorry."

"He hasn't been here for three months. Where the hell is he?"

"Maybe he's decided younger women are more fun, and he is lying on a beach with some blonde babe, while she rubs lotion on him."

"You came to London with me, to tell me that?"

"Maybe he got sick of looking at your pictures?"

Annabella and Stephanie slowly make their way down the stairs. The housekeeper is waiting at the bottom of the stairs.

"May I tell you something?"

"Yes, please do!"

"When I first came to work here two years ago, I was given instructions by him, about that room. I was not to touch anything, except the pictures on the wall, and that I was to take special care to make sure they are cleaned properly. The first time I cleaned all the pictures on the wall, I felt a deep sadness in my heart.

I thought you were his wife and that you'd died. The pictures on the wall were a shrine to you. I deeply respected his wishes. When I saw you outside I was so happy that you were alive and I was wrong. Please don't tell him I showed you the room, I might lose my job."

"I promise. Not a word of this."

"Thank you. May I ask you another question?"

"Yes."

"Were you two married?"

Annabella's eyes start to fill up, she is about to cry again.

"I met him for the first time for a few hours, a few weeks ago."

"But the pictures have been on the wall for two years."

"Maybe he has a crush on me."

"I don't think so. I think that he is totally and completely in love with you."

"Please don't mention to him that I was here."

"Oh my God! You are in love with him."

"Does it show?"

"Yes, your eyes speak love."

"Thank you."

Annabella walks towards the front door, Stephanie takes out fifty pounds, from her purse and hands it to the housekeeper, she resists, but Stephanie insists and she puts the money in her hand.

"Thank you for allowing us to see the room."

"I hope they find each other. It would be such a shame for a love like this to not be together."

"Thank you! They better find each other! Otherwise, I'm stuck with her!"

Stephanie walks out the front door.

Chapter Twenty Five

Posturing

On the first floor of the Eiffel Tower, Gabriel is sitting alone facing the outside world, having lunch in at "Restaurant 58" Paris can be seen through the large windows that go from floor to ceiling in the restaurant, Gabriel takes advantage of the beautiful view.

Santiago, approached him from the back of the restaurant, he's dressed very sharply. He pulls up a chair, places his cane next to him, and sits near Gabriel, who pretends he has not seen him.

"We need to talk."

"About what?"

"How is she?"

"Distraught, unhappy and suicidal."

"Me too! The only difference is I feel worse."

"How the hell can you feel worse than being suicidal?"

"I'm actually thinking about doing it."

"Good! That sounds like a symphony to my ears."

"Be nice please. I have feelings. Has she settled?"

"She is settled in the barn, her husband has agreed to give her a divorce, on the condition that she does not ask for anything except for the furniture she took from Paris to Morocco. I have paid his lawyer some money to expedite the process.

"I will reimburse you the money!"

"I spent your money!"

"Without asking me?"

"As I recall, it was you that said; "Make her divorce transition as smooth as possible." "Spending some of your money was what the transition called for."

"When are you leaving for South of France?"

"I have retired from the firm. I came here for the last time to have a quiet meal and reflect on my life. We are leaving next week."

"Good! Roberto and Maria will be happy to see you both!"

"They have started to receive their first batch of the guests. Painters, writers, poets, I hope they behave themselves and Roberto does not end up shooting one of them."

"I need a favour it's concerning Annabella."

"I'm warning you Santiago, stay away from her! You've done nothing but make her life   miserable."

"I'm miserable too! What about my life? Don't I count?"

"No. Did I ever mention that my late father in law was in the French resistance?"

"No."

"He kept a handgun until he passed away. I inherited that gun."

"Where are you going with all of this? Are you suggesting that you're going to give me the gun, to kill myself?"

"No, I am telling you, I am going to shoot you myself! In fact, I think I will do the job properly and shoot you twice!"

"I'm super serious here! I need your help!"

"There is no known doctor or medicine that can cure you Santiago. I'm warning you, I will intentionally shoot you!"

"Gabriel, please!"

"She is a broken woman Santiago. For God's sake, leave her be. Right now, she has peace and quiet there at the barn. She has started painting again, and in good company she has Venus, Roberto, Maria, and she will have me and Stephanie next week."

"Well, what about me?"

Gabriel leans closer to Santiago

"What about you? You need to get a life! What good is having everything when the only thing that matters is her? Stop all these stupid games Santiago!

Can't you see what you two are doing to each other? You are both destroying the very thing you love the most, each other! It's time to make up or let it go!

Do you have any idea how painful it is for Stephanie and me to watch all of this madness?"

"Well, how do you think I feel? I can't eat. I can't focus. I can't function. Gabriel, my friend, my advisor, I feel like I've died and gone to hell!"

"Good! That's because you are a STUPIDO!"

Santiago breaks out into a big smile.

"Stupido" is catchy you must have picked it up from her! Annabella is the only one who calls me that! All I tried to do was to do something good Gabriel. I need to see her. I'm dying!"

"Did I tell you that we are putting up signs round the property?"

"No, what signs?"

"Trespassers will be shot on sight!"

"Gabriel, I've come to the realization that I can't win."

"What are you talking about?"

"When I had nothing, living in that room, all I dreamed and wanted was to be with Annabella. Now that I have everything, I only dream and want to be with Annabella. Maybe it's time to quit. I mean it's coming up on six years that she and I have known each other, most people get married and divorced within six years."

"Think of it as a blessing. You have your freedom. I hear you are a "ladies man." There are literally thousands of women, beautiful women that would love to be with you!"

"I have not promised anybody, anything in the world, least of all my undying love. Can you imagine life without Stephanie?"

"That's going too far   Santiago!"

302

"No, I can see it in your face that the mere thought of what I said, created a grief with you that cannot be denied. You could not handle your life now without the "Love of Your Life" by your side. Yet you condemn me Gabriel, when you can leave this table and go to her, hold her in your arms, kiss her lips, look in her eyes, smell her hair, and tell her that you love her.

I live with the same grief and emotions day after day; her voice is in my ears, her smile in my mind, her soul connected to me through starlight and moonbeams. Annabella is my soul mate, as Stephanie is yours!

I would die a happy man if I could only tell her before I die, the gift she gave my soul.

The treasure she bestowed on me with each of us is sound of her voice, I would indeed die happy if she could hear this from my heart and look into my eyes. You are a divorce lawyer for God's sake; don't you have any advice on how to save a relationship?"

Relationships, like everything else in the world Santiago, are saved through negotiations and compromise. By sitting down, face to face and talking about everything. In your case you must bare your soul if you are to stand a chance of saving yourself and Annabella.

"Is that the best you can do?"

"Santiago De Le Cruz, you have been more of a headache to me, than twenty clients combined. Give me a break. I retired today."

Santiago stands up and starts walking off with his walking cane leaving Gabriel to ponder their conversation a while.

Chapter Twenty Six

Garden of Eden

<u>Six Months Later</u>

In the South of France, "The Global Arts Foundation" is up and running. Gabriel and Stephanie have settled into the penthouse, Roberto is in charge of all the outdoor production of organic foods that are frozen for consumption in the house. Fruits are turned into jam, and the bees are happily producing honey. Some of all of this will be kept for everyone in the house and some of them put into small jars and sold at the local market, as well as the vegetables grown on the property. This provides money to buy other things they need for food and supplies. Annabella and Stephanie can be seen with Maria in the kitchen helping with the evening meals.

Paris and Venus have become the stars of the house. Everyone loves them as they roam around the house freely now.

Gabriel takes care of all the financial transactions of the house as well as the legal matters concerning the house, the land, everything.

The chateau runs like clockwork especially first thing in the morning when the rooster starts his incessant crowing!

The evening meals if the weather is nice, are, outside under the stars in the garden. Everyone has a routine. Early to bed, early to rise.

The artists are given the privilege of staying for two months at a time, and then they must leave, giving chance to another aspiring artist.

This is the place to come to focus on artistic talents, it's beautiful, no, and it's breath-taking and full of constant inspiration. Everyone works four hours a day. It makes everyone's life much easier and less stressful. There are plans for the future to add ten log cabins on the grounds and build a larger, more self-sustaining greenhouse that is totally "eco-friendly" and can house some of the plants in the winter.

Annabella has taken up painting again. Sometimes she encourages Maria and Stephanie to paint with her when she goes out to do a beautiful landscape close to the house. They can often be seen sitting by the pool having a glass of wine at night and talking.

Roberto and Gabriel play chess and discuss philosophy. Sometimes Gabriel goes fishing and game hunting with Roberto. Life is incredibly beautiful all around.

Stephanie drops into the barn to see Annabella. Relaxing on the sofa drinking tea, Annabella checks her phone messages

"You are still checking your messages?"

"Habit"

"It's been seven months Annabella; he's not going to come."

"He will come."

"What makes you so sure?"

"Because he is my soul-mate, I can feel Santiago. He will come."

"Maria, Roberto, Gabriel, and I, we all want you to be together."

"Thank you Sissy!"

"I'll see you at the house   later?"

"Yes, of course you will."

Roberto is on horseback taking Annabella to the waterfall to do some painting. They stop at the top of the mountain before the climb down. There is a white horse by the lake and a knight in shining armour all dressed in shining silver. There's a pallet out and he appears to be painting the waterfall, Annabella looks at Roberto.

"He better be a mirage otherwise, I am going to shoot him for trespassing and I don't care what century he is from!"

As they approach the lake this is no mirage. He is real and standing there, facing away from them. Clearly, he is enchanted by the beauty of the waterfall.

Roberto takes out his shotgun, "Shall I shoot him?"

"No! Wait. What kind of lunatic would wear such an outfit on a cold morning like this? One must ask the question; what kind of an idiot could end up in a place like this, trying to paint wearing all that armour? A real mystery is now in our hands here brother!"

They approach him slowly. As they get close to him, he turns, but his face is covered by the helmet.

"No one knows this spot. How the hell did you get here?"

The man in the silver armour points to his head as if to say he cannot hear, then he indicates with his index finger; One moment. He turns to the pallet and takes the single red rose that is lying neatly at the bottom of the canvas board and looks at Annabella.

Handing her the red rose, she is feeling inquisitive and amazed. Stepping forward, she slowly opens the mask upwards, and sees Santiago. The first words out of his face were: "I LOVE YOU!" she slammed the mask shut.

Annabella turns on her heels, storms past Roberto and commands

"SHOOT HIM!"

"WHAT?"

"SHOOT HIM TWICE!"

Roberto points the gun to the sky and shoots. Not expecting this, Santiago loses his footing and falls backwards. He is lying on his back on the stones.

Annabella rushes to him with the rose still in her hand.

"Oh my God! You've killed him!"

"Not quite"

"Oh Santiago! Speak to me!"

She opens the mask again looking at his eyes.

"I am cold and my arthritis hurts. Above all else, my pride hurts. I've had enough. I'm going home."

"Oh Thank God you're not hurt! What do you mean you're going home?" You've just arrived here."

"Give me your hand."

Santiago takes Roberto's hand, and he pulls him to his feet.

"Take that stupid thing off your head. Anyone would think you two were ten years old kids playing fantasy hero games with a maiden in distress."

Santiago takes off the helmet and looks at Annabella

"I've run out of ideas how to make a fool of myself."

"You don't have to anymore!"

"Here give me a hand."

Roberto helps him take the top part of the armour of his chest and shoulders, Annabella looks at him curiously.

"Santiago, where did you get this outfit from?

"I rented it. I should have rented a gun and shot myself!"

Annabella giggles, takes his hand, smiles.

"I am sorry."

Roberto turns his eyes up.

"I'll leave the gun with you two; to scare off bears. Try not to shoot each other."

As Roberto is getting on his horse, Annabella and Santiago are holding hands and walking to a rock to sit down. Roberto gets on his horse Beauteous and heads back up the mountain. Taking the last look out to the waterfall he turns Beauteous around and looks down.

There by the lake, two horses, Annabella and Santiago sit on a rock talking and a huge rainbow across the falls rest in the background. Roberto smiles and turns Beauteous and goes around the mountain.

Once out of view, he nudges Beauteous into action and he starts galloping towards the house.

Roberto stops outside the house, jumps off the horse and charges into the house into the living room where everyone is gathered. Some of the guests, Maria, Gabriel and Stephanie are all watching on the big screen, a drone shot from above the waterfall looking down on Santiago and Annabella, sitting on a rock talking. Roberto stops near Stephanie and Maria. Turning to Stephanie,

"Has anything happened?"

"No, they're just sitting on a rock talking like a pair of kids."

"What? He hasn't kissed her yet?"

"No."

"Are you sure?"

"Roberto, we have been here watching this for the past twenty minutes. She hasn't seen a kiss, I haven't seen a kiss, and no one else here seen a kiss!"

"Thank God they're not teenagers. They would never have any kids at this rate."

Roberto, se non hai niente di carino da dire, allora stai zitto, Ti amo Amore mio! (Translation): Roberto, if you do not have anything nice to say, then shut up, I love you my love!"

Back at the waterfall, Annabella and Santiago sit on a rock talking, the horses are drinking water.

"You never told me why you wrote the book."

"I wrote the book in the hopes that I would forget you. It made things even worse. I missed you terribly. The one dream that had never died was that; one-day we would be together in a beautiful place like this and in total harmony."

"I am going to try my best to make you happy starting with no more arguments or tantrums."

"I've been single for so long, that I don't know if I will make a good soul-mate. I'm willing to try. I am out of practice with all this stuff myself."

The reason why I get so emotional, is that I get butterflies in my stomach when I hear your voice or see your face, most especially when you are in front of me. I can't control my feelings and what I say sometimes always seems to be the wrong thing.

I always regret it after. Like asking Roberto to shoot you or telling you to get out of the barn, you make me emotional."

"You make me nervous too! I've never been like this with anyone. What I mean is being here with you, completes me as a human being. I know my worth in life, and I know I am nothing without you. You brought me here because we fell in love a long time ago."

Santiago leans and softly kisses Annabella's mouth. It's a beautiful, tender kiss. Annabella responds by putting her hand on his face as she is kissing his mouth.

Back at the house everyone watching the large screen drone footage. Upon seeing the kiss, they all start clapping and cheering as if they were watching a successful Mars landing. Everyone is smiling. Gabriel looks at Stephanie, Maria, and Roberto

"This is evidence that he has proposed to her."

Back at the waterfall they look into each other's eyes. They kiss again, hug again, and then look into each other's eyes deeply.

"I love the insecure little girl in you, I love the adult you, and I love you!"

"My Hero, My Santiago, I love you!"

Santiago smiles at her and leans in kisses her mouth softly, looking in her eyes, and then turns and they watch the waterfall together, holding hands on the rock.

Chapter Twenty Seven

Written in the Stars

<u>One Week Later</u>

Outside the house, the sun is rising. There are six horses packed and ready to go on the lead horse Roberto. As always, the horses are tied together, making a chain. Annabella second in line, Santiago third, Stephanie fourth, Gabriel fifth, and at the back of the chain, is Maria. All the horses carry extra things on them for the BBQ they'll have.

In the garden one of the guests who know how to fly drones remotely controls the drone and it lifts off. He watches the drone rising high over the house on a laptop that has been set up in the garden. There are a few other guests watching. It's a beautiful picture looking down on the horses all in a line going down the old track that will lead them to the waterfall. The second camera is switched on as the drone passes the horses overhead, they can also be seen from the second camera as the drone moves away from them.

The drone flies over the last mountain and below is the waterfall and lake. The drone slowly flies around the lake and the waterfall and then slowly comes back to find the horses on the side of the mountain going down to the lake. The drone takes up a new position above the waterfall and the lake. As the ceremony begins, the drone slowly comes down closer so everyone can be seen.

Annabella is dressed in a long white summer dress with flowers in her hair is holding some lavender flowers as well as jasmine that has been stitched through a cotton thread and they circle the lavender flowers.

Annabella is on Roberto's arm. Roberto walks her over to Santiago, who is waiting with Maria to perform the ceremony. Gabriel and Stephanie standing a few feet away. Roberto delivers Annabella to the altar, then moves back and takes his place on the side. Annabella and Santiago look into each other eyes and smile. Maria will be residing over the ceremony. Maria begins

"The journey to be here today started long ago. It started with uncertainty, hopes, dreams, and wishes. It began with fear, self-doubt, and the unknown of where this adventure would end up. This odyssey, this pilgrimage, in their crusade to discover the "Holy Grail" in life that is called "Love."

They didn't know what shores they would be shipwrecked on in life. There have been a few derelict outcomes that have left them disappointed, souls bruised and their trust diminished. Nature rewards us with persistence, diligence, integrity, sincerity, and truthfulness. The pursuit and the quest for love have brought them here today. In doing so, they begin their new journey to heal each other, to give love and appreciation to one another.

This is a time to embrace a new beginning in the name of love; it is now my honour to unite these two beautiful souls.

We are gathered here today to witness two souls, in their devotion, allegiance, and dedication to each other in this ceremony to have their love blessed.

Do you Santiago De La Cruz take Annabella Beaulieu as your lawful wedded wife?"

"I do!"

"Do you Annabella Beaulieu take Santiago De La Cruz, as your lawful wedded husband?"

"I do!"

"Standing here before God, before nature, and before the witnesses here, I happily pronounce you man and wife. You may kiss your bride!"

Santiago softly kisses Annabella on the lips

Gabriel's best man speech:

"We stand here in this beautiful little patch of heaven to celebrate and bless these two amazing souls. I hope life will bless them with many years of joy, love and all things beautiful to unite them for eternity. God Bless You Both! We love you!"

Roberto plays the song *"Do You Love Me"* by Sharif Dean, it was their song. Santiago and Annabella start dancing slowly looking into each other's eyes.

Maria hands out the home-made wedding cake she made. She offers Gabriel and Stephanie a piece of cake, Stephanie takes it and starts eating, Gabriel joins her, Roberto takes a piece and he starts eating the delicious cake. (Stephanie to Maria)

"You don't think I put too much of a certain ingredient in there do you?"

We'll find out soon enough!"

Gabriel and Stephanie finish their cake and start to dance together to the song.

Roberto looks at Maria they gravitate together naturally and into each other arms as they begin to dance Roberto Grabs Maria bottom and squeezes it hard, she opens her eyes and slaps him on the shoulder giggling. Everyone is happy, relaxed, and dancing with their true love in each other's arms; it was a gathering of Soul-mates.

THE END

Printed in Great Britain
by Amazon

83684217R10182